The Anglesey Murders: Book 6

What Happened to Rachel?

CONRAD JONES

ISBN; 9798645082208

COPYRIGHT @ CONRAD JONES 2020

The Detective Alec Ramsay Series
The Child Taker
Slow Burn
Criminally Insane
Frozen Betrayal
Concrete Evidence
Desolate Sands
Three

The Inspector Braddick Books (follows on from Ramsay)
Brick
Shadows
Guilty
Deliver us from Evil

The Anglesey Murders (runs alongside Braddick)
Unholy Island
A Visit from the Devil
Nearly Dead
A Child from the Devil
Dark Angel

Soft Target Series (feature Tank from The Child Taker)

Soft Target

Tank

Jerusalem

18th Brigade

Blister

Standalone Novel

The Journey

CHAPTER 1

Rachel Evans looked out of the window. It was already nearly dark. Black clouds were gathering over Snowdonia; the white-topped peaks seemed to glow against the gloomy sky. She wasn't looking forward to leaving school today, which was unusual as she hated school. If she'd had the choice, she would never step through the gates again. She welcomed the fact that the school was closing because of the Covid-19 outbreak. Rachel was very bright, but she didn't enjoy the regimented regime.

It started to rain, and she watched droplets running down the window, blurring her view of the outside world. It was quickly fading into dusk. The clocks had gone back at the weekend and walking home had changed dramatically; the balmy strolls of summer had gone. It was cold and windy. She would be battling against the rain while the school traffic splashed surface water onto the pavements, their headlights piercing the gloom. Winter nights on the island could be long and dreary and boring. The opportunities to hang outside with her friends were limited by the weather and the light. They would be even worse soon if Boris enforced the lockdown everyone was talking about. Her stepdad didn't like her being outside after dark; he still thought she was a little girl, but she could look after herself. He wasn't her real father, which she reminded him of as often as possible. She didn't care what he thought, in fact she couldn't care any less if she tried. He had no idea who she was as a person. He was no one to her. She was as polite as she could be and towed the line to keep her mum happy, but it was hard work at times. She didn't like him and that was that; she disliked his son even more. He was a creep with a capital C. She knew things about him that her mum didn't. The internet was a mine of information, but her mother was blissfully unaware of how times had changed. Rachel drifted inside her mind, her thoughts casting back to the time before the long summer holidays when her life had changed dramatically.

'Rachel,' her maths teacher said. His eyes looked ridiculously big through the lenses of his glasses.

'What?' she asked, startled by his interruption of her thoughts.

'Are you still with us?'

'Yes, sir,' she replied with a nod. She blushed a little. Sniggers rippled across the classroom.

'Are you listening?'

'Yes. I'm listening.'

'Good. In which case, you can tell us the answer to the question.'

Rachel blushed crimson. She had no idea what he'd been prattling on about for the last hour. Maths was such a shit lesson. If she needed to work something out, she used the calculator on her phone, simples. She twisted her dark hair with her forefinger; most of it was tied up in a long ponytail, but she had strands dangling near her ears. Her best friend, Sandra, kicked her foot under the desk three times.

'I think it's three,' Rachel said. Mr Roberts looked disappointed that she was right. Sandra smiled behind her hand. 'Definitely three, sir.'

'Good. Well done.'

Rachel smiled and nudged Sandra in the ribs with her elbow. Sandra nudged her back and tickled her. Mr Roberts was about to say something to them, when the bell rang.

'Okay. That's it for the foreseeable future,' he said, over the racket of chairs scraping on tile as the class stood up, eager to get away. 'Remember this is not a holiday. This is social distancing to slow the spread of the virus. I still need you to complete the exercise on page sixty-two for your homework. I want it back to my email address on the school website on Thursday, without fail. It's going towards your final grade.'

'Sir,' the class said in unison.

'Philip Noonan,' Mr Roberts shouted above the noise.

'Yes, sir?'

'If your dog eats your homework again or you tragically lose another relative before Thursday, you'll be on report to Miss Miles and you will fail this subject. Are you clear on that?'

'What about the virus, sir?'

'That includes the virus, Noonan. Are we clear?'

'Yes, sir.' Noonan coughed into his hand. 'Wanker,' he snorted.

The sound of laughter filled the air. The pupils rushed for the door, pushing and shoving their way through. Outside the classroom, Rachel headed for her locker, which was further along the corridor. Her friends were gathering by the exit doors, waiting to walk home together.

A couple of them had umbrellas at the ready. The others had fur-lined hoods pulled up to protect them from the wind and rain. They chatted incessantly about the virus while they waited; their voices merged into one. Rachel unlocked the padlock and opened the locker door. She put the books she didn't need inside and grabbed her leather satchel. It was old and distressed and very cool. Her Nain had given it to her not long before she died; she treasured it and had it with her most of the time. She had butterflies in her stomach, not good ones. Her nerves were jangling, and she wanted to turn the clock back twelve months; things seemed so simple back then. Everything had become very complicated and what was once fun and exciting was now toxic and frightening. It had changed in the blink of an eye and she couldn't change it back. The genie was out of the bottle and she'd run out of wishes.

She closed her locker and headed for the girls' toilets; she planned to remain there until the others had tired of waiting and set off for home without her, then she would exit through the rear doors and use the playing fields as a shortcut home. She needed to avoid the road. Rachel went into the cubicle furthest from the entrance and locked the door; the air was thick with the overpowering smell of pine disinfectant. It was obvious the caretaker had recently mopped the floors, so he could get off on time. She put the toilet seat down and sat on it and switched her phone on; the school banned them until lessons were finished. Her phone vibrated immediately, and she checked her messages, nervously. She relaxed. It was Sandra.

Sandra. *Where are you, doll?*

Rachel: *I need to see Miss Miles before the school closes. You lot go ahead. Catch up with you later.*

Sandra: *What've you done now, knobhead?*

Rachel: *Nothing, bitch. No worries. See you later.*

Sandra: *Have you been on Insta and FB yet?*

Rachel: *Not yet, why?*

Sandra: *Your stalker, David Laws, has been liking all your pics again; I bet he's playing with himself while he's ogling you. Dirty birdie, yeah.*

Rachel: *OMG. I told him to f-off. He's been sending me dick pics again. He's disgusting. SUCH a geek. Makes me puke.*

Sandra: *Don't lie. You fancy the arse off him. I think you want to do him big time.*

Rachel: *Really? You can't talk. You snogged Delwyn Evans and let him feel your tits. Your opinion doesn't matter anymore! Dirty dog.*

Sandra: *That's a low blow and it was only one tit so it doesn't count. Wounded.*

Rachel: *Lol. Later, knobhead.*

Sandra: *Laters.*

Rachel chuckled and shook her head. She checked her Instagram and Facebook accounts and Sandra was right; David Laws had trawled through every picture of her and clicked on like, love or wow. He'd written *'smokin' hot'* under some of them. It must have taken him hours. The thought of a horny boy ogling her photos had been such a buzz at first. It was amusing and creepy at the same time, dependent on who it was. It was such a rush when hundreds of likes appeared on a photo, although some of the comments could be a bit lewd. Some men were clearly desperate; David was one of them. David Laws was in the year above her and thought he was God's gift to females, but he was far from it. He wasn't bad looking, but he was a knobhead. One of her friends had kissed and made out with him after a prom and said he had bad breath and a little dick; the pictures he'd been sending of his penis confirmed that. Her friend didn't go all the way with him; none of her friends had done it yet, not that Rachel was interested in him, anyway. He was an immature prick with blackheads on his nose and cheap shoes. He was way behind the trend. His interest in her was unwelcome; very unwelcome indeed. She'd been polite, but he clearly wasn't listening. It had gone too far and needed to be nipped in the bud quickly. She typed a message to him in Messenger:

Read this very carefully. I've told you to fuck off and I can't be any clearer. Stop stalking my photos, weirdo, and stop sending me disgusting pics of your tiny penis. Leave me alone, you creep, or I'll tell my brother to kick your head in and I'll share your pics on the school pages. This is your last warning F-OFF.

She sent it, blocked him from all her social media accounts and then put her phone away. Her friends would be gone now. She opened the door and checked the toilets were empty. They were. She straightened her hair in the mirror, pouted and applied cherry lip gloss; then she took a mirror pic and uploaded it. Her followers went into a frenzy when she had her hair up. The pout was perfect. David Laws and a few hundred others would react in minutes. They would message that they dreamt about her lips. In reality, they had zero chance of getting anywhere near them. The truth was she didn't like men; it was her secret for now, but she knew she was attracted to females. The thought of being near a male sickened her.

She left the toilets and reached the corridor and looked towards the front exit. The school was empty and quiet, only a few stragglers were about. She fastened the zip on her bubble jacket and headed to the back doors. The rain was pouring, and a cold wind was blowing across the island from the north. She shivered, pulled up her hood, and ran across the playground; she kept her head down and went towards the rugby pitches. The grass was muddy, and progress was hard going, but she eventually made it to the reasonable shelter of the woods. It had taken her about ten minutes. She was soaked. Rainwater dripped from the upper branches, feeling like drops of ice when it touched her skin, but the trees offered some shelter and took the cold sting from the wind.

Rachel slowed to a trot and followed the narrow path through the undergrowth; it ran parallel to the road which led to her estate but was far enough inside the treeline to make it impossible to be seen from a passing vehicle. The light was fading quickly, and a gloom descended on the woods. Usually, the dark made her nervous but today it gave her the cover she needed. It shrouded her and made her invisible.

She was too old to believe there were ghosts and ghouls prowling the woods. There were far more frightening things in play at the moment. The living are more terrifying than the dead could ever be. She felt alone; more alone than she'd ever felt before. There was no one she could confide in and no one could help her. She'd brought it on herself and she was the only one who could solve the problem, but she didn't know how to. The problem seemed to be insurmountable. It had snowballed and become an unstoppable force. The damage was done. Some things could never be fixed.

The sound of a breaking twig behind her made her stop in her tracks. Rachel turned her head, but there was no one there. She looked to her right, but the darkness was too deep to see much more than a few yards. No matter how she tried, she couldn't penetrate the gloom. The shadows seemed to shift and merge as her eyes tried to adjust to the dark. Degrees of darkness melted into one another; inky shadows blended into different shades of black. There was another sound. It was a branch snapping this time. It was to her left, but closer now. She held her breath in her chest and listened. Leaves crunched underfoot to her right. There were more footsteps to her left, or was it in her imagination? Someone was there, approaching from the darkness. There was a rustling behind her. Was there more than one person there? Why would there be anyone there at all?

Was it because of what you've done, Rachel?

She wished she'd taken the normal way home. She'd picked the woods because she thought she could use the trees for camouflage. No one used the path through the woods in the winter. It was longer and more treacherous. There was only the sound of dripping rain now. Her mind was playing tricks on her. She took a deep breath and moved to the next tree, keeping low. Her footsteps sounded ridiculously loud in the darkness. She cursed as another twig snapped beneath her feet, giving away her position. There were demons beyond her vision. She swore and scolded herself. *Giving her position away to who?* she thought.

Could he be there, following her? She could feel her heart beating in her chest and the blood pumping through her veins as she listened, her senses ultra-aware. There was nothing but the sound of her breathing and the raindrops falling from the trees. Drip, drip, drip.

Her breath was visible now as day turned to night and the temperature dropped sharply. She moved to the next tree, following the path which was barely visible anymore. Her mobile had a torch function but she daren't turn it on. Not while there might be someone out there, hiding in the blackness between the trees. Stalking her. Hunting her.

The sound of a twig snapping echoed through the darkness; she turned around quickly. She caught a movement to her left and stared at it, but it was gone; the darkness pressed in on her making it difficult to breathe. The smaller trees were like dark skeletal creatures lurking beyond the path, the branches reaching for her like bony fingers. Her breathing settled a little as she told herself it was all in her imagination. She closed her eyes and took a deep breath, letting it out slowly, trying to calm herself. But another snapping sound pushed her into a panic. She bolted and ran as fast as she could. There were footsteps behind her; she was sure of it. She was running blind and low branches struck her in the face and scratched her legs. Blood trickled down her shin. The path weaved through the trees, but she lost her bearings. Blind panic forced her on. She ran full speed into a tree and the blow to the front of her skull sent a lightning bolt through her mind; her knees buckled as her mind switched off. She staggered backwards and tripped, crashing into another tree, and the bang to the back of her skull stunned her further. She crumpled to the floor and unconsciousness smothered her.

CHAPTER 2

DI Alan Williams parked his BMW next to the custom's sheds at Holyhead port. Blue lights strobed the area and a cordon had been made of traffic cones and police vehicles. He could see Pamela Stone's CSI van near the gates at the rear of the sheds. Two uniformed officers walked towards his vehicle. He recognised them as sergeants Bob Dewhurst and April Byfelt. A camera flash caught his eye from a few hundred yards away. On top of the rocky outcrop which overlooked the harbour, three cameramen were huddled next to a stone obelisk called Skinner's Monument, sheltering from the rain. He could just about make them out. The fact they looked cold and windswept made Alan smile. There was a god somewhere, even if he appeared not to be around at the moment. Covid-19 was spreading across the planet and there were no signs of it slowing down anytime soon. Thousands were dying. The police force had been briefed that a lockdown was imminent and that it would be up to them to enforce it. The only way to stop the spread was to minimise human contact.

Things were bad enough, but the call about what had been found at the harbour enforced the old adage that things could always be worse. It was going to be a tough scene to analyse. He'd seen lots of bad crime scenes, too many to recall. When women and children were involved, it made them much harder to process. They climbed out of the BMW, opened the boot, and donned their forensic outfits. Bob and April neared.

'Evening,' Bob said.

'Hello, Bob. How the hell did the vultures get wind of this so quickly?' Alan asked, pointing to the hill where the journalists were gathered. The thinning dark hair on his head stood on end in the breeze. He patted it down with his hand to no avail. The pea shaped growth on his forehead looked purple and angry in the cold.

'Your guess is as good as mine,' Bob said. 'It will be a tip off. Someone has made a few quid from the paparazzi. All it takes is one text or phone call and they can double their weekly wage. Christmas is just around the corner. Things are tight and if Boris enforces this lockdown, things will get a lot tougher.'

'Millions will be out of work.'

'It will be a disaster for a lot of families. I get that, but it's no excuse to tip off the press. If I find out who it is, I'm going to kick them up the arse,' Alan said.

Detective Sergeant Kim Davis was staring at the journalists on the hill. She thought she recognised one of them. His name was Peter Cecil and he'd been a huge mistake from her past. Alan pointed to them.

'Is that prick Cecil up there?' he asked.

'Yes. I think so.'

'Do me a favour. Run up there and tell him to bugger off,' Alan said.

'He's not on your Christmas card list?' Bob said.

'No. The last time he covered one of our cases, he printed a few untruths and we were both nearly suspended.'

'He's an arsehole,' April added.

'I'm unlikely to forget that, thank you for reminding me of the obvious,' Kim said. 'Run up there yourself and tell him what an arsehole he is,' Kim said, smiling. 'I'll keep everything moving down here.'

'I've got a bad knee,' Alan said. 'The doctor said I can't run up hills.'

'It's bad when it suits you,' Kim said. She tied her long blond hair up behind her head.

'You're a cruel woman.'

'Only when I have to be. Let's have a look at what we've got, shall we?'

'Is Pamela still in there?' Alan asked April.

'Yes. She's still processing the bodies,' April said. 'It's a bad one.'

'I'm told they're all female?' Alan asked.

'Yes. She suspects some of them are only teenagers,' April said.

'How many bodies, so far?'

'Thirty-nine.'

'Jesus,' Alan, muttered.

'What has the driver said?' Kim asked.

'He's a Bosnian. Claims he can't speak English. We're waiting on an interpreter.'

'He can speak English,' Alan said. 'He's buying time. We'll wait for the interpreter.'

'That's the plan, but I'm not holding my breath. He's unlikely to give us anything useful, anyway.'

'Let's go and talk to Pamela,' Alan said. He felt sick to the stomach. 'How desperate must these people be to put themselves in this predicament?'

'Very desperate indeed,' Kim said. 'And I don't see it ending anytime soon.'

They headed into the customs' shed and the smell of death drifted to them. A black tractor unit was attached to an articulated refrigerated trailer. The load had been partially removed onto the concrete, exposing the corpses of young women, who had dared to find a better life but were tricked by evil men. Pamela and her team were working among the dead, removing them one at a time, clearing a path deeper into the trailer. The refrigeration units had been left on to slow decomposition. Pamela spotted Alan and waved a gloved hand. She walked over to him.

'Thirty-nine so far,' she said. 'According to the paperwork, the lorry was heading for a distribution company in Manchester,' she added.

'Why was it stopped?' Alan asked.

'It was a routine stop and check. The heat sensors in the customs' shed spotted a warm zone at the centre of the load, which looked suspicious. They opened it up and found the migrants, but it was too late. They died of hypothermia or suffocation, probably both; there's no sign of foul play. They've been in the refrigeration unit too long and used up all the oxygen. Someone got their calculations wrong.'

'Where are they from?'

'There's no ID on any of them, but my initial guess is they're eastern European. Some of them have tattoos which look like they're written in Czech or possibly Slovakian. I can't tell for sure yet, but I'll let you know as soon as I do.'

'They travelled a long way to suffocate in the back of a truck,' Alan said. 'Who owns the lorry?'

'It's registered to a company in Dublin, but I think it's a spurious registration,' Pamela said. 'I've sent all the details to you,' she said, turning to Kim. 'I've sent them to you, Kim. I know you check your emails and he doesn't. Can you forward them to him, please?'

'Will do,' Kim said. Alan shrugged and looked mildly offended, although he didn't argue the fact. 'Richard Lewis is working on tracking the vehicle's movements. I'll pass the information on to him.'

'He's the best man for the job,' Alan said. 'If there's anything to find, he'll find it.'

'We have another conundrum,' Pamela said. She picked up a vial containing an indicator strip. The tip was blue. 'We've tested for drugs in the vehicle. It lit up like a Christmas tree.'

'Where?' Alan asked. He frowned. There was no obvious storage place for a shipment to be hidden.

'Here,' Pamela said, pointing to pools of liquid near the bodies. 'Urine has leaked from some of the deceased. I've tested it. It's all positive.' She walked over to an evidence case. 'See here,' Pamela said, pointing at some bottles of amber liquid. 'They used these empty bottles to urinate in. They've all tested positive for cocaine.'

'They have drugs inside them?' Alan asked.

'It would explain the positive results. We'll know more once we get them back to the lab, but I can't see any other explanation.'

'Why are there no men here?' Alan said. 'They're all young women and girls and they've been forced to be mules. I don't think they're migrants, do you?'

'No. I don't,' Kim said. 'They were destined for the sex industry, in my opinion.'

'I agree. If they're Czech, they could travel here legitimately. They've been offered lucrative jobs in the UK, lured somewhere were their passports were taken and their families threatened. They were kidnapped and forced to swallow class-A's. The next part of their journey doesn't take much imagination, but they wouldn't have been working as nannies.'

'They probably offered them a fortune to leave their homes for jobs, which don't exist. They didn't think they would be swallowing condoms full of cocaine as part of the deal,' Kim said. 'They were not in a position to argue.'

'You can't argue with people like that,' Alan agreed. Pamela walked them through the scene. The grey faces of the dead became engrained on his mind; their glassy stares looked at him accusingly. The younger girls were huddled close to the older ones. Their last few hours on the planet must have been cold and frightening, suffocating to death with no way to escape. Alan had seen everything he needed to see.

'Okay. We'll let you get on with your work. Thanks Pamela.' They walked back to the car and took off the forensic suits. There was a welcome silence while they stripped and stored away their gear. 'It shouldn't take long to trace who is responsible for this,' Alan said, closing the boot. 'Let's find out who they are and pass this over to the NCA. Are they on their way?'

'Yes. They're liaising with Pamela direct.'

'Good. I hope they crucify the bastards.'

CHAPTER 3

Pauline Evans checked her watch again and then looked at her phone. They both told exactly the same time and that meant her daughter, Rachel, was over an hour late home from school. The kitchen clock on the wall agreed. Rachel could be a little late on the odd occasion, if she was walking with her friends, gossiping and messing about, but no more than fifteen or twenty minutes. This was completely out of character. Rachel was the type of girl who couldn't wait to change out of her uniform after school. She was probably fine and safe, but something niggled at the back of Pauline's mind, making her more worried than she should. The schools were shutting down to combat the spread of the virus, so maybe they were keeping pupils behind to organise their home schooling. Rachel hadn't mentioned that, and she was never late.

Rachel was fourteen and very savvy for her age; sometimes a little too savvy. She was fourteen going on forty. Despite all that, Pauline was worried. Rachel was probably with her friends. Probably didn't feel like it was enough today. Pauline needed to know where she was. She checked her phone again. It was blank. She hated calling Rachel and asking her where she was. Her own parents had been pedantic about knowing where she was and what she was doing, and it had been stifling. She was determined not to give her daughter any reason to resent her as she grew up and became an adolescent. It would drive a wedge between them, and she wanted to avoid that.

The sentiment was admirable but letting go of the reins wasn't that easy. She stirred her chilli and turned down the heat and checked her watch again. Her youngest daughter, Annie walked into the kitchen. Her long brown hair fell to her shoulders. She looked more like Rachel every day.

'I can't believe they've shut the school,' Annie said. 'I'm so happy. I think this might be the best day of my life.'

'People are dying, Annie,' Pauline said. 'This isn't a joke. Thousands of people are very sick, and the government are closing the schools to try to save lives. Please don't make light of this, it makes you look uncaring and unintelligent.'

'Okay, calm down,' Annie said, rolling her eyes. 'Mary Harris reckons the virus was invented in a lab in China to wipe out the over sixties because the population is too high and it's causing global warning.'

'Warming.'

'What?'

'It is global warming, not warning,' Pauline said, shaking her head. 'And Mary Harris needs to listen to the news and stop believing everything she reads on Facebook.'

'Whatever. What's for tea, Mum?' Annie asked, uninterested.

'Chilli,' Pauline said, checking her phone again. 'Did you see your sister on the way home from school?'

'Erm, I don't think so,' Annie said, shaking her head. 'I can't remember.'

'You can't remember if you saw your sister or not?'

'Well, I thought I might have but then I remembered that might have been yesterday. One school day is much like another. They merge into one big boring day. School sucks. That's why I'm happy.'

'School will educate you. Your future depends on what you do in the next few years. Some people might not have a future.'

'Whatever. It still sucks and I'm glad it's shutdown. When are we eating? I'm hungry.'

'Did you see any of Rachel's friends on the way home?'

'I don't think so.' Annie opened the fridge and snapped a chunk of cheese off a block of cheddar. She pushed it into her mouth before her mother could tell her not to.

'Don't eat cheese now,' Pauline said. 'You'll ruin your tea.'

'It won't ruin my tea because I'm hungry. I haven't eaten much today. School dinners are so boring. School sucks.'

'Yes, you said. Did you speak to Rachel at all today?'

'Nope. It's school, Mum. We avoid our siblings at school. They're so not cool. What time are we eating?' Annie mumbled through a mouthful of cheese.

'When your sister decides to show up,' Pauline said, quietly. She felt a shiver run down her spine; it felt like ice-cold fingers had touched her soul. Something wasn't right.

'It smells good in here. I'm starving. No more school until September. Crazy times,' Rob said, walking into the kitchen. He was handsome, tall, and filling out. His hair was cut short to his scalp.

'That sounds so good,' Annie said. 'No more school until September.' She turned to Rob. 'Mary Harris says the virus was made in a lab in China to kill all the wrinklies over sixty and stop global warning.'

'Do you mean global warming?' Rob asked, laughing. 'Your friend Mary is a dunce,' he added. He opened the fridge and snapped some cheese off the block. 'What's for tea?'

'Chilli. Don't eat any more cheese. It'll ruin your tea,' Pauline said.

'It won't, Mum. I'm starving.'

'Did you see your sister after school?' Pauline asked.

'Which one?' Rob said. 'The orange one who pouts like a duck on Instagram or the little gobby one who farts like a bloke?'

'I'm here thank you and I don't fart like a bloke,' Annie said, blushing.

'You fart in bed when you're asleep. I can hear you through the wall.'

'You're such a dick.'

'Don't call your brother a dick, please. I don't like that language in this house. It's crude, Annie.'

'I'm just telling the truth. He's a dick and I do not fart in my sleep. He's being crude first.'

'Sorry, Annie. Of course, you don't fart in your sleep,' Rob said, pretending to cry.

'Shut up, Rob the knob,' Annie mumbled, still chewing the cheese. 'You really are a dick.'

'Pack it in, the pair of you,' Pauline said, frustrated. 'You drive me around the bend. Why can't you just get on?'

'Because he's such a dick. Simples.'

'I won't tell you again, Annie. Pack it in.' Pauline checked the clock again. The feeling of impending doom was worsening. 'We can't eat until Rachel decides to appear. Are you sure you haven't seen her on the way home?'

'Definitely not,' Rob said. 'I saw her orange friend, Sandra and the other pouters walking home but Rach wasn't with them. I don't think so, anyway.'

'Ring her on your phone please,' Pauline said. 'Tell her I'm dishing up in five minutes or tea will be ruined.'

'Why me?' Rob asked, whining. 'I've only got a bit of credit on my phone.'

'Don't argue with me, Rob,' Pauline said. 'Just ring her, please.' Rob rolled his eyes and stabbed at his screen. 'Your nails need cleaning,' Pauline noted. 'Are either of you listening to what's going on around you? You both need to wash your hands before you sit at the table.'

'Don't stress, Mum. I will.' He called Rachel and waited for her to answer. After several attempts, he gave up. 'There's no answer,' Rob said. 'It's gone straight to voicemail.'

'What does that mean?'

'Her phone is off.'

'She never has her phone off,' Pauline said, biting her bottom lip.

'She might have run out of battery, probably drained it pouting on Instagram.'

'Oh, for God's sake,' Pauline muttered under her breath. 'Give it a rest, will you, Rob?' Her anxiety peaked. She turned off the gas. 'Annie, ring her friends, please.'

'Which one?' Annie said, frowning.

'All of them until we know where she is.'

'I'll ring Sandra first,' Annie said. 'She'll know where she is.' Pauline took a garlic bread out of the oven and sliced it up. Rob washed his hands in the sink, sensing her distress. He didn't like seeing his mum stressed out. She'd had a hard time bringing them up on her own after their father died of cancer. Her relationship with her current partner, Norman was only a few years old. He'd moved in eighteen months ago with his teenage son, Ricky, and the dynamic within the family had shifted; not for the better. They had a big house; all the kids had their own room, but it was not harmonious. He listened to Annie talking to Sandra, trying to find out where Rachel was.

His mum was worried; it was written all over her face. The virus was unsettling her, and she was addicted to watching the BBC news. It was making her anxious about the slightest thing. He thought she was overreacting again; sometimes her anxiety stopped her thinking clearly. Losing her husband at such a young age had made her overprotective of her children and the virus had frightened her. He heard Annie end the call.

'Sandra said that Rach texted her after school to say she had to go and see Miss Miles after school.'

'Why would she be seeing the head?' Pauline asked.

'I bet she's in detention,' Annie said. 'Can we eat now before I pass out from starvation?'

'Why would Rachel be in detention?' Pauline asked. 'She's never been in any trouble at school and the school is closing for God's sake.'

'I don't know. I'm not psychic.'

'Don't be cheeky with me, young lady,' Pauline said, wagging a finger. 'I've had just about enough of you.' Annie looked at the floor and blushed. 'Now, can you please tell me what Sandra said, exactly?'

'She said, Rachel sent her a text saying she wasn't walking home with them because she had to see Miss Miles,' Annie said, shrugging. 'You have two other children, Mum, and we're both Starvin Marvin. I'm thinking of calling Childline to report you for neglect.'

'Grow up, Annie.' Pauline checked the time again. She felt partly relieved. At least she knew where she was or, did she? The school was closing. Rachel had sent a text to her friend, but the school wouldn't keep a pupil behind for more than an hour. Sometimes they had after school competitions, like the chess club and a gaming society but those events were all prearranged and Rachel wasn't a member of either. It didn't feel right.

'Can we eat, please?' Annie moaned.

'Put the knives and forks on the table and stop moaning, Annie,' Pauline said, abruptly. Annie was about to answer back but the look on her mother's face warned her not to. She dished out five portions of rice and chilli and put two of them in the oven. The other three plates were put onto the table. 'Get the drinks, Rob,' she added. Rob poured three glasses of orange juice from a carton and took them to the table; Annie sat down and ploughed into her chilli, like she hadn't eaten for a week. Pauline took out her phone and scrolled through the numbers.

'Are you not eating with us, Mum?' Rob asked, shovelling food into his mouth.

'Not yet,' Pauline said. She found the number for the school and dialled. It rang out a dozen times before it was answered.

'Ysgol Bodedern,' an irritated voice answered.

'Hello. I'm sorry to call at this time but my daughter had to see Miss Miles after school and she hasn't come home yet,' Pauline said, quickly. 'I wonder if you can tell me what time she'll be there until.'

'What is your daughter's name?'

'Rachel Evans,' Pauline said. 'Her sister Annie and brother Rob are pupils there too,' she added, nervously.

'Yes. I know exactly who she is. I'm speaking to Pauline, right?'

'Yes.'

'Hello, Pauline. We've met a few times at parents' evening. This is Beverley Miles. I'm a little confused. Rachel didn't come to see me after school.' There was a nervous silence.

'She didn't?'

'No, Pauline, she didn't. Who said she was coming to see me?'

'Her friend, Sandra. Sandra Thomas.'

'What did she say?'

'She said that Rachel sent her a text saying that she wasn't walking home with her friends because she had to see you about the school closing down.'

'I have no idea why she would say that, but I'm the only person in the building. There're no after-school activities today because of the shutdown.' Another tense few seconds ticked by. 'I don't know what to tell you. Have you contacted her other friends?'

'No. Not yet. When Sandra said she was with you, I didn't want to bother anyone. I thought she was there.'

'Okay, that's perfectly understandable.'

'I'm worried sick.'

'I'm sure there's a perfectly reasonable explanation. I'll help you find her, Pauline. Don't worry. I have a good idea who her friends are, and I have their contact details to hand. I'll make some calls from this end. I suggest you do the same with her non-school friends and family. If either of us track her down, we'll call the other. How does that sound to you?'

'It makes perfect sense, Beverley. Thank you very much for your help. It's much appreciated. I'll ring you back shortly. Thanks again.'

'It's absolutely no problem at all. Don't worry, we'll find her.'

The call ended but Pauline kept the phone to her ear, her mind in a spin. An ice-cold shiver ran through her soul. She instinctively knew something terrible had happened.

CHAPTER 4

Walter Dallow sat in his Range Rover on Walthew Avenue, looking down the hill at the sea. The avenue was wide and sloped gently to the marina. He could see the lighthouse at the end of the breakwater; its beam of light turned relentlessly, piercing the night. Three-storey buildings lined the road. Most of them were once guest houses, the hub of the town's bed-and-breakfast offering but those days were long gone. Premier Inns, the expansion of caravan parks and a Travel Lodge absorbed the visitors now. Times had changed. Floral quilts, pot-pourri, shared bathrooms, and toast racks were a thing of the past.

To his left, spotlights illuminated the park across the road. At its centre, built on a grassy knoll was a new skateboard park. A group of teenagers were riding their boards up and down the half-pipes, turning and spinning and performing stunts that would make their parents uneasy, were they watching. One of them spotted his vehicle. She waved and peeled away from the other skateboarders, riding her board down the path towards the park gates. He lost sight of her behind some trees.

'Is that her?' his companion, Dave, asked. Dave was wearing a dark leather jacket which covered his substantial frame. His nose was flattened against his face, giving him the look of a pugilist.

'Yes. That's Louise Lee.'

'Do you want me to bring her here?'

'No need. I'll go to her. I want her to trust me. You'll frighten the life out of the girl.'

'What are trying to say?'

'That you look like a thug and you're too heavy handed.'

'I am a thug. That's what you pay me to be. And you can't talk.'

'You do exactly what it says on the tin. Don't change a thing.'

'I don't intend to.'

'You just stay in the car. I need this to go smoothly.'

'What, like the last one?'

'Shut up, Dave.'

Dave grumbled something and tilted his seat back. He closed his eyes. Walter opened the door and climbed out. A cold wind was blowing from the direction of Holyhead Mountain. It touched his exposed flesh with icy gusts. He liked coming to the island and staying in the cottage but it was windy. Especially at this time of year. Winter was well underway. Every time he came across the Menai Bridge, he felt cold. It seemed that the further across the island he drove, the windier it became. Ultimately, it was a rock in the middle of the Irish Sea, a pretty rock but a rock, nonetheless. The business made it a worthwhile journey, cold or not. This was the last stop of the day and once he'd finished here, he would drop Dave off at the station and it was less than twenty-minutes back to the cottage. Despite a few hiccups, by the end of the day, he would be ten-grand better off. Dealing with teenagers had its ups and downs but it wasn't as dangerous as working the city. If the lockdown happened, the lowest levels of society would suffer the most. There would be no money and no drugs and that would make the streets a powder keg waiting to explode. As he approached the park, he heard the gates creaking; the hinges needed oiling.

'All right, Walter,' Louise said, bumping his elbow. 'No shaking hands anymore. I don't know where you've been.' Her baseball cap was back-to-front. Louise was fourteen. She was already taller than him. Her cheekbones were high and defined and her blue eyes sparkled. She held her skateboard under one arm and looked around nervously. She shifted her gaze from one end of the road to the other.

'You look nervous. What's up?'

'The cops have been patrolling all night. Let's go into the park where they can't see us from the road.'

'Are they looking for someone?' Walter asked, looking up and down the road. The hinges squealed again as they went into the park.

'They're always looking for someone. We'll be fine in here.'

'Let's go over there,' Walter said, pointing to the bowling green. There was a wooden clubhouse shrouded in shadows. The street lights didn't penetrate the night that far. 'The clubhouse looks safe enough.'

'No. Not there. Come this way,' Louise said, taking the other path. She gestured in the other direction. 'The houses on Porth-y-Felin overlook the bowling green. They're owned by wrinklies who spend their time looking out of the window. Some of them keep a log of what they see and give them to the police.'

'Some people can't mind their own business, Louise,' Walter said. 'Live and let live, I say. At home in Liverpool, we call them nosey bastards.'

'Same here. My uncle lives on that street and he's a nosey bastard. He told my mam he'd seen me smoking in the park last week.'

'Did she go mad?' Walter asked, following her towards an old toilet block. He could see a dull yellow glow inside it.

'Nah. She knew I smoked anyway. I've been smoking since I was ten. She doesn't give a toss what I do. Half the time she's bumming them off me when she's skint,' Louise said, spitting into the bushes. She cleared her throat and spat a second time. Walter sensed it was an act to make him think she was tough. He wasn't impressed. He didn't need tough, he needed obedient.

'How's business been?' he asked.

'I've had a good week. I nearly ran out of weed. I'm going to need more this week.'

'Good girl. What kind of feedback are you getting?'

'It's all good stuff, especially the weed. My mates are loving the skunk; best they've had, they reckon.'

'That's good to hear,' Walter said. 'I told you it was all good gear. Stick with me, and you'll go far. This is just the start. Once you've grown your client list, you'll be minted. Just make sure you keep it all under wraps. Don't sell to anyone you don't know and don't go bragging to your mates or online and don't go spending your money like a prick. People will notice if you start buying watches and designer gear. Keep it all hidden for now.'

'I will, don't worry about that. I'm not stupid. My mam watches me like a hawk. I can't get away with anything.'

'That's not a bad thing. Just be smart.'

'Don't worry. Nothing goes home with me and everything is well hidden.'

'What about the cash?'

'Do you mean my till?' she said, chuckling. Walter called her takings the *till*. She didn't have a clue what he was talking about the first time he said it. She had to ask him to explain what he meant. 'The only person who knows where my till is, is me,' she said, pointing to her chest. They elbow bumped again. 'I've got most of your money.'

'Most of it?'

'Yes. I split it up,' she said. 'Never keep it all in one place, you said.'

'Smart girl,' Walter said, smiling. She was a protégé.

'I do listen to what you say,' she said. 'Let's go in here, Wally.'

'Lead the way.' He didn't like being called Wally but she was cute so he would put up with it for now. He needed to earn her trust. Slowly, slowly, catches the monkey.

'No one will see us in here.'

Louise turned off the path and headed into the ladies' toilets. Walter smiled and nodded. He was impressed. The kid knew there was little chance of being disturbed in a public toilet after dark, especially if they used the ladies' side.

'Very smart kid,' Walter said. He took a quick look up the path towards the street lights. There wasn't a soul around. As he walked into the ladies, the smell of urine, excrement, and disinfectant was overwhelming. 'Bloody hell. The drains need sorting out in here.'

The concrete floor was wet and the paint on the walls was peeling in places. Louise was waiting at the far end, next to the last cubicle. She was taking a roll of twenty-pound notes out of her underwear.

'I like the look of that, kid. How much is there?' Walter asked.

A tall figure stepped out of the cubicle. He stood over six-feet-four, wearing a dark tracksuit and a beanie hat. The hat was Stone Island, the tracksuit Hugo boss; the grin on his face contained no mirth in it. Walter took a few steps backwards but was stopped by three other men who had come out of the cubicles behind him; all built like gorillas. A hard shove in the back pushed him forward.

'Where are you going, Wally?' one of them asked.

The tall man took the roll of money from Louise. 'Look what we have here,' he said, waving the money. 'We have a little Scouser on our patch, selling his shit to kids from our town. We can't have that, now can we?'

'What are you doing here, little Scouser?' one of the men behind him asked, slapping him across the back of his head. 'This isn't Liverpool. Are you lost?'

'Are people looking for you?' Another laughed. 'You've got your own books. Where's Wally?'

'What is going on, Louise?' Walter asked, shrugging. 'This isn't good. Did you set me up?'

Louise blushed and stared at the floor. She was scared. Her eyes filled with tears.

'It's not her fault. She's just a kid.'

'Kid or not, setting up a mate is out of order,' Walter said. 'I'm very disappointed.'

'Get lost, Louise,' the tall man said, putting the roll of notes into his pocket. Louise looked confused. 'What are you waiting for? I said, get lost.'

'What about my money?' Louise asked.

'Piss off, Louise,' the man said. He slapped her across the back of the head. 'Go now before I break your head.' Louise walked quickly, passing Walter with her head down. When she got to the door, she ran. They waited until she'd left. 'My name is Mike. Mike Smith. People call me Smithy.' Smithy pointed to himself. 'Have you heard of me?'

'Yes.' Walter nodded. 'I have heard of you.'

'Good. What have you heard?'

'Only bad things,' Walter said, shrugging. He half-smiled. 'No point in lying to you, is there.'

Smithy laughed and nodded. 'You're a funny man. He's funny, isn't he?' The men behind Walter chuckled like they had grit in their throats. 'Did anyone warn you that I run things over the border?' Smithy waited for an answer but didn't get one. 'Let me explain the situation to you. Across the border in England, you lot can do as you please. You can sell your shite to kids wherever you like. We don't care what you do to each other. You can make your alliances; you can shoot each other; you can steal each other's gear and stick it where the sun doesn't shine but you don't cross that border and trade without our knowing about it.' He paused again. 'There's three and half grand in there,' he said, patting his pocket. 'Louise is a nice kid. Not too bright but a nice kid. Her mother is a real scumbag, isn't she, lads?' The men behind Walter agreed. 'She's always pissed, and she'll do pretty much anything or anyone for the price of a bottle of vodka, less when she's strung out. Louise has done well getting this far to be honest. She's a lovely girl.'

'I'm not a social worker. Why are you telling me this?' Walter asked.

'I'm curious how an outfit from over a hundred miles away has recruited a young girl from here to sell your gear?'

'It's not rocket science. They all want to earn money.'

'Enlighten me how you found Louise.'

'Facebook. The internet makes the world a smaller place,' Walter said, shrugging. 'I gave her an opportunity and she took it. That's all. It's not a big deal, is it?'

'It is a big deal to me. Because when you step into a small town and recruit a fourteen-year-old girl to sell drugs for you, every man and his dog will know about it the next day.'

'I may have underestimated that.'

'Oh, you did indeed. This is a small town and reputations count for everything. Everyone knows what everyone else is doing.' Smithy laughed and shook his head. 'I don't know how you thought you could get away with it. We knew she was dealing the day after she started, so obviously, we needed to know who she was dealing for, which didn't take long and here we are just a week later having this little chat.'

'Okay, it's a small town and I've stepped on your toes. I didn't mean any disrespect. It's just business.'

'You didn't mean to disrespect me. What did you mean to do?' Smithy asked, shaking his head. 'We were always going to find out and we were always going to be pissed off by someone trading on our patch. A fourteen-year-old girl operating on my patch is dangerous. The next thing you know, they'll all be at it.' Smithy lit a cigarette. 'Do you watch the news, Walter?'

'Sometimes. All this virus stuff is hard to avoid.'

'There's more than one virus, Walter,' Smithy said. 'You should keep up with what's going on. Teenagers are stabbing each other to death in London and all over the place. Knife crime is through the roof and do you know why?'

'I'm sure you're going to enlighten me.'

'I will. They're knifing each other because twats like you are turning them into drug dealers. They're stabbing each other for turf; turf which would otherwise be controlled by people like us. We maintain the balance, Walter, not teenagers. We maintain the peace. Teenagers can't control their rivals without stabbing them. I'm not having that here in our town. You're crossing the border and bringing the plague with you.'

'That's a bit dramatic,' Walter said. A cold silence answered him. Smithy glared at him with contempt. 'Look, I've apologised. What more can I do?

'You have apologised, and your apology is worth shit.'

'What else can I do?' Walter shrugged.

'You seem to be taking this very lightly. Do you realise how much trouble you're in?'

'It's a few grand. I'm sure we can smooth things over.'

'I doubt it.'

'Look, keep the money and I'm gone. I won't tread on your toes again,' Walter said. 'We shouldn't have come to your town. Lesson learned and no harm done.'

'I'd like to believe that, Wally but unfortunately, I don't.' Smithy shrugged. 'You see, we're going to take your money and your drugs from you and that will cause problems with your employers.'

'It's nothing I can't handle. There's no need to overreact. Like I said earlier, it's just business. I meant no offence.'

'It's not you I'm concerned about because the drugs and money we're taking from you, don't belong to you.'

'What do you mean?'

'You're way down the ladder. You haven't paid your boss for them yet. You're just a puppet for some tinpot gangster in the big city who is trying to sell their shit to kids along the coast. Our coast and our kids.'

'That sounds like a fair description,' Walter agreed, reluctantly. 'In reality, I just do as I'm told. I was told to recruit down the Welsh coast, so I did.'

'Do you know why people from the cities are targeting rural areas and the coastline?'

'Easy money,' Walter replied.

'Easy money?' Smithy asked, calmly. 'It isn't looking that easy from where I'm standing. How did it work out for you, Wally?'

'It's not been my best day at work, to be honest.' Walter shrugged and blushed.

'I'm guessing your boss crosses the border because they haven't got the bollocks or the muscle to sell it on your own patch. Liverpool is a tough patch.'

'You've got that one wrong. You're way off the mark. She does okay,' Walter said.

'She?' Smithy looked surprised.

'Don't underestimate her just because she's female.'

'It isn't me who is underestimating people,' Smithy said. 'Your boss is recruiting kids in North Wales because she'd be crushed like a cockroach by the real dealers in the city.'

'You're wrong. She's been around as long as I can remember,' Walter said. 'But things have changed in the cities, hence the expansion.'

'Explain it to me,' Smithy said, playing dumb.

'The drug squad and Matrix teams have got so many undercover officers that we don't know who we can trust and who we can't anymore. It's making business difficult.'

'I understand. The police don't have teenage undercover officers so you know you're safe using kids to move your shit. So, she sends jokers like you to recruit kids to sell it for you along the coast. Our coast. You can bully them because they're kids but you've come too far this time.'

'Pretty much.'

'The way I see it, we can send you home with a good hiding and take your money,' Smithy said. 'Your boss might kick you out of the job but then she'll just send another dick-head here next week to take your place and we can't have that, you see. I haven't got the time to be chasing you all over North Wales. I'm going to have to send a stern message to your boss. She needs to know coming onto our turf is a fatal mistake.'

'Fatal?' Walter said. 'Oh, come on. There's no need for anyone to get hurt. I'll tell her to stay off your patch,' Walter said, starting to panic. He didn't like where this was going.

'I don't think she would listen to you. You're clearly shit at your job, so why would she?'

'I'll tell her not to dabble here. I'll make her listen. If she sacks me, she sacks me. I could leave the company and go it alone, maybe come and work for you?' Walter said, trying to lighten the situation.

'Now, you are joking,' Smithy said, laughing dryly. 'You're an amateur. You wouldn't last five minutes with the big boys. That's why they sent you to bully the kids. No, I'm afraid there's no position for you here and we really need to let your employer know that we don't tolerate people trying to operate here; especially using kids.'

'I'll take the message back to her for you,' Walter said. 'You don't need to do anything stupid. She'll understand that we've crossed the wrong people.' He waited for Smithy to answer but he didn't. 'You clearly have a handle on everything here. She's a smart lady. She'll listen.'

Smithy rubbed his chin in thought and shook his head. 'That's not how these things work, Wally. This is a dangerous game and the penalties for screwing up are dire. She should have explained that to you.'

'She didn't explain how tied up you have it here. I thought North Wales would be a mishmash of one-man bands.'

'It pays to do your homework, Wally. That was a fatal mistake.'

'Look, Smithy, I just want to go home. I don't want any trouble. This is the very last job I'm doing for her. I'm out.'

'It's too late. You're not going home today,' Smithy said with no emotion in his voice. His eyes were ice cold. 'You're not going home ever.'

'Come on, Smithy,' Walter pleaded. 'I've made a mistake recruiting here but I haven't hurt anyone and there's no threat to your operation.'

'I'll tell you what I'll do for you,' Smithy said, raising his forefinger.

'What?' Walter said, sensing some hope. 'I'll do anything to sort this out.'

'You tell us where the rest of your gear is stashed, turn over your till and give me all the information about who you work for and where she operates from and we'll work something out so you get home in one piece. How does that sound?'

'She'll kill me,' Walter said. 'The guy who's with me is a total nutcase. He has some of the gear and money on him. If I ask him for it, he'll kill me before we get off the island, but I'll give you what I have on me.'

'Your minder was taken care of before you entered the park, Wally. You don't have to worry about him; he's gone and so is your Range Rover.'

'Gone where?'

'Gone, Wally. Use your imagination. He won't be seen again.'

'Oh shit,' Walter said. He felt his knees tremble. 'Have you done him in?'

'Don't worry about him. What you need to worry about is us. You need to think about your next words very carefully,' Smithy said.

'Here's the money I have on me and here are the drugs I was going to give to Louise.' He handed two rolls of notes to one of the men behind him. The man counted it. The second man took several bags of drugs.

'Seven grand,' he grunted. 'Coke and skunk bagged up ready for sale.'

'And I'll tell you whatever you want to know.' Walter sighed. Any hope that Big Dave would come running to his rescue was dashed. Dave was a big man and mad as a bull with a wasp on its arse. He also carried a gun. If they'd taken him out of the equation, he had no chance on his own. All he could do was tell them what they wanted to know and hope they would be true to their word. 'You've got all the gear and money and I'll tell you what you want to know. That must count for something?'

'What do you think, boys?' Smithy asked. 'Do we let Wally go or do we throw him off the mountain?'

'I vote we throw him in the sea.'

'Yep. Toss him off the breakwater. Don't let him walk away.'

'Throw him off the mountain and let's bet on how long he floats.'

'If he floats. Reedy didn't float.'

'Don't throw me off the mountain, please,' Walter said. 'I have a wife and three kids.' He lied. 'I've said sorry and you'll never hear of me again.'

'I think the boys want to throw you off the mountain. It's their favourite, to be honest.'

'Please,' Walter asked, lips quivering.

'I'll think about it. In the meantime, strip him.'

'There's no need to do that,' Walter protested. He didn't struggle as he was stripped to his underwear. His body began to shake with the cold and fear.

'It's got to be done, I'm afraid. Tie his hands and feet and put him in that stall,' Smithy said. The man pushed him into a cubicle and fastened his limbs with duct tape. When they were done, they sat him down on the floor between the toilet and the wall. Smithy came to the stall and looked at him. He closed the door.

'Put the cocaine in his pocket,' Smithy whispered.

'Why are you doing that?'

'It just seems fair to me,' Smithy said, smiling. 'Make yourself comfortable until we get back. If you move, you're going for a long swim, understand?' Walter nodded his head. 'Tape his mouth and his eyes.' The men followed orders. 'I'll be back in ten minutes.'

They pulled the door closed and he heard their footsteps leaving the toilet block. Their voices were hushed, but he knew they were discussing whether to kill him or not. His muscles were aching but he daren't move. All he could do was wait.

CHAPTER 5

Pauline put the phone down and felt the knot growing in her stomach. She felt like she was going to vomit. There was no one left to contact. She'd exhausted all close family members, extended family members, and casual acquaintances. Beverley Miles had called everyone in Rachel's social circle and beyond, with the same result. No one had seen Rachel leave school or heard from her since. She'd simply vanished.

'Any news, mum?' Rob asked. Her expression answered his question without words. She shook her head. 'Alright, then I'm going out to look for her. She must be out there somewhere,' he said. 'Annie will come with me, won't you?' Annie nodded, reluctantly. 'Let's go to the school and walk the route back here together,' he said. 'What did Miss Miles say to do?'

'She said to send out family and friends around her usual haunts and in the meantime, notify the police,' Pauline said. The front door opened and her heart stopped beating for a second. 'Rachel, is that you?'

Norman walked down the hallway, whistling tunelessly. His cheeks were glowing and his eyes were bleary. He sensed the atmosphere and frowned.

'What's the matter?' he slurred a little.

'Are you pissed?' Pauline asked, shaking her head. 'That's all I need.'

'I'm not pissed,' Norman said, slurring slightly. He was trying hard not to appear as drunk as he was. 'What's wrong with everyone? You've got a face like a smacked arse.'

'Rachel hasn't come home from school,' Rob said. 'Mum is worried.'

'If she hasn't come home, she'll be with her friends,' Norman said, checking his watch. He walked into the kitchen and sniffed the air. 'I can smell chilli. Nice one, I'm starving. Have you saved me some?' he asked, opening the oven.

'Ignore him, mum,' Annie said. 'We'll go and look for her. You call the police.'

'You're not calling the police because she's a bit late, are you?' Norman called from the kitchen. 'Don't overreact. She's with one of her mates or a boy, guaranteed.' The sound of plates clinking came through. 'Did you do any chips with this?' he asked. 'You have to have chips with chilli.'

'No. I didn't make chips and Rachel isn't with a boy, Norman,' Pauline snapped. She had an idea her daughter was gay, but she'd kept it to herself. 'She wouldn't go anywhere without letting me know.'

'Whatever you say. You're still overreacting.'

'Mum is very worried, Norman. So, wind your neck in,' Rob said, poking his head into the kitchen. 'We're going to the school to look for her. Mum is going to phone the police. Try not to wind her up anymore than she already is, please. She's very worried.'

'I don't need relationship advice from a kid, thank you,' Norman mumbled. 'Everything has to be a crisis in this house.'

'That's the perfect attitude to have right now,' Rob said, sarcastically. He put a thumbs up sign. 'Nice one, Norman. Make it look like you actually give a shit, why don't you?' Rob walked away before Norman could reply. He gestured to Annie. 'Let's go and have a look for her before I punch him in the face.'

'Don't start please, Rob,' Pauline said.

'I'm not starting. He's a dick and he's getting on my nerves. Give the police a call, Mum. It can't hurt to ask them to help.'

Pauline nodded and picked up the phone. Her hands were shaking as she dialled.

CHAPTER 6

Walter's muscles were beginning to cramp. His legs were numb, and his fingers had pins and needles in them. He needed to move, despite what he'd been told to do. His throat was dry, and he was starting to gag. If he was sick, he would choke, and he was dead. Trying to quell the feeling he was going to vomit was proving difficult. He twisted his hips and wriggled his legs to try to get his circulation moving but the space between the toilet bowl and the cubicle wall was minute. Footsteps echoed outside. He could hear people on the path, and he froze. They were coming back; probably to kill him. Deep voices talked in hushed tones as they neared. There was a burst of noise, like static and the sound of a voice on a device of some kind. It wasn't them. He heard people entering the toilet block and he started to kick his feet at the door to attract attention. Voices were raised and he heard boots splashing in the water on the floor. The door opened and the voices became alarmed. He felt hands on his shoulders and under his armpits, pulling him up roughly. The tape was pealed from his lips and he inhaled deeply.

'Thank you,' he gasped. He felt the tape being pulled from his eyes, painfully. His vision was blurred, and he could see police uniforms. 'Oh shit,' he muttered.

'What's your name?' a female officer asked him.

'Walter,' he said.

'Okay, Walter,' Kim said. 'I'm DI Davies. We're going to get you out of this cubicle. Are these your clothes?' she asked, holding up his jeans, jumper, and jacket. Walter nodded. 'You're absolutely sure they're yours?'

'Yes. They're mine.' Uniformed officers removed the tape from his hands and legs. The blood flowed back to his extremities. They put a silver thermal blanket around him. 'I'm so glad you're here. How did you find me?' Walter babbled. 'They said they were going to throw me off the mountain. I thought they were going to kill me.'

'Who was going to kill you, Walter?'

'I don't know who they were. I came in to use the toilet and they jumped me.'

'Really. You're in the ladies'.'

'Am I? My mistake.'

'Don't try to bullshit me. You know who they were,' Kim said, nodding. 'Where are you from, Walter?' the DI asked, searching the pockets of his clothing. She checked his ID and rifled through his wallet.

'Liverpool,' Walter said.

'That's a coincidence because we've just arrested a man in a black Range Rover outside on Walthew Avenue. His name is Dave Timpson and he's from Liverpool too.' Walter swallowed hard. He couldn't comprehend what he was hearing. 'Do you know him?'

'Dave is still outside in the car?' he stuttered.

'Yes. He's exactly where you left him. Why, does that surprise you?'

'I'm not surprised,' Walter lied.

'You look surprised.'

'No. I'm just glad he's okay.'

'He was sleeping when we got there.'

'I'm still not surprised.'

'Would it surprise you to know he had a gun on him?'

'Yes. It would.'

'He had a gun on him, so he's in a lot of trouble. You both are.' She held up the bags of cocaine and a roll of money. 'Are these yours?'

Walter shook his head. 'I've never seen them before. Someone must have planted them in my pocket.'

'That's another coincidence,' she said. 'Your friend Dave said the same thing. He also said the drugs in the vehicle must belong to you and that he didn't know they were there. He said he just works for you and everything in the vehicle belongs to you.'

'He's a liar. I don't know anything about any drugs in that motor,' Walter said. Kim held up two mobile phones. She scrolled through the contacts and recent calls. 'They're not mine either.'

'Walter,' Kim said, sighing. 'We're going to contact every number in both phones. We'll dump all the GPS information for today to see where you've been, and we'll analyse the social media and email communications. It won't take long to identify the phones belong to you.' Walter blushed and looked at the floor. 'So, let's not bullshit each other or this will take a lot longer than it needs to, okay?'

'Okay. How did you know I was here?'

'We had a tip off that there was a drug deal going on in the park toilets and that the Range Rover parked on Walthew Avenue was involved and that the passenger in the vehicle would be armed.'

'A tip off, eh?' Walter muttered beneath his breath.

'Yes. A tip off. Now then, who do you think made that call?'

'I've got no idea,' Walter said. 'And I don't know anything about any drug deals.'

'Okay, have it your way. We've already contacted the Matrix unit in Liverpool. They have your vehicle on their books and your friend Dave Timpson is fairly high up on their watch list, as are you. I'm not sure exactly how Matrix work but here in Wales, we would say Dave Timpson is fucked. You both are. We'll be handing you over to the drug squad from St Asaph and you'll be transferred and charged depending on whatever they come up with from your phone records.'

'They're not mine.'

'Matrix are saying they've been watching that vehicle in connection to child exploitation enquiries along the Welsh coast.'

'I don't know anything about their enquiries.'

'It's called 'child exploitation' for a reason, Walter. They call it County Lines nowadays and people caught exploiting vulnerable children are being sent to jail for a very long time. My advice to you is to limit the amount of time you're going to serve.' Walter looked at her and nodded. 'Take him to Caernarfon. The officers from St Asaph are already on their way to pick them up.'

The uniformed officers let him put his shoes and trousers on and then led him away. Kim followed them, hanging back a little. There were a group of youths on the skateboard park at the top of the knoll, sitting on the concrete ramps, smoking cigarettes. The tips glowed red in the darkness. She could hear them laughing on the wind. They were too young to be pulling the strings. Whoever had made the call to the tip-line was much older and much wiser. Walter and his associate were on enemy soil and someone wasn't happy with that. The best way to dispose of the opposition without murdering people was to throw them under the bus. Handing them to the police was simple. The judicial machine would take them out of circulation for a while. There were a handful of suspects locally, who were capable of that and they would be long gone by now, sitting in a pub laughing about it. She knew they were fighting a losing battle. The drugs business would always be around even if the faces of those in charge changed periodically. Ventures from the big cities into her jurisdiction were becoming increasingly more frequent and the use of children was on the rise. This one had ended quickly and peacefully but she didn't think all of them would. Not a chance. There would be retaliation and it would be swift.

CHAPTER 7

Alan and Kim arrived at the Evans residence at ten o'clock in the evening. A family liaison officer, Julie Caldwell had been there for an hour and Bob Dewhurst had balled together half a dozen uniformed officers and a dozen or so volunteers to do an unofficial walk through the playing fields and woodlands behind the school. Bob approached Alan and Kim as they reached the driveway which was full of vehicles. It was a big house with five bedrooms and a double garage attached to the side. The gardens were illuminated by security lights; they were expansive but not well kept. It looked like a keen gardener had once lived there but hadn't been there for a long time. The borders had lost their shape and were full of weeds. People were coming and going through the front door as friends and family rallied around. Alan noticed a boy in his teens leaning against the wall, one foot raised behind him, smoking a cigarette. No one was interacting with him and he appeared to be oblivious to what was going on around him. His disinterest made him stand out.

'Any sign of her?' Alan asked Bob.

'Nothing yet. I've set up a search party. We're concentrating on the fields and woodland behind the school and checking the paths between there and here. It's dark and the undergrowth is thick, so it's slow going.'

'Why are we searching there in particular?' Kim asked.

'There're no sightings of her leaving the school grounds or walking her normal route home along the road. We're still checking the school CCTV in case we've missed anything but we're sure she didn't leave through the front gates. So, we're guessing she may have cut across the rugby pitches behind the school and gone through the woods. The path would bring her out at the end of the lane over there,' Bob said, pointing to a gap in the hedges further down the road. 'If she's fallen and hurt herself, she might be stuck in the woods. If she is, we'll find her.'

'She's been missing about six hours,' Alan said. 'Could this be a domestic issue?'

'No.'

'Are we sure we're not jumping the gun?'

'I don't think so. There's been no arguments or fallouts at home or at school. Rachel is never late home from school. She's a good kid from a good family and this is completely out of character.'

'Okay, that's good enough for me. What's Mum saying?' Kim asked.

'Her mother told me that she always answers her mobile within a couple of rings and on the odd occasion she's missed a call, she calls back straightaway. Her phone is switched off. That's unheard of.'

'Okay. What's the domestic situation?' Alan asked. 'Tell me what the family set up is.'

'Rachel's mum is Pauline. She has an older brother, Rob, he's fifteen and a younger sister, Annie, she's twelve. The stepdad is

Norman White, originally from Manchester; he's a self-employed builder and his son, Ricky, he's seventeen. Between us, we get the impression all is not a bed of roses between the siblings and stepdad. There seems to be an atmosphere.'

'When is it ever simple?' Alan said. 'Where is her real dad?'

'Died when the kids were young. Cancer apparently.'

'I want the siblings, stepdad, and his son spoken to and run through the system. Let's eliminate the family members first. Let's prepare for the worst and hope for the best.'

'I'm already on it,' Bob said. 'Richard Lewis is recovering whatever information Manchester have, just in case the Whites are known to us. Julie Caldwell is the FLO on this. She's in the living room with Mum.'

'Have the rest of the family been spoken to yet?' Alan asked.

'The sister Annie has been spoken to briefly because she called Rachel's friend earlier. The friend told her that Rachel said she had to go and see the headmistress after school, which wasn't true. That's why her friends walked home without her.'

'So, Rachel told her friends she had to be somewhere after class and that was a lie?' Kim said, frowning. 'Why would she lie to her friends?'

'No one can answer that at the moment.'

'So, clearly she was going to do something she didn't want anyone to know about,' Kim said.

'Are there any boyfriends, current, potential, or previous?' Alan asked.

'Not as far as we know. Mum says definitely not but you know what teenagers are like for telling lies,' Bob said. 'Mine could look me in the eye and tell me my name isn't Bob without blinking.'

'Let's hope Mum is wrong and she's with a boy or sulking about something somewhere,' Alan said.

'Fingers crossed. I'll leave you to carry on here. I'm going to catch-up with the search in the woods,' Bob said. 'Call me if you need anything.'

'Thanks, Bob,' Alan said. He looked at Kim and they walked towards the front door. The young man he'd noticed earlier didn't look up as they approached. He pulled deeply on his cigarette and stared at his trainers. 'I'm guessing you must be Ricky,' Alan said. Ricky looked sheepish and nodded.

'Yes, I'm Ricky. Are you police?'

'Yes. We're detectives.'

'You look like police,' Ricky said.

'Thank you.'

'It wasn't a compliment.'

'I'm sure it wasn't. Are you staying out of the way?' Alan asked, smiling.

'Something like that.'

'Can't say I blame you. It must be panic stations in there?'

'Everyone is stressing and I feel like I'm a spare part,' Ricky said. 'I think it's best if I stay out of the way. Not that anyone will notice,' he added.

'Didn't you want to help with the search?' Alan asked. He studied the boy's reaction. He was skittish; very skittish. His cheeks reddened and there was a flash of anger in his eyes. 'There're quite a few volunteers helping to look for her. How come you haven't joined them?'

'I haven't been back from work very long,' Ricky said, shrugging. 'They'd already gone when I got home.'

'What time was that?' Alan asked.

'Pardon?' Ricky looked offended.

'When you got home. What time was it?'

'About nine. Maybe a bit later.'

'That's quite late, isn't it?' Alan pressed. 'What do you do?'

'I work as a trainee commis chef in Beaumaris.'

'Where?'

'The Liverpool Arms. I was on an 8-8 shift, but someone called in sick and I had to stay later. You can check with my boss if you like,' Ricky added.

'We will check. We check everything,' Alan said, nodding. Ricky blushed again. This time, he looked annoyed. There was something about his attitude bothering Alan, but he wasn't sure what it was. 'Shall we go and talk to the rest of the family inside,' Alan said to Kim. 'We'll need to speak to you again at some point. Don't go far away.'

'I'm not going anywhere. I live here,' Ricky said. He flicked his cigarette into the air, and it landed in a shower of sparks.

'Good man,' Alan said, nodding. The detectives walked into the house and closed the door.

'He looked dodgy,' Kim commented as they went inside.

'He was uncomfortable being questioned,' Alan said.

'I got that impression.'

'Makes me think he's been questioned before and it wasn't a pleasant experience.'

'Could be.'

'If he's telling the truth, he was on the other side of the island when Rachel left school, but we need to confirm that. Call Richard and have him check with Ricky's employers.'

'No problem,' Kim said, making the call.

They walked further into the house. The hallway was tastefully decorated in grey and white; laminate covered the floor and a carpeted stairway led to the upstairs. Photographs of local beauty spots were framed on the walls.

'Someone has an eye for a photograph,' Alan noted. 'Look at that. The Milky Way over Llandwyn chapel. That's incredible.'

'Very talented,' Kim agreed.

They reached the door to the living room and stepped inside. Julie Caldwell greeted them.

'Pauline. This is DI Alan Williams and DS Kim Davies. They're detectives,' she said, smiling. Pauline didn't look impressed. Her eyes were haunted. Alan had seen that look a hundred times. Nothing would comfort her until her child was returned unharmed. Trying to reassure her was a pointless task. She didn't need meaningless reassurance she needed her child safe at home. Alan had seen it too many times. Cases involving missing kids rarely ended well. The sad truth was, the longer time ticked by, the less likely it would end happily. The first hour following a child disappearance is called "the golden hour", outside of that, the odds of recovering them unhurt, tumble as the clocks tick by.

'This is Pauline's partner, Norman White,' Julie added as an afterthought. Her eyes indicated that he was a fly in the ointment. He was standing in the doorway to the kitchen and looked like he didn't want to be there. Alan sensed a barrier between him and Pauline; there was a tense atmosphere in the house. The smell of stale beer drifted to him. Norman looked as edgy as his son had. Something about them wasn't right. They were nervous around police officers. He could sense it a mile away.

'Why don't you take Norman into the kitchen and have a chat with him?' Alan said to Kim.

'What if I don't want to have a chat in the kitchen,' Norman said. He was a handsome thick set man with dark curly hair and a gold loop in his left ear. He was an older version of Ricky. Alan thought they could have Romany genes in them. He put Norman in his late thirties. 'I'm not a child.'

'Then don't behave like one,' Pauline said, shaking her head.

'What does that mean?' Norman asked, offended.

'Just don't be obnoxious,' Pauline said. She was an attractive woman, older than Norman; petite with a dark bob framing her face. 'I'm sorry. He's had a few pints and he's a prick when he's had beer.' Norman looked offended again but didn't argue. She turned to face him. 'Unless you haven't noticed, they've got a job to do. Go into the kitchen and speak to the lady or piss off out of my house.' Norman tutted and stormed out of the room into the kitchen.

'It's always your house when it suits you,' he muttered from the next room. 'I'll remember that the next time something needs fixing.'

'Grow up, Norman,' Pauline called after him. Kim and Alan exchanged glances and Kim followed him into the kitchen. 'Sorry but I can't be doing with his attitude tonight,' Pauline said. 'My nerves are shattered.'

'I understand. It's not a problem,' Alan said. He sat down on the armchair opposite her. 'Are you okay to answer a few questions?'

'Yes, of course.'

'Was Rachel okay when she left for school this morning?' Alan asked. Pauline looked confused. 'I mean was she behaving normally, acting the way she always would or was she anxious or worried about anything?'

'No, she was fine. She's been worried about this virus kerfuffle but who isn't? She was the same as always,' Pauline said. She looked thoughtful. 'At least, I think she was. It's so hectic here in the morning. Norman and Ricky are getting ready for work; the kids are getting ready for school and everyone wants the bathrooms at the same time. Rachel was her usual self, rude to Norman and Ricky and winding her sister up. She has a sarcastic sense of humour.'

'Are the kids close?' Alan asked.

'Rob and Rachel are like twins. Their banter is good natured. Annie idolises both of them,' Pauline said. Alan noted that she didn't mention her stepson. 'I made her a piece of toast to walk to school with. She kissed me and said she'd see me later like she always does.' A tear ran down her cheek. Alan gave her a chance to compose herself.

'What about in the past few days, any change in her mood or behaviour?' Pauline shook her head. 'She wasn't moody or brooding about anything?' Another shake of the head and a touch of uncertainty in the eyes. 'You've noticed nothing out of character?'

'No. Nothing.'

'How are things at school?' Alan asked.

'Good. She has good grades and lots of friends.'

'She gets on with other pupils, no bullying or arguments with anyone?'

'No. It's a good school. They don't allow any nonsense.'

'Okay, that's good. Does she have her own room?'

'You mean bedroom?' Pauline asked, confused. Alan nodded. 'Yes. They all do.' She paused. 'My husband had a good job before he died; he worked away on the rigs. Pancreatic cancer killed him when the kids were very young. Annie was eighteen months old when he was diagnosed. He was dead before her second birthday.'

'I'm very sorry to hear that,' Alan said. 'It must have been a very difficult time for you.'

'It was, but he was a practical man. He had life insurance, which paid for this place and a bit more,' she said. 'It's been a struggle, but my kids are all healthy and we do okay.'

'Rachel is fourteen?' Alan asked. He knew the answer but needed to get Pauline to open her mind and keep talking. She nodded. 'Don't take this the wrong way but I need to ask the question,' Alan said. 'Is she sexually active?' Pauline looked shocked but didn't answer straightaway. 'Does she have any boyfriends?'

'No. Not as far as I'm aware and she'd tell me if there was a boy on the scene.'

'What about previously?'

'No. She hasn't shown any interest in them, although she isn't short on offers online. She doesn't have much time for boys in the real world.'

'What about anyone interested in her?'

'There are plenty of them,' Pauline said. She shook her head. 'She's always posting selfies online. I used to look at her Facebook page to see who she was talking to. She's always mithered to death by boys, some much older. Some of them were men. We fell out about it a few times. I used to go mental.'

'I can imagine you would. What made you concerned?'

'There were too many comments for a mother to cope with. Some of them were very suggestive from older men. We had a few arguments about it. She blocked me in the end because I went on about it all the time. The truth is, she was far more capable of fending them off than I would have been. She puts a lot of pictures of herself online; some of them too provocative for my liking. I told her to curb it but that's what young girls do nowadays. They're selfie mad, aren't they?'

'My nieces are the same,' Alan said. 'The pictures they put online are so filtered, I don't recognise them. They don't look anything like they do in real life.'

'Rachel attracted a lot of attention. The more likes she got, the happier she was. She stopped telling me about the comments in the end because it caused arguments. Eventually, I stopped asking, to keep the peace.'

'Has she mentioned being bothered by anyone in particular?'

'No. She hasn't mentioned anything to me and I'm sure she would tell me if she was having trouble.' Pauline looked uncertain. 'At least, I think she would.'

'Does she use a tablet, iPad or laptop?'

'Yes. She has a Samsung. It's in her room. I think.'

'We'll need to look at it.'

'Okay.'

'Would you mind if I take a look at her room?' Alan asked.

'No. Of course not,' Pauline said. 'What are you looking for?'

'Nothing in particular,' Alan said. 'Anything out of the ordinary.'

'Out of the ordinary, like what?'

'I don't know until I see it. You might not notice something out of the ordinary that we might find as unusual. Sometimes people become oblivious to what they see every day. There may be something there which appears odd to me, that may not be odd to you.'

'I see.' Pauline looked confused. 'At least, I think I do.'

'You can show me where it is if you want to or you can tell me where it is, and I'll find my own way?' Kim stepped in from the kitchen. Her poker face gave nothing away. Pauline hardly noticed her arrival. She was focused on Alan. 'Just in time. I'm going to have a look around Rachel's bedroom.'

'Excellent. That was good timing,' Kim said. 'I'll come with you.'

'It's at the top of the stairs. First on the right,' Pauline said. 'Shall I show you?'

'There's no need, Pauline,' Alan said. 'We'll find it.' Pauline looked blankly at them as they left the room. They walked along the hallway and up the stairs. Norman watched them from the kitchen doorway. He looked as shifty as he had earlier. Rachel's door was half open. The smell of designer perfume from the cheaper end of the market, drifted to them. They stepped into the room and studied it. 'What did Norman have to say?' Alan asked, quietly.

'He's been working on a conservatory all day in Holyhead, Wian Street. He had an early finish today and went for a few beers in the Bull, Valley with his labourers. One of them has just had a baby, so they had more to drink than they normally would. He left his car at the pub and got a taxi home. He's definitely had a few. We can check out his whereabouts easily enough. Did Mum have anything useful to say?'

'Nope. Apart from the fact Rachel doesn't get on with Norman and Ricky, everything appears to be hunky dory. No problems at home and no problems at school.' Alan pointed to a Samsung tablet on the dressing table. 'We'll need that. You take that side of the room. I'll take this one.'

The single bed was unmade; the quilt had been thrown back. A paper tissue was balled next to the pillows. There was mascara smudged on it.

'It looks like she's been crying,' Kim said. There was more mascara on the pillowcase.

'I wonder what she was crying about?' Alan said. 'That's not a good sign.'

Kim noticed a paperback on the bedside table. The cover was a striking picture of a black woman crying; the backdrop was the African continent. It was titled, *The Journey*. Kim had read it the month before.

'She was reading this,' Kim said. 'It explains the tears.'

'Why, is it a tearjerker?'

'And some,' Kim said. 'I cried all the way through it.' She looked under the bed. There was a plate with a stale piece of pizza on it and a couple of pairs of trainers. Kim checked inside the shoes for anything hidden but they were empty.

Alan opened the wardrobe. It was crammed to bursting with clothes on hangers. A shelf at the top was overflowing with jumpers and jeans folded neatly into piles. He felt beneath each pile and found two, twenty-pound notes, leaving them where they were. At the bottom, beneath the clothes were shoes, a pair of boots, and some shoe boxes. He took them out and opened them. One of them was full of old birthday and Christmas cards, signed from Mum and Dad. A small teddy bear stared at him with button eyes. There were items of christening jewellery sat on top of the pile. A tiny silver bracelet looked old and tarnished. He put the shoebox back into the wardrobe and opened the second one. Inside was a Michael Kors shoulder bag. He unzipped it and whistled. Kim looked over his shoulder.

'What is it?'

'Money. All twenty-pound notes.'

'How much do you think is there?'

'About eight hundred,' Alan said, making a quick assessment, without touching the notes.

'That's a lot of money for a fourteen-year-old,' Kim said.

'It is a lot of money for me never mind a teenager,' Alan agreed. 'We need to ask her mum where it came from, but I'll be surprised if she knows it's there. Take the tablet. We need to dump what's on it and go through it. I think the answer to this is going to be online either on this or on her phone. Let's go and ask about the money.'

'Sorry. I overheard you. You need to ask me about what money?' Pauline asked from the landing.

'We've found something we need to ask you about.'

'What have you found?'

'There's quite a lot of money in a bag in the wardrobe,' Kim said. Pauline frowned and walked into the room. Alan pointed to the shoebox. 'Approximately eight-hundred pounds, all in twenty-pound notes. Did you know it was there?'

'No,' Pauline said, shaking her head. 'I don't know where she's got that from. Little bugger. She borrowed a fiver from me yesterday.' She tried to smile, but it didn't work. 'What's she doing with that much money?'

'She couldn't have saved it up?' Kim asked. Pauline shook her head again. 'Christmas money, birthday money; that type of thing?'

'No. She spends it as soon as she gets it. I've got no idea where she got that from.'

'We might find out something from her social media. We need to dump the information from her tablet,' Kim said. 'Is it okay if we take this?'

'Yes. Of course,' Pauline said, staring at the money. 'Do you think this could be linked to her not coming home?'

'Do you?' Alan asked. He watched her expression. There was nothing but anguish in her eyes. She wasn't hiding anything. 'Don't jump to conclusions. You're probably thinking the worst at the moment,' he said, trying to reassure her. 'When young people have a lot of money, people will automatically think they're up to no good; usually drugs or criminal activity of some kind but we need to keep all options on the table,' Alan said. 'Teenagers can be very entrepreneurial. It's way too early to be blinkered by anything at this stage.' His mobile rang. It was Richard Lewis calling from the station. 'Excuse me,' he said stepping out of the room. He answered the call on the landing. 'Hello, Richard.'

'Alanio,' Richard said, using his standard greeting. 'Bobio asked me to run a couple of names through Manchester's database.'

'And?'

'Ricky White is on the system.'

'Hold on a minute. I can't talk here,' Alan said. He walked into one of the other bedrooms to make sure no one could overhear the call. 'Go on.'

'He's on the sex offenders' register.'

'For what?' Alan asked. A knot formed in his stomach. He had a gut feeling something was not right with Ricky White and his father.

That was why they were so skittish. They knew his record would come out.

'Underage sex. He claimed it was consensual. They were seeing each other for a few months. He was fourteen, but the girl was only twelve, below the consenting limit. He was given a suspended sentence and put on the register. Part of the files have been sealed. Manchester are sending everything they have over to me now.'

'That puts a different perspective on things,' Alan said. 'We don't want this getting out to the press yet. Who else knows?'

'Just me and you and the DI in GMP for now.'

'Let's keep it that way,' Alan said. 'Did you contact Ricky's employers?'

'I did,' Richard said. 'The shift manager confirmed Ricky stayed on a few hours to cover a sickness.'

'Okay. What time did he leave?'

'After eight o'clock.'

'Okay. Despite the record, that rules him out of the picture.'

'Not necessarily,' Richard said.

'Why not?'

'I asked him what time Ricky took his break and how long they give their employees to eat. Breaks vary, depending how busy they are but the kitchen staff get an hour minimum, more if it's quiet.'

'And how long did he have?' Alan's pulse quickened.

'He doesn't know because he didn't take over the shift until six o'clock.' There was a pregnant pause. 'The dayshift manager authorised the dayshift breaks, and he isn't back on until six in the morning so, I'll have to speak to him directly tomorrow.'

'Can't we get hold of him sooner?'

'He said he tried to contact him on his mobile, but he didn't answer, and he doesn't have an up-to-date address.'

'Oh well. We'll have to wait then but that rules him back in,' Alan said. 'Call me when the files arrive from Manchester. Good work, Richard.' The call ended. Ricky White had just been catapulted to the top of the suspect list, despite there being no proof a crime had been committed; yet.

CHAPTER 8

Rob Evans shone his torch on the path in front of him. The path curved to the left. Bare branches dangled from the trees, swaying in the breeze like skeletal fingers trying to reach the searchers. Another path forked to the right, which he knew led to the road. He looked around at the line of searchers. Beams of light probed the trees which surrounded him, and a dozen voices called Rachel's name. They were answered by silence. He'd seen similar events on the television and the endings were never good. This wasn't television, it was real life. It was a surreal scene, police officers, friends, and strangers searching for his younger sister in the pitch-darkness, soaked by the rain. He felt sick as they walked on, Annie at his side. She was unusually quiet; it was cold and wet and she wanted to be at home warm and dry, watching the television with her sister safe in her room. He heard someone approaching from behind.

'Hello,' a police officer said. 'I'm Jake. Are you Rob?'

'Yes.'

'You know these woods well?'

'Yes. We've played in here since we were very young.'

'Where does that path lead to?' Jake asked him.

'The road into Bodedern, eventually but it's really muddy that way. When it's been raining, it floods,' Rob said. 'Rachel wouldn't go that way. Not without wellingtons on. She knows these woods. This is the quickest way.' Rob pointed left. 'If she came this way, she would have used this path.' Jake nodded.

'Okay, let's go that way. We can check the other way in the daylight when we've got more officers,' he said. He shone his torch along the left-hand path. They moved forward in a line, twigs and branches breaking underfoot. Their torches picked out footprints in the undergrowth. Ahead, some of the grass was flattened. Rob saw it too and walked towards it. 'Don't trample the area, please Rob,' the officer warned. 'Stay back and don't touch anything.'

Rob stopped walking. He knew the policeman was thinking 'crime scene' and that frightened him. He skirted the area staying a few metres shy of the tracks in the mud. He shone his light on the flattened patch of earth, desperate to rush in and take a closer look. The tracks weaved through the trees, leaving the path here and there. Someone had been that way recently. The policeman knew it and so did Rob. He searched the surrounding area and the torchlight revealed another patch of flattened grass but this one was the shape of a human and about the size of Rachel. Someone had been lying there for a time. There was a dark patch at one end, which looked like blood. It was congealing and glistened in the rain. Rob searched the area with the torch, probing the long grass, desperate to find Rachel. Something glinted near the roots of a tree, reflecting the light.

'Jake. There's something near that tree,' Rob said, pointing. 'Look there.'

The officer approached with caution. He knelt and picked up the object with a gloved hand. Rob could see it was a Samsung Galaxy. The screen looked damaged.

'What type of phone does Rachel use?' Jake asked.

'A Samsung Galaxy, like that one,' Rob said. 'Is the screen smashed?'

'Yes.'

'Oh shit,' Rob murmured. Annie started crying and hugged him tightly. Tears filled his eyes too. 'Bloody hell, Annie. How are we going to tell mum?'

'Don't you worry about that, son,' Jake said. 'We'll tell her what we've found. Don't make any assumptions. We haven't found a body and that's a good thing. She could have banged her head and become confused and gone wandering in the woods. If she's in here, we'll find her.'

CHAPTER 9

Alan and Kim approached the area where the blood had been found. It was cordoned off with tape. The family members and volunteers had been ushered away, so as not to contaminate the scene. A canopy had been erected and tripod lights illuminated the scene to enable a forensic search to be carried out. The sound of petrol generators echoed through the trees. More uniformed officers had been dispatched to continue the search further into the trees in case Rachel was injured and unable to move. It was quickly turning from a rescue mission to a recovery mission. Despite the search continuing, the hope of finding Rachel alive was fading. Pamela Stone was already on scene, studying the evidence. She was guiding the forensic photographer through her findings. Another CSI approached them. His expression was dour.

'Hello, Bryn,' Alan said. 'What do you think?'

'It doesn't look good. There're at least two sets of recent footprints in the mud, leading through the woods to that path over there. The stride appears to be normal up to there. Once the footprints reach that path, the stride becomes much wider and more erratic.'

'Why would that be?' Kim asked.

'We think they broke into a run there,' Bryn said, illuminating the tracks with his torch. 'Both sets indicate they started running for a short distance.'

'One chasing the other?' Kim asked. 'What about the size of the feet?'

'One set is significantly bigger than the other. We're estimating a size five and a size eleven.'

'A grown man and a teenage girl?' Alan asked.

'Possibly. There's blood and hair on that tree and blood and skin on that one. It looks like someone ran into one tree, were stunned and then fell backwards against the other, landing on the ground there, where the grass is flattened. There's not a lot of blood, certainly not enough to be thinking the injured party has bled to death. Of course, a blow to the head could mean their injuries were fatal, but it's unlikely.'

'It is unlikely in the absence of a body,' Alan said. 'Okay, in summary. We've got at least two people running through the trees in the dark. One of them crashes into a tree and collapses onto the floor,' Alan said. Bryn nodded in agreement. 'Where was the phone found?' Alan asked.

'Over there in the long grass.'

'It's definitely Rachels?'

'Yes. We turned it on, and her brother identified it as hers.'

'How did it end up so far away from the point of impact?' Kim asked.

'We don't know.'

'If she had it in her hand when she ran into the tree, could it have catapulted so far?' Alan asked.

'We don't think so. It couldn't have landed so far away by accident, in my opinion.'

'So, it might have been thrown,' Kim said.

'That's what we think.'

'Has the phone gone to the lab?' Alan asked.

'Yes. It's been sent marked as urgent. It shouldn't be difficult to access the data once it arrives at the lab. The screen was cracked, but it was in full working order,' Bryn said.

'It was working okay?' Alan asked. 'Her mother said the phone was off.'

'It was off. Cracking the screen wouldn't stop it working. Someone turned it off manually,' Bryn said.

'Whoever was chasing her turned it off and tossed it?' Kim said. 'So, it couldn't be tracked.'

'It looks that way,' Bryn said.

'That is worrying,' Alan said. 'Pamela said there were tracks leading away from the impact site.' Alan peered into the trees where the search was continuing. He could see torchlight slicing through the darkness and hear her name being called.

'The search is following the tracks as far as they go.'

'We're certain there's only one set leading away?'

'Yes. The path heads west towards the old A5. It splits a bit further on. The second path heads east towards the lake at Llyn Llwenan.'

'It's a long walk to the lake from here,' Kim said.

'Yes.'

'If there's only one set of tracks, she was carried away by whoever was chasing her?'

'There's no other explanation.'

'If she was unconscious, she would be a dead weight. You can't carry an unconscious person very far and it's a long way to the road,' Kim said. 'Which would suggest we're looking for a male who is physically fit.'

'Agreed. We need to find out where she was carried to,' Alan said. 'And we need to do it quickly. I feel that time is running out for Rachel Evans.'

CHAPTER 10

Louise Lee didn't sleep well. In fact, she hadn't slept a wink. The dawn chorus was late today as heavy clouds blocked the sun. Violent threats had been made via text message. They had come from Walter's boss. Louise had to assume that when Walter Dallow had arrived at the custody suite at St Asaph, he'd used his phone call to ask his employer in Liverpool for legal representation.

His employer was clearly not a happy lady. In reality, she'd questioned him about what went wrong and how they managed to get arrested. Walter explained that he had been set up by his young contact in Holyhead and mugged by the local outfit, headed by Mike Smith. The sting had resulted in two of her men being arrested in possession of drugs and a firearm. They would be banged up, looking at serious time. Losing two employees that she could trust was bad enough. The loss of a substantial amount of money, product, a Range Rover and a firearm meant that she had several reasons to be pissed off. They were all valuable assets. She wanted Louise Lee and Mike Smith punished severely and she wanted it done now. They would not get away with what they had done. She would make sure of that. No one took liberties with her business. Her reputation was built on trust. There was a guarantee that there would be a brutal response to any infringement on her operation. Walter was one of her best employees and he was organised. He'd stored all his county lines contacts on a memory stick and given her a copy. She had Louise Lee's mobile number.

To say she was angry was an understatement and she'd sent a nasty text to Louise in the early hours, telling her that she wouldn't be walking unaided for much longer. At the time, Louise didn't know she was a she, not that it mattered. She asked her what she meant by that and the answer was quite descriptive. When someone threatens to cut your legs off with a chainsaw, gender is irrelevant. Louise was frightened and angry. Smithy had forced her to set Walter up, but it wouldn't matter to whoever was Walter's boss. Louise thought that the betrayal would fall on her and her alone. She was frightened to go out and didn't want to leave the house to walk to school for fear of being kidnapped and mutilated. Being a drug dealer had lost its appeal overnight.

She showered and got dressed and ran things over in her mind. The school was set to close because of the outbreak of Covid-19 and there was only one more day. Another positive was that Walter didn't know where she lived. He'd tried to follow her once, but Louise spotted him and cut through the lanes to lose him. She was so glad she had. It was the only light in a very dark tunnel. If she kept her wits about her, she could make her way to school and back without using the main roads. Walter had never met her without her wearing a baseball cap, which was another good point. In her green uniform with her hair down, she looked like all the other kids swarming around the school. The pavements and playgrounds swarmed with kids in green. It would be nigh on impossible for a stranger to spot her and she didn't think Walter would be getting out of the cells anytime soon. In the meantime, she needed Smithy to protect her. He promised he would, not that his promises counted for shit. He promised to give her a cut of the money too but then when she asked for it, he told her to piss off and smacked her across the head. Her venture into the drug business had been fraught with disappointments.

She peered through the curtains to make sure there were no vans with blacked-out windows waiting for her. Her mood was gloomy and there was a dark cloud hanging over her. When she'd composed herself, she left through the back door and jumped over the fence into the alleyway behind her home. Next door's cat jumped off the wheelie bin and nearly gave her a heart attack. Louise hissed at it, but it didn't move. It stared at her nonchalantly.

She made her way to school, passing the park where it had all gone wrong, the night before. The skateboard ramps were empty now. It would be wise to avoid the place for the foreseeable future. If they came to Holyhead to find her, they would go there looking for her, without a doubt. It was where she always met Walter and would be the first place, they would go to ask questions about where she lived. She didn't think her skateboarding friends would tell them where she lived; not unless the price was right. Everyone had a price. Someone would crack eventually. It wouldn't take them long to find her; hence she needed Smithy to step in. This situation was not her fault. She was about to step through the school gates, when a restored Ford Capri pulled up at the kerb. The passenger door opened and one of Smithy's goons climbed out. She knew he was called Monkey or something animal like. Smithy was driving.

'Get in, squirt,' Smithy called. Louise walked to the car and reluctantly sat in it. The door slammed closed and Smithy accelerated away, tyres squealing. 'Do you like the motor?'

'It's great,' Louise lied.

'Have you been in one of these before?' he asked.

'Can't say I have,' Louise said. 'There aren't many about.'

'That is very true. This is an absolute classic,' Smithy said. 'Two-point-eight injection engine and pepper-pot alloy wheels.'

'Nice.'

'How much do you think it's worth?'

'I've got absolutely no idea.'

'Guess.'

'I don't know.'

'Come on. Don't be shy. Have a guess.'

'Fifty grand?'

'Fifty grand. Don't be stupid,' Smithy said. 'Not that much. It's worth a small fortune but not that much. That's a stupid guess.'

'I told you I had no idea about cars and I really don't care, if I'm being honest,' Louise said. 'In fact, I couldn't care any less if I tried.'

'Are you still mad with me?' Smithy asked, sarcastically.

'Yes. I am, actually,' she said, folding her arms.

'Tell Uncle Smithy what's the matter.'

'It's not funny. Listen, I had a text last night from Walter's boss,' Louise said, bored with the vehicle history lesson and Smithy's 'don't give a fuck' attitude. 'He said he's going to cut my legs off with a chainsaw.'

'She,' Smithy said. He grinned and patted the steering wheel.

'What?'

'She. Walter Dallow's boss is a she,' Smithy said.

'You're joking?'

'Nope. Her name is Amie Muir and apparently, she's a nutcase.'

'What do you mean, nutcase?'

'You know what it means. She's a psycho, mad, bonkers, off her head,' Smithy said, smiling. 'She put one bloke, who crossed her, through a tree shredder.'

'OMG. That's just sick. The poor man,' Louise said.

'And from what I'm told, she has a thing for chainsaws. She likes to watch while her enforcers do their thing.'

'Oh great. Thanks for cheering me up. I feel much better now.'

'I'm telling you how it is. I've been doing my homework. There's no need to panic.'

'Are you kidding me?'

'Nope. She's hardcore but I'll sort it.'

'OMG. What have you got me into?' Louise moaned. 'Everything was fine until you came along and ruined it all.'

'Everything was not fine, Louise. You were selling skunk for an outfit from Liverpool. That doesn't happen here. You need to understand how these things work. You're lucky.'

'I don't feel very lucky. You need to protect me, Smithy,' Louise said, in a panic. 'Walter was an all right bloke. I didn't want to stitch him up. You made me do it and now I've got some bitch psycho texting my phone!'

'No one made you take gear off Dallow and sell it to your mates,' Smithy said. 'I didn't make you do that. You did that all by yourself.'

'I didn't intend to rip him off though. You could have just told me to stop and I would have,' Louise protested. 'That's why his boss is pissed off with me because I set him up. You've dropped me right in the shit. She said she's going to cut my legs off and you said she's a nutcase. What if she comes here to get me?'

'Okay, okay,' Smithy said. 'Calm yourself down. I'm going to smooth things over with her. You don't need to worry your pretty head. I will fix it.'

'How are you going to do that if she's mental?'

'I'll talk to her. She'll realise she's out of her depth. She might be a big fish in Liverpool but this is my island.' He pulled the car to a stop and turned to face Louise. 'Here's your cut of the money. There's two-hundred there.' Louise was going to protest but thought better of it. 'Now, count yourself lucky I'm giving you anything at all. Stay away from the park until I can speak to Amie Muir. We don't want you losing your legs, do we?'

'No. We don't,' Louise said, stuffing the cash into her coat pockets. 'Thanks Smithy. I need you to sort it out. I didn't sleep last night.'

'I will sort it out,' Smithy said, turning the car around. He drove back towards the school. 'Trust me. I'm not having some bigshot from away thinking they can throw their weight around here. That isn't happening. In the meantime, keep your head down and your mouth shut. Understand me?'

'Yes. Thanks again.'

'When is school closing?' he asked.

'This is the last day, I think. They've been talking about it for weeks. I think all the other schools on the island have already shutdown. We're the last.'

'Crazy times,' Smithy said. 'You take it easy. I'll be in touch.' Smithy stopped before the zebra crossing, and Louise climbed out.

'See you.'

His associate climbed in and the car sped away. Louise felt relieved as if a huge weight had been lifted from her shoulders. She felt better having spoken to Smithy and the money was a bonus but there was still a nagging doubt at the back of her mind. She wanted away from it all, completely. The money was great, but she wasn't cut out for what came with it.

'Hey, Louise,' her friend Jaki called to her. She ran across the road, out of breath, a worried look on her face. 'Have you heard about your cousin Rachel?'

'No. What about her?'

'I thought your mum would have told you last night,' Jaki said.

'My mum was wasted last night when I got in,' Louise said. 'What's happened?'

'Rachel didn't go home from school yesterday. The police are involved,' Jaki said, excitedly. 'I reckon she's run off with that lad who always comments on her pics. David Laws. He's all over Facebook. I bet they've absconded.'

'Shut up. Rachel hasn't run off with a lad, Jaki,' Louise said, frowning. 'If she didn't go home, she's in trouble.'

CHAPTER 11

Richard Lewis doublechecked the information. The traffickers were not amateurs. They had done this many times before. The lorry stopped at the port had been shuffled around through multiple cardboard companies, which didn't exist. They made it virtually impossible to trace. It had him going around in circles, hitting a dead end each time. The current registered owner was a company which didn't exist, based in the Isle of Man. There were no company accounts registered at Companies House, no tax records, and no list of directors. It was a professional shroud, designed to stop the police discovering who was responsible for trafficking people and drugs. They were clearly experts at what they did. He'd hit another dead end when he decided to change tack.

The vehicle wasn't legitimate so normal means of tracing it to the owner were defunct. He had to think out of the box. He contacted the CSI company and asked Pamela stone to send all the photographs they'd taken of the vehicle to him and after studying them closely, he called the compound where it had been taken to be inspected. Some of the engine parts looked new and the storage cages inside were custom built. If he could trace them back to where they were made and who paid for them, he might have a chance of identifying the owner. It was a long shot but worth a try. Everyone makes mistakes and he had to find what they'd missed.

***

Alan arrived home as daylight was creeping up on the horizon. The night sky was turning to orange tinged with red. The search of the woods hadn't turned up anything further. Initial tests on the blood showed it was group O, a match to Rachel's but DNA results to confirm it was one-hundred per cent hers wouldn't be in for hours yet. They couldn't say for certain it was hers until then, although it was highly unlikely to belong to anyone else. There was no sign of her in the woods or along the paths, which led to the street where she lived. A more thorough search would be conducted in daylight. He was convinced that Rachel was either dead or being held against her will. There was no other rational explanation. His eyes were sore, and his knees were aching. He needed a shower and a change of clothes before joining the investigation again.

The dogs were doing their usual welcome home performance, scratching at the patio doors and barking in unison. They did the same each night when he pulled into the driveway. He opened the front door and let them mob him for a while, before letting them out onto the fields at the back of the house. They sprinted off at a million miles an hour, Henry much slower than Gemma, nowadays. He watched them run over the hill out of sight and then filled a glass with water from the tap. The bungalow was quiet now the boys had gone. A bottle of whisky looked tempting but he couldn't have even a little one. His brain needed to be sharp. He was thinking about using the toilet when his mobile rang. It was the station.

'DI Williams.'

'Alanio,' Richard said.

'Richard?' Alan asked, checking his watch. 'Have you been home yet?'

'Nope. Not yet.'

'What are you doing still there?'

'Busy, busy, busy, trying to track that lorry. They know what they're doing. I've been going around in circles all night,' Richard said. 'But I've got a few ideas I'm exploring.'

'Good man.'

'The reason for the call is that the lab has been on. They've got something interesting from Rachel's phone. I thought you'd want to know straightaway.'

'Yes. I do. What have they found?'

'To use the technical term, they have found dick-pics,' Richard said.

'What?'

'Dick-pics. Pictures of penises for want of a better explanation; one penis in particular. She clearly wasn't happy receiving them.'

'Ah, that is interesting,' Alan said. 'Do we know who the pictures belong to?'

'Yes. They all belong to the same guy. He's in the year above Rachel. His name is David Laws.' Alan recognised the name. A local solicitor had the same surname. 'Yesterday, she threatened to have her brother beat him up if he didn't stop bothering her and she blocked him on social media.'

'Yesterday?' Alan asked. 'Just before she went missing.'

'Yep. It looks like he's been stalking all her social media profiles, sending her pictures, and she's pissed off with him.'

'Where is he from?'

'Holyhead. He lives in Harbour View.'

'Okay. That is Colin Laws' son.'

'The solicitor?'

'Yes. He lives in Harbour View. It must be his son. I'll be there in an hour.'

'Do you want him bringing in?'

'Usually, I'd say no until we have all the information from her devices, but she could still be alive somewhere. Let's tell him we want to ask him a few questions. Bring him to Holyhead station with his dad. We'll shake him and see what he has to say for himself.'

'Okay. I'll send a car. Sending the pictures should be enough to arrest him if we need to.'

'Agreed but I don't want to arrest him just yet. Although, sending pictures of your penis to anyone should be an arrestable offence, in my humble opinion,' Alan said. 'What on earth are people thinking?'

'Apparently, it's all the rage,' Richard said. 'I remember when aftershave and roses were used to attract the finer sex, now a picture of your genitals seems to be standard practice. The lab boys were saying they see it all the time when they're dumping phones and laptops.'

'My mother didn't like my father wearing shorts. She thought showing his knees was obscene,' Alan said. 'Can you imagine what she would have thought if he'd sent a picture of his bits and pieces when they were dating?'

'You wouldn't be here, that's for certain.'

'She would be spinning in her grave if she could hear this conversation.'

'Likewise. I'm trying not to be single, but I won't be attempting it to attract a mate.'

'Stick to the roses, Richard,' Alan said. 'Please don't be tempted to mimic the younger generation.'

'Goodness me, no. I can't see it anymore let alone photograph it,' Richard said, a serious tone to his voice. 'It would take the clever use of a mirror to do that, nowadays.'

'I don't want that image in my mind, thank you. Please don't talk to me about it anymore. It's making me queasy,' Alan said, shaking his head. 'I'll see you at the station.'

'Okay,' Richard said. 'There's one more thing.'

'Go on.'

'The ACC has sent out an email to all North Wales departments.'

'About the virus?'

'Yes. They want all the caravan parks closed and holidaymakers told to return to their homes. He wants it enforced from today. That's going to eat into our resources somewhat.'

What Happened to Rachel?

'Unless we put machinegun towers and checkpoints on the A55, I'm not sure how that will work. It will be uniform's headache for now. I'll see you later. Go home and get some sleep,' Alan said.

'Will do, see you later.'

CHAPTER 12

The sun came up slowly, shrouded by low clouds. As the search party set off in a staggered line, rain began to fall. A mixture of uniformed officers and suited CSI's combed the undergrowth for any sign of Rachel Evans. They skirted the area where the blood was found and continued deeper into the woods. Every piece of litter and Coke can was assessed; discarded cigarette buts were bagged and a marker left in their place. The woods were frequented by youngsters and dog walkers in the warmer months. It was a popular route home from school during daylight hours. There would be plenty of irrelevant items to sift through and rule out. Identifying relevant pieces of evidence was sometimes more luck than judgement. The footprints leading away from the impact site were easier to see in the dull light of day. They were erratic and not always on the path; at one point, they veered off and went full circle through the bushes and back to where they started. Kim couldn't explain why. Maybe the darkness had caused disorientation or maybe they went back to retrieve something.

A cry echoed through the trees from the far left of the line. The line stopped advancing while they waited for the order to move on again. Kim walked towards the source of the shout. Two CSI officers were crouching near the base of a tree.

'What is it?' Kim asked.

'A boot,' one of them said. 'A grey Ugg boot, to be precise.'

'Bag it, please and call the DI. That's what she was wearing when she went to school.'

***

David Laws checked his phone again. His social media sites were buzzing with chitchat about Rachel Evans going missing. Her brother Rob and sister, Annie had posted several appeals for information on Facebook and hundreds of local people had responded. The rumour mill was running at full tilt. It didn't take long for conversations to turn sour and the finger pointing to begin. One of Rachel's friends had mentioned David on Facebook, saying he was bothering Rachel. Another had mentioned the fact he'd been stalking her photographs on Instagram and a third mentioned that he'd actually sent unsolicited dick-pics and that Rachel was disturbed by them. She also mentioned that he continued to send them despite being asked not to by Rachel herself. That single comment was like lighting the blue touch paper of a firework. It provoked a barrage of abuse from her friends, family, and the wider community. He was now the target for everyone's anger. His phone lit up with text messages, Facebook Messenger, and WhatsApp groups, telling him what would happen to him if anything had happened to Rachel. Even his best friends were pretending to be outraged at his behaviour. The strength of feeling was so strong it would be foolish for them to defend him. Things quickly got out of hand. He was overwhelmed with abuse. There were several death threats made before he decided he'd had enough and logged out. It crossed his mind to unlike all her photographs, but it was too late; the damage was done on that front. It would take hours and hours anyway and he was already running behind getting ready for school.

His mum and dad hadn't seen the kerfuffle online, but he was sure people would bring it to their attention as soon as they could. People were good at making sure everyone knew what was going on, good or bad. His parents would lose their minds when they did. They were ultrasensitive about people's perception of the family. His dad was a solicitor in Holyhead and his mother worked on the ferries as a manager. It's a small town and everyone knows everyone and what other people think, counts. They tended to look down their noses at people who earned less or didn't work at all, which was embarrassing sometimes. David was told who he could hang about with and who he couldn't. They were very materialistic and the age of the car someone drove could dictate if his friends were welcome in their home or not. They never actually said the reason why they didn't like one of his friends, but they didn't have to. As he grew older, he saw the patterns in their behaviour. It had caused plenty of arguments growing up.

His sister knew what was happening online and was in the same year as Rachel. She was vehemently trying to defend her brother on her social media platforms, although earlier that morning when they were discussing it in whispers, there was an uncertain look in her eyes. She was questioning him silently. The accusations on social media reached fever pitch and she was fighting a losing battle. Trying to stem the tidal wave of abuse was impossible.

His mobile rang. It was his new girlfriend, Bethan. She was a college student in Bangor but lived in Trearddur Bay. He'd been chatting to her for months before they started dating. She was reluctant to date a boy still at school, even if he was in his final year. Her friends were all dating boys older than them. They had cars and money and could go into pubs, but his persistence paid off and she finally agreed to a date. They'd been out four times in three weeks which was akin to becoming a couple in her mind. She was becoming possessive and monitoring his Facebook newsfeed, sulking if there was any interaction with other females. Bethan had never called him before school. It was obvious she'd seen the chaos online. He took a deep breath and answered the call, needing to hear a friendly voice.

'You lying, cheating bastard,' she said as a greeting.

'Good morning, Bethan.'

'Don't *good morning* me, you paedo.'

'That's a bit harsh.'

'Not from what I'm reading it isn't.'

'Thanks for giving me the benefit of the doubt.'

'I can't believe you've done that to me.'

'I haven't done anything, Bethan,' David said. He felt sick to his stomach. He really liked Bethan. She was older than him and he knew she'd slept with a few guys. The chances of him having sex were much higher with a girlfriend at her age. He didn't want to blow his chances. 'Don't believe everything you read on social media. People are blowing this out of all proportions. It isn't what it looks like.'

'Really?' she asked. 'According to your Facebook, you've been bothering a girl who's gone missing?'

'I messaged her a few times, but that was months ago. I've got nothing to do with it, honestly.'

'Did you just use the word, honestly?' she said, sarcastically. 'I've seen your comments on her photos, telling her how hot she is. You couldn't spell the word 'honest' if you had to.'

'I like lots of photos on Instagram. That's what it's for.'

'Really and do you write 'hot' under them all or just on the underage kids?'

'No. That was ages ago.'

'The picture I'm looking at was posted the day before yesterday. You're nothing but a liar,' Bethan said. 'Her friends are saying you've been stalking the poor girl and sending her pictures of your tiny knob.'

'There's no need to be nasty.' That hurt his feelings. She'd felt him through his jeans a few nights ago when they were kissing.

'I bet she was as impressed as I was. It might get bigger as you grow up. Not. I feel sorry for the poor little girl. And now she's gone missing. It sounds to me like you're in big trouble.'

'She's not a little girl,' David said, embarrassed and a little angry now. 'She's fourteen and I don't know anything about her going missing. She's probably just had an argument at home.'

'Yes, lots of girls her age just don't go home from school. Not. She's a kid and you were stalking her pictures. You make me want to puke. You're a paedo.'

'I'm not a paedo, Bethan. That's out of order.'

'Sending pictures of yourself to kids is out of order. I hope you get locked up. You're a paedo.'

'Stop saying that and for your information sending the pics was just a joke.'

'A joke?'

'Yes.'

'You've been stalking all her selfies and telling her she's smokin hot and I'm supposed to believe that it was all done as a joke?' Bethan fumed. 'She's a child, you absolute sicko.'

'It was just a joke.'

'Well, you might think it was a joke, funny but I'm not laughing,' Bethan said. 'My friends told me you were an immature prick when I started seeing you. I don't know why I even bothered with a kid like you. Don't ever contact me again. I'll be blocking you when I get off the phone. I read some of the comments people are making. I hope someone cuts your bollocks off, paedo!'

The call ended. David lay back on his bed and stared at the ceiling, feeling like he'd been kicked in the guts. Suddenly, going to school didn't seem like such a good idea. He was contemplating feigning illness when his sister, Steph burst into his room. Her face looked red. Her eyes were angry.

'You are so embarrassing!'

'What now?' He sighed. 'I really don't need any more shit, thank you. You're supposed to be on my side.'

'Sandra has posted online that you sent Rachel dick-pics. Did you really send her dick-pics?' David rolled his eyes and shrugged. He couldn't see the point in lying although he felt mortally embarrassed now. It seemed like fun at the time. 'Aren't you even going to deny it?'

'What's the point?' he said. 'It was just a laugh. I was flirting with her.'

'Flirting?' Steph said, incredulous. 'OMG, Rob Evans is going to batter you. He's well hard.' She closed her eyes and bit her bottom lip. 'This is so embarrassing. Everyone in school is going to blank me. My brother is a massive pervert.'

'I'm not a pervert.'

'You sent pictures of yourself to a girl in my year. You are such a perv.'

'Loads of guys do it.'

'No, David, loads of pervs do it.'

'It was just a joke.'

'That is not funny. I've been sticking up for you and you are actually a massive pervert.' She stormed out and slammed the door behind her. 'This is so embarrassing. I'm telling Mum what you've done.'

'I'm not a pervert,' David called after her. He heard her stomping down the stairs. She would definitely tell his mum and then a whole new level of shitstorm would begin. He waited a few minutes and heard the doorbell. Then he heard voices chattering for a few minutes and then there were footsteps climbing the stairs. The door opened again, and his mother stood there, looking shellshocked.

'What on earth have you been doing?' his mum said. Her eyes looked wide and teary. He could see two men standing behind her.

'I haven't done anything, Mum,' he said.

'Well, you must have done something. There are two detectives here and they've come to talk to you about Rachel Evans going missing.'

David froze for a second and then launched himself across the room. He opened the window as wide as it would go and tried to scramble through it. The detectives pulled him back, pinned him to the floor, and cuffed him. He could hear his mother crying as they took him downstairs and bundled him into their car.

CHAPTER 13

Smithy read the text message on his phone and grinned. It was from an old cellmate from HMP Walton, who owed him a favour and he had come good. He'd sent him the mobile number where Amie Muir could be reached. He stood near the kitchen window, which overlooked the sea at Porth-y-post and watched the waves crashing into the small cove. It was mesmerising. All that natural power was forced into the narrow space between the rocky headlands and it created waves bigger than a house. Storm Brian had been impressive, but this one took the biscuit. The road was covered with boulders and seaweed again for the third time this winter. It had taken four council workers and a JCB to open the road last time; this time was worse. He sipped black coffee from a KitKat mug and dialled his adversary from Liverpool. A male voice answered the call.

'Yes?'

'I need to speak to Amie please,' Smithy said. The line remained silent. 'Tell her it's Michael Smith from Anglesey. I want to talk to her about Walter.' He heard mumbled voices in the background.

'She's said fuck off,' the man said. He hung up the call. Smithy swore and redialled the number. It went directly to voicemail. He hung up and called again; this time he left a message.

'Amie, this is Michael Smith from Anglesey. You can either talk to me on the phone or the next time one of your goons crosses the border, I'll pin a message to his chest with a steak knife and send him back to Liverpool in pieces. Call me back on this number.'

Smithy put the phone down and went into the kitchen. He boiled the kettle and made another brew. The wind was picking up, driving the waves into a frenzy. Tons of water crashed onto the road in front of his flat and foam floated through the air like bubbles. It was hypnotic watching the storm. His phone rang, the number withheld.

'Michael Smith speaking,' Smithy answered sarcastically. He chuckled to himself. 'I'm assuming this is Amie?'

'You're a cocky bastard,' Amie Muir said, her accent thick and guttural. She was from the deepest darkest streets of the city on the Mersey and she sounded like a heavy smoker. 'You've got two minutes to tell me what you want.'

'I want to appeal to your better nature, Amie,' Smithy said. 'You've threatened a young girl who Walter hired to sell your shit.'

'And what?'

'She's very young and she's frightened.'

'She should be frightened. She's cost me a lot of money.'

'She's a school kid, Amie.'

'She's old enough to sell gear and take the money, then she's old enough to take the consequences.'

'Come on, Amie. You're actively recruiting school kids to sell your gear; they're going to make mistakes.' Smithy waited for a response, but none was forthcoming. 'It's my fault she stitched up Walter. I made her do it.'

'What do you want, a medal?'

'No. I don't want any repercussions. I want a truce.'

'A truce?' she said. 'There's an interesting concept.'

'Let's be reasonable. Your boys came onto my turf and they were sloppy. They were lucky they didn't get hurt. You would do the same if someone stepped into your area.'

'Probably. But I doubt they would still be in one piece.'

'Exactly. We could have thrown them into the sea, and you'd be none the wiser.' She didn't speak. 'Let's draw a line in the sand and leave it at that. No hard feelings. Leave the girl alone.'

'Thanks to you, the legal fees are going to cost me thousands and my Range Rover has been confiscated,' she said. 'You and your little rat have cost me dear and made me look silly. I can't show weakness, Smithy. You know that; show weakness and the sharks will eat you up and in this game they're always circling.'

'We're one hundred and twenty miles apart. You haven't lost face here or at home. Stay away from here and there's no mither. Neither of us wants a war,' Smithy said. His comments met silence. 'Wars get messy and cost more in the long term. Better to sort this out peacefully.' There was another long silence. 'My little rat didn't have any choice in the sting; that's on me. This is a small town, Amie. Walter was never going to get away with selling gear without me finding out. I found out the day after Walter hired her. I leaned on her and made her set him up.'

'And I'm supposed to do what exactly?'

'Leave her alone; she's just a kid and no threat to your reputation. Come on, Amie. You know it makes sense?'

'Fifty thousand and I'll walk away,' Amie said.

'Fifty thousand. That just rolls off the tongue. You and I both know that isn't happening,' Smithy said. 'Look, I understand why you cross the border and employ teenagers but there are hazards in playing that game. Like I said, this is a small town, everyone knows everyone. Your man Walter crossed the line and that's going to cost you. He got turned over; it happens. If you're going to be pissed off with someone, be pissed off with him. He screwed up.'

'You set him up, Smithy, and you called the Dibble. That's dirty. I can play dirty with the best of them.'

'Oh, I'm well aware of what you're capable of, Amie. I do my homework. Don't make this bigger than it needs to be or we both lose. The fact we're having a conversation tells me there's mutual respect. We could help each other out if we're clever.'

'You think so?' Amie didn't sound interested.

'Definitely. How much are you paying for a kilo at the moment?'

'I'm not getting into that.'

'Come on. You're on the phone, I'm on the phone. We both sell product. How much are you paying for a kilo?'

'It depends,' she said.

'It depends because you're reliant on someone else bringing it in, right?' Smithy said, lighting a cigarette. Amie stayed quiet. 'I bring in my own. I can guarantee uncut product at sixty-thousand a kilo, direct from darkest Peru.'

'I have a supplier,' Amie said. 'I don't know you and I don't like you.'

'We don't have to like each other. Your prices are about to go up.'

'What makes you think that?'

'There was a lorry stopped here in the port. There were thirty-nine mules being trafficked in a refrigerated unit only someone kept the door closed too long. They're all dead. The police have the lorry and the gear inside it. That's going to hurt someone in your area.'

'When was this?' Amie sounded shocked.

'You didn't know already?' he said, smiling. He could hear the concern in her voice. 'It was yesterday. The NCA will be all over it like a rash. Rumour has it, that lorry was heading for Manchester. It was a big shipment and it will hit the supply chain in your area. The price will go up until they can reopen the supply line and with the NCA sniffing around, that will be a long time coming.' She stayed quiet. 'My supply line is open all year around because I live on an island.'

'We all live on an island.'

'Granted. When was the last time you went on a boat, Amie?' Smithy asked, laughing. 'My supply comes in all year around. If you find yourself paying over the odds or short of product, you have my number and I'll help you out as a gesture of goodwill. It's my way of making an apology.'

'Don't hold your breath.'

'The offer is there and it's a genuine one,' Smithy said. 'Are we cool on the other business or do I have to order a dozen stab vests for my boys?'

'I'll think about it.'

The line went dead. Smithy inhaled deeply on his cigarette and finished his coffee. He had a feeling Louise would be safe and that he wouldn't hear from Amie Muir again.

CHAPTER 14

Alan and Kim walked into the interview room; it was grey and grim and drab and had an unwholesome odour to it. The scent of sweat tainted the air. The human body doesn't respond well to being incarcerated and interrogated; its natural scent turns sour and lingers. David Laws was already there, sitting next to his father, Colin. His eyes were red and swollen from crying. His father looked shaken and angry. Alan could sense his temper was simmering beneath the façade of calm, that he was trying but failing to maintain. Alan shook hands with Colin and sat down opposite David. Colin was younger than Alan by fifteen years or more, but the men had known each other since Colin was a boy and they were in the same Masonic lodge for many years. Lately, Alan's interest in all things Masonic had waned. The pomp and ceremony no longer belonged in this world; it was from a different time. Kim nodded hello and put her laptop on the table.

'Okay, gentlemen, let's dispense with the small talk,' Alan said. He turned to the boy. 'David, your father and I have known each other for many years. That might be a good thing, or it might be a bad thing; we don't need to beat about the bush with formalities. One thing for certain is this situation is an awkward one for all concerned so let's be honest with each other and get this over as quickly as we can, okay?'

'Okay.'

'You know why you're here?'

'Yes,' David said, quietly.

'Can you tell me why we've brought you in?'

'Because of Rachel Evans.'

'What about Rachel Evans?'

'She's gone missing.'

'Good. When, my officers came to speak to you, you tried to jump out of the bedroom window,' Alan began. Colin shook his head almost imperceptibly; disappointment was etched into his face. 'That's very odd behaviour for an innocent person.' David blushed. 'Can you tell me why you did that?'

'I'd been threatened online. My girlfriend kicked off with me and my sister was upset. I was scared and I just wanted to run away.'

'Scared of what?'

'Have you seen what people are saying online?'

'Some of it. It must be very uncomfortable for you. But I don't see why that would make you want to run away from the police.'

'I was scared that if I talk to the police, people might think I've hurt Rachel.'

'People already think that,' Kim said, bluntly. Colin threw her a withering glance which she ignored. 'They're very quick to judge, especially online.'

'Your father tells me people have made threats against you?' Alan asked.

'Yes. Some of them have said they're going to kill me.'

'We're not going to let that happen and we'll speak to the people who have made threats.' Alan took off his glasses. 'Why do you think people have singled you out?'

'I don't know why because I haven't done anything wrong. I certainly haven't done anything to Rachel.'

'People are very concerned about Rachel Evans and her whereabouts. She is only fourteen and she's missing, and we need to find her.'

'I understand that, but I haven't done anything.'

'Do you know anything about her disappearance?'

'No,' David said, shaking his head. His eyes were focused on the table. He glanced at his father, but he was looking the other way. 'I know nothing about it at all.' The detectives remained quiet; a ploy to make him ramble. 'She's probably fell out with her mum and dad and stayed at a friend's house. She doesn't get on with her stepdad,' he added. 'She's always slagging him off online.'

'Do you think we haven't explored that avenue?' Alan said. David shrugged and looked sheepish. 'We're detectives and part of our role as detectives is to detect,' Alan paused. 'We look at the evidence available to us and explore all the possibilities.' David seemed to shrivel in is chair. 'We know for a fact that she's bleeding, and she only has one boot on. You don't need to be a detective to analyse those clues. In my experience, they would suggest she's not staying at a friend's house following an argument. Some harm has befallen her.' He paused to let it sink in. 'You can see that, can't you?' David nodded. 'Now we have that straight, when did you last see her?' Alan asked.

'At dinnertime yesterday. I saw her in the corridor after geography. She was with her friend Sandra and some others.'

'Did you speak to her?'

'No.'

'Why not?'

'She was with her friends. They don't like me. We don't get on.'

'When was the last time you spoke to her?'

'I haven't spoken to her for ages. She's been blanking me.'

'Why was that?' Kim asked.

'Why was what?' David asked, blushing.

'Why was Rachel blanking you?'

'I messaged her a few times on social media, asking her out. She didn't like it.'

'That's not quite right, is it?' Kim said, turning the laptop to face him. 'You didn't just ask her out. You sent pictures of your penis to her on Facebook, WhatsApp, and Instagram,' Kim said. She looked at him, but he didn't make eye contact. His father looked furious and embarrassed. 'You sent them fourteen times to be exact,' she added.

'Fourteen times?' his father repeated looking at him in disgust. David avoided his glare. 'What on earth were you thinking?'

'I don't know. It was a joke,' David said, muttering.

'Why did you keep sending it?' his father asked, shaking his head.

'It isn't just, one picture,' Kim said.

'What do you mean?' Colin asked.

'He hasn't sent the same picture fourteen times,' Kim said. 'He sent fourteen different pictures from varying angles. Very artistic.' Colin looked at her, his face like thunder. He looked at his son with shame in his eyes. 'That's what she didn't like. It wasn't the fact you asked her to go out, it was the pictures. That's why she wasn't speaking to you, isn't it?'

'Is there a question for him, detective?' Colin asked, eyebrows raised. He looked annoyed; embarrassed and very uncomfortable indeed.

'Yes. The question is clear,' she said, half smiling. 'Is that why she was blanking you or not?' Kim asked.

'Yes. I suppose so.'

'You suppose so?' Kim pushed. 'We've recovered several communications between you and she's pretty clear that she doesn't want to go out with you and she didn't appreciate your dick-pics,' she said, folding her arms.

'I shouldn't have sent them,' David said. 'I know that now.'

'Did you see Rachel after school yesterday?' Alan asked, changing tack.

'No. I told you.' David blushed again. 'I saw her at dinnertime and that's it. I don't know anything about her being missing.'

'Are you sure you didn't see her?'

'Positive.'

'Which way did you walk home?' Kim asked.

'Along the road. The way I always walk.'

'You left school through the front gates?'

'Yes.'

'Who did you walk home with?'

'No one.' David shrugged.

'Don't you walk home with your mates?' Alan asked.

'I stayed behind for a bit, sorting my books out for my homework. The school is closing down.'

'Yes. We know that.'

'I was sorting out my home study and my mates had walked on.'

'Why didn't they wait for you?' Kim asked.

'I don't know,' David said. 'Probably because it was pissing down with rain.'

'Mind your language, David,' his father snapped.

'Sorry. It was raining heavily.'

'What time did you leave?'

'I don't know. School finishes at half three, so about fifteen minutes after that.'

'Rachel sent you a message threatening that her brother Rob would beat you up if you didn't stop stalking her photographs.'

'Yes.'

'That was sent at three, thirty-five,' Alan said.

'Yes. Roughly.'

'You read it immediately?' Alan said.

'I don't remember.'

'It says here when you read it,' Kim said, pointing to the laptop. David blushed again. 'It was three thirty-five.'

'If you say so.'

'I don't say so. Messenger says so,' Kim said. 'You can see the time the message was read here.'

'Okay. Sorry.'

'What's your point?' Colin asked, frustrated.

'Did her message annoy you?'

'Not really. I've got a girlfriend, so I wasn't bothered about Rachel anymore,' David said. 'Or I did have a girlfriend until this morning.'

'Your girlfriend has finished with you?' Alan asked.

'Yes.'

'Because of all the social media activity, I assume?'

'Yes.'

'Did you read the message and then follow Rachel across the rugby pitches into the woods to have it out with her?' Kim asked, ignoring his answer.

'No. I told you, I saw her at dinnertime, and I haven't seen her since.'

'Someone chased her through the woods,' Kim pressed. 'Were you angry with her?'

'No. I wasn't angry, and I didn't follow her. I didn't see her.'

'Are you sure?' Alan asked.

'Yes.'

'David, this is very important,' Alan said. 'There's a young girl missing. We've found her blood and one of her boots in the woods. She sent you a threatening message shortly before she went missing so, you can understand why we're asking you questions?' David shrugged but didn't answer. 'Do you know where she is?'

'No. I'm sorry I sent those pictures, but it doesn't mean I've done anything to hurt her. Why would I want to hurt her?'

'I don't know,' Alan said. 'Being rejected can make people do strange things.'

'I understand why you need to ask me questions. I shouldn't have sent those pictures, but I haven't done anything to Rachel.' David started sobbing. He looked like a little boy at that point, even Kim felt sympathy for him.

'My son has answered all your questions,' Colin said. 'Sending her messages of such an inappropriate nature was wrong and I'll deal with that and he's recognised that it was a mistake. He's told you that he didn't see Rachel after school, and I believe him. So, unless you have any direct evidence of any wrongdoing on his behalf, we're finished here.'

'Okay. Just one more question,' Alan asked. 'What time did you get home from school?'

'After four o'clock,' David said. His eyes flickered when he answered.

'Was anyone in when you got home?'

'Nope,' David said. 'Mum and Dad were working, and Steph went to her friends for tea. She didn't get in until about six.'

'Okay. I suggest you keep your body parts in your pants from now on, young man. That's all for now,' Alan said. 'Interview terminated.'

Alan and Colin shook hands again and the Laws left in silence. Alan and Kim waited until they were out of earshot. Kim chewed her pen and grimaced.

'What do you think?' she asked.

'I think he doesn't have an alibi when Rachel went missing,' Alan said. 'I also think he's going to struggle for the foreseeable future. The whole family will. The online reaction shows the strength of feeling and if people think he's to blame, mud sticks.' Kim nodded her agreement. 'Emotions are running high. Until we find Rachel or lock someone up, he's going to be in the firing line.'

CHAPTER 15

Richard Lewis squeezed in a few hours' sleep on the old settee in the staffroom. He woke up with a dry mouth and a stiff neck and a head full of unanswered questions. He checked his mobile. There were two messages. He would listen to them once he'd been to the toilet and put the kettle on. The events of the last forty-eight hours had been disturbing. Thirty-nine dead migrants and a fourteen-year-old girl missing. The villages on the island had tightknit communities that felt the loss as if it was their own; the news of a young girl missing had rocked the community to its core. Rachel Evans was the subject everyone was talking about and she would continue to be until there was some resolution to the matter. Fourteen-year-old girls don't often vanish of their own volition.

He yawned and went into the kitchen; his phone rang. It was the CSI he'd sent to the compound where the lorry was being examined.

'DS Lewis,' he answered.

'It's Elaine.'

'Hi, Elaine. What did you find?'

'I checked over the engine like you asked,' she said. 'You were right about some of the parts looking new. The radiator has been doctored. So has the diesel tank and the oil sump. They're new parts that have been dismantled and rebuilt with compartments welded into them and stuffed with drugs. We've recovered another fifty kilos.'

'Fifty kilos, what a result. I thought they looked new,' Richard said, pleased with himself. 'What about the serial numbers, can we trace them?'

'We've traced them back to the manufacturer. They supply those parts to Europarts, who work on an account basis. You'll be pleased to hear that the tank and the radiator were purchased from Europarts three weeks ago on account.'

'By whom?'

'A garage in Warrington, who specialise in diesel engines, mostly lorries and buses. I've spoken to them and they fitted the parts new for a haulage company in Manchester.'

'Text me the name and address,' Richard said, excited. 'This could be the breakthrough we need. I'll send the details to the NCA. Well done, Elaine.' He whistled tunelessly as he walked into the kitchen and put the kettle on. There was no milk, so he made his coffee black. His mobile rang again.

'DS Lewis,' he answered.

'Hello, Detective Lewis. This is Sean Edwards from the Liverpool Arms at Beaumaris. My boss gave me your number and asked me to call you.'

'Hello, Sean. Thanks for coming back to me.'

'No problem. My manager said you need to ask me some questions about the day shift yesterday.'

'Yes. I do.'

'How can I help?'

'Ricky White was on your shift yesterday, wasn't he?'

'Sort of,' Sean said. 'He was an 8-8 shift in the kitchen but he had to go to a dentist appointment. I told him to rearrange it, but he insisted he had to attend. We had some cross words, not for the first time. He should have booked the day off, really. He left me short staffed, selfish bugger.'

'Some people don't care,' Richard said. 'What time did he leave?'

'About three. His appointment was three-thirty and his dentist is at Valley.'

'Tell me,' Richard said, thoughtfully. 'How does he get to work?'

'He has a crash helmet with him when he comes in, so I presume he rides a motorbike. I don't know him that well, to be honest so I've never asked him.'

'Okay. What time did he get back to work?'

'It was after half five, closer to six,' Sean said. 'I told him he was taking the piss and that he wasn't having a break as well as taking three hours off, which he didn't mind. To be fair, he did stay on because someone called in sick for the nightshift, so he's not all bad. Some of the staff here won't lift a finger to help out when we're short of staff. They don't give a shit about the business, half of them.'

'Right you are. It must be frustrating for you. That's been very helpful,' Richard said, trying to get off the phone. 'If I need any clarification, you don't mind me calling you on this number, do you?'

'Not at all. Anytime.' Sean paused. 'Is this anything to do with that girl who's gone missing from Bodedern?'

'Oh, I can't discuss anything like that,' Richard said. 'But thanks again for calling me back.'

'I understand,' Sean said. 'But I will say this. I had to have a word with him about making inappropriate remarks to female staff.'

'I see,' Richard said, not wanting to get into it. 'Please keep this to yourself. I don't want you jumping to any conclusions from our conversation. Please don't mention it to your other staff members. You know what gossip is like. It spreads like wildfire.'

'My lips are sealed. Nope, not me,' Sean said. 'I'm not one to gossip or judge people but I will tell you he's a wrong one, between you and me.'

'Yes, you've said as much. I appreciate your candour.'

'I'm more than happy to help. Do you need me to make a statement to help you charge him?'

'We're not charging anyone at the moment.'

'So, you don't want a statement?'

'Not at this point, no, but thank you.'

'Mark my words, he's not right in the head.'

'Right you are. I'll bear that in mind. I might need a few more details from you at some point, Sean,' Richard said, trying to end the call politely. 'Thanks again for calling me back. I'll be in touch.'

The call ended. There was a niggle in his head, like a dog barking in the distance. He needed to speak to the DI. Richard scrolled to Alan's number and pressed dial.

CHAPTER 16

Kim walked into the Valley dentist. The surgery was converted from a row of terraced houses, knocked through into one. Inside, it was bright and clinical with a coffee machine and a mineral water station; glossy magazines were strategically scattered on high-gloss tables and a sixty-inch plasma screen was showing an episode of Homes Under the Hammer. The receptionist greeted her with a brilliant smile which revealed a set of perfectly white teeth. She was obviously a walking advert for the practice. Kim didn't recognise her, but her name badge said she was called Amber. She showed her warrant card and the smile turned to a frown. Amber looked concerned.

'I'm Detective Sergeant Davies,' she said. 'There's no need to worry, you're not in trouble.'

'How can I help you?' Amber asked.

'It's very quiet, isn't it?' Kim asked.

'We're shutting down from this afternoon,' Amber said. 'Because of the virus. We've cancelled all appointments until May.'

'It's terrible. I'm glad I caught you before you closedown. I need to confirm the whereabouts of one of your patients.'

'I'm not sure I understand?'

'Sorry. Let me explain. His name is Ricky White and he had an appointment at three-thirty on Wednesday just gone.'

'I'm not sure how I can help,' Amber said.

'I need to know if he attended his appointment.'

'Oh. I'm not sure we can divulge that information. I can ask Mr Greenman if it's okay when he gets back from his meeting. I'm sure he won't mind but I'll need to ask his permission.'

Kim looked around. The waiting room was empty. She leaned closer to Amber. 'Have you heard about the young girl, Rachel Evans going missing?' she whispered.

'The girl from Bodedern. Yes. It's awful. Everyone is talking about it,' Amber said, in her quietist voice, as if the waiting room was full. 'Her mum is my auntie's second cousin.'

'Really?'

'Yes.'

'Then you'll understand how time sensitive this is. I'm investigating a line of enquiry, which is vital to finding her. I could come back with a warrant but you're closing and that would slow us down and hinder any progress.' Kim looked around again, as if they were conspirators discussing a secret plot. 'Or you could just look on your screen and nod if Ricky White attended or shake your head if he didn't. It would be a huge help and technically, you haven't told me anything.' Amber bit her lip, unsure. She wanted to help but didn't want to compromise the rules. 'Rachel's mother is distraught, as are the rest of the family. I'm sure you can imagine what they're going through.' Amber nodded and tapped at her keyboard. She looked at the information and shook her head. 'You're absolutely sure he didn't attend.' Amber nodded. 'Thank you, Amber,' Kim said. 'You have lovely teeth,' she added as she walked away. Her heartbeat quickened as she took out her mobile and dialled the DI.

Amber went to the window and watched Kim getting into her car. She waited until the detective had gone from view before ringing her mum to share the gossip.

***

Alan was sitting at his desk, mulling over the information they had so far; it was precious little. Emily from the tech department knocked on the door. She looked flustered, which was unlike her. Alan took off his reading glasses and smiled.

'You look like someone who's got a lot on their mind,' he said. 'Have you had any results back?'

'Yes. But there's too much to tell you, I need to show you.' Emily shrugged. 'If that makes sense.'

'Okay. Yes, it makes sense. What have you found?'

'I'm not quite sure what to call it. You won't believe it when you see it,' Emily said, shaking her head. Her Doctor Martin's boots caught his eyes. He had a pair thirty-years ago when they were less cool and more thug-like.

'I'm sure I will believe it. Nothing surprises me anymore. Take a deep breath and tell me about it.'

'You remember you said to prioritise the devices connected to the Rachel Evans case.'

'Yes.'

'Obviously, we wanted to get her evidence analysed as quickly as possible.'

'Obviously.'

'We outsourced her Samsung tablet to a laboratory in Cheshire called Evolve. They're the best around and can hack firewalls that we can't. Their technical capability is way beyond ours. Their equipment is the latest design with an incredible spec compared to what we have to work with.'

'I see,' Alan said, not seeing at all.

'There's no comparison between them and us be honest. They can retrieve content that has been deleted. I don't know how they do it, but they do,' she rambled.

'Emily,' Alan said.

'What?'

'You're waffling,' he said, smiling.

'I am, aren't I.'

'Yes, you are. Slow down and tell me what you found.'

'Okay. We sent the tablet to them and they ran what is called an evolution check.'

'What does that entail?'

'It's software which searches for the source of any content and tracks any interaction with it. It follows how content evolves on the internet.'

'Okay. Are we talking about photographs?' Alan asked.

'Yes.'

'Rachel's mum said she was concerned about her selfies.'

'She has good reason to be. The evolution software tracked some of Rachel's pictures and it identifies anyone who interacted with them online, then it tracks if anyone shares them and where it went to and any further interactions any other users made. It's like a spider's web.'

'I see. This sounds like it could get messy.'

'It has become very messy indeed. One image can have almost infinite notifications. Anyway, some of the content she is linked to is off the scale and the sources are dubious.'

'Sources?' Alan said.

'Yes. That's where the content was actually first uploaded from.'

'Okay.'

'I'll explain later. The MD from Evolve called me this morning. He never calls anyone, but he was so concerned about what they found, he felt he had to call us himself to explain the severity of what they've found.'

'It sounds concerning.' Alan's detective senses were tingling. It sounded like they were onto something.

'It is concerning. It would be best if you and your team come to my office and I can go through it all with you. It might take us some time.' Her face was unusually pale, emphasised by the dark brown hair which fell halfway down her back. 'I know you're busy, but this will blow your mind and it will have a bearing on the way you treat this case.'

CHAPTER 17

Pauline Evans was standing in the woods, staring at a patch of grass that was stained with blood. More than likely, her daughter's blood. Rachel had been there, cold, wet, and bleeding. It broke her heart to think of her lying there alone in the dark being stalked by a predator. Crime scene tape flapped on the breeze, but the police officers and crime scene investigators were gone now; their job was done. The evidence had been photographed and removed for testing as they pieced together the jigsaw of what happened to Rachel.

Pauline had wanted to come to the spot to feel closer to her, but she couldn't feel anything but emptiness. Her daughter was not in the woods anymore; she was gone, where to, no one knew. Her son, Rob was standing next to her, his arm around her shoulder, trying to comfort her; in reality, there was no comfort to be had. Someone had taken one of her offspring and she'd never known a feeling of pain and loss like it; not even when her husband had died, ravaged by cancer. This was a different type of loss and she didn't feel that she could cope with it. It was totally overwhelming.

She was weeping into a tissue and she knew her son felt just as helpless as she did. As much as he tried, he couldn't take the pain away from her; no one could. She hadn't had any sleep or any food since Rachel went missing. Family and friends had surrounded them and supported them as much as they could, but their pity didn't help and was suffocating at times. She'd spent a lot of time alone in her bedroom, seeking solace away from the endless speculation and cups of tea, preferring to be alone.

Earlier, Pauline had said she needed to see where Rachel had fallen, and she needed to go alone. She wanted some space to clear her thoughts, but Rob wouldn't hear of it; he insisted on walking with her. Pauline didn't have the energy to argue. Inside her mind, was a bubbling caldron of what ifs and maybes. Her thoughts were dark and desperate, and she could find no peace or quiet. She couldn't settle or relax. The police liaison officer had said it was imperative to stay positive, but it was easier said than done. One of her children had been taken by force; it was obvious. There was no other reasonable explanation that anyone could come up with. Rachel had been taken. She wasn't lost and she wasn't somewhere else. She'd been taken against her will and there was nothing Pauline could do about it. She'd never felt so desperate in her life. Despair enveloped her very being like a dark shroud. She was surrounded by people yet terribly alone.

The wind blew through the trees and cut through her soul like a knife through butter. A raindrop touched her cheek and mingled with her tears; its touch was like a pinprick of ice. She closed her eyes and tried to feel Rachel but there was nothing but a deep black void. Her mind tried to replay what had happened to her. The police said they thought Rachel had been running away from someone; if that was true, she must have been terrified, alone in the dark being chased by some lunatic. Pauline felt her daughter's fear, felt her sense of panic, felt her pain as she crashed into a tree and fell. Sensing her child's emotions shattered her heart. Rachel had been in a terrifying place and Pauline hadn't been there to protect her. She still couldn't protect her, and the helplessness was debilitating.

What bothered her the most was the fact that she couldn't feel Rachel anymore. She was numb inside. It was as if Rachel's energy had been snuffed out; the mortal coil which attached them was broken. She had an overwhelming feeling of dread. She'd felt it from the moment Rachel hadn't arrived home for her tea. The questions were never-ending. Where was she? Was she alive or dead? Who would want to hurt her? Why would they choose Rachel? Why not someone else? There were so many questions running around in her mind that she couldn't think straight. Rob sensed her distress and squeezed her hand, but it had no effect. Nothing could soothe the pain. The emptiness inside her was crippling.

'It will be all right. Everyone's looking for her, Mum.'

'I know they are, son,' Pauline said, 'but that doesn't help me feel any better. I need to know where she is. I need her home safe.'

'She will be. They'll find her,' he said. 'I know they will.'

'You can't know that, son,' she said. 'None of us can predict the future. All we can do is hope she's still alive.' Pauline lost her control. She let go of all the pain and angst that was bottled up inside. Her body was racked with sobs. Her face was soaked by the tears she was crying. She could barely breathe. Saliva ran from her lips and dangled from her chin. She was broken.

Long minutes passed until her trembling settled. Rob supported her as best he could. It felt like hours before her sobbing faded and she could finally support her own weight. Eventually, her breathing slowed to near normal. Rob held her as tightly as he dared; she seemed so fragile, he feared she would shatter into a million pieces. He wiped a tear from the corner of his own eye; he wasn't crying for Rachel. Not this time. He was crying because he couldn't bear to see his mother's sadness anymore. His mother looked up at him, delving deep into his eyes, searching for the truth. She was looking for answers. She was looking for anything more than she had, which was nothing but questions and anxiousness and the deep sense of loss which filled every molecule. Her expression hardened as if something inside her had switched.

'I need you to tell me the truth, Rob.'

'What do you mean?'

'You know the police took eight-hundred pounds from her bedroom,' she said. Rob nodded and sniffled. He wiped his nose on his sleeve. 'Where do you think she got that much money from?'

'I don't know, Mum,' Rob said. He looked away. 'Honestly, I don't know where it's from. If I did know, I would tell you.'

'You two have always been like two peas in a pod. You were like twins, thick as thieves since you were babies.' The memory let a smile touch her lips momentarily. One second it was there, the next it was gone. 'There's no way she could have been doing something dodgy without you knowing about it,' Pauline said. 'What was she up to?'

'Nothing. Nothing I know about it anyway.'

'She must have been. Money doesn't grow on trees.'

'What makes you think she was doing something dodgy?'

'How else does a fourteen-year-old get that much money?' she asked. 'Was she selling drugs?'

'What are you talking about?' Rob asked. 'Rachel wouldn't do anything like that.'

'It's too much of a coincidence.'

'What's a coincidence?'

'You must have heard the rumours about our Louise?' Pauline asked, watching his expression, looking for the telltale signs of a lie. 'It's all around Holyhead that she's been selling drugs to her mates on the skateboard park.'

'I've heard whispers.'

'They're much more than whispers and you know it,' Pauline said, shaking her head. 'Has she got Rachel involved in something?'

'Rachel isn't like Louise. Louise has always been a wild one,' Rob said. 'That's aunty Jen's fault for being a pisspot all her life.'

'Don't say things like that about Jen,' Pauline said, softly. 'She's had mental health problems since she was a little girl. I know that doesn't excuse her but a lot of it isn't her fault.'

'It hasn't helped Louise though,' Rob said. 'I've heard the rumours, but Rachel wouldn't do anything like that. She's not like Louise.'

'So, the rumours about her are true?'

'I think so,' Rob said, looking away. 'I don't know for sure.'

'You either know they're true or you don't,' Pauline said. 'Which is it?'

'I know they are true,' he said, reluctantly.

'How can you be sure?'

'Why does it matter?'

'Because it matters to me,' Pauline said, calmly. 'How do you know Louise was selling drugs?'

'I just heard she was.'

'Bollocks,' Pauline snapped. Rob looked surprised at his mum's choice of words. She rarely swore and bollocks wasn't part of her usual repertoire. 'Tell me the truth, Robert Evans. I can tell at a glance when you're lying to me. How do you know for sure?'

'It doesn't matter how I know. I just know.'

'It matters to me. How do you know?'

'Why does it matter?'

'Because your sister had been kidnapped,' Pauline said, pointing to the blood on the grass. 'Can you see that?'

'Of course, I can.'

'That's your sister's blood. Someone's taken her, and I don't think it was random. There must be a reason for it, Rob.' She paused and touched his face. 'Don't you see? I'm racking my brains for the reason why Rachel isn't here. I need a reason to make sense of it all and the only thing which doesn't make sense is that money. Can't you see that?' Rob rolled his eyes. 'Look at me when I'm talking to you.' Reluctantly he turned his head, tears flowing freely now. She could see he was hurting too, but she needed answers. 'Where did she get that money from, Rob?'

'I don't know, Mum. If I knew, I would tell you,' he answered.

'That money has something to do with her going missing,' Pauline said. 'I know it has. Tell me, Rob. What was she up to?'

'I don't know,' Rob said. 'If I'd known she had all that money, I'd have borrowed some.' Pauline looked into his eyes as he spoke. 'Maybe she borrowed it for something.'

'Borrowed it for what?'

'I don't know. She was always on about getting her lips done and a boob job. Maybe she borrowed it from a mate.'

'Where would her mates get that kind of money?' Pauline asked. 'They're fourteen. When did she ever mention getting a boob job, for Christ's sake?' Pauline asked, shaking her head in disbelief. 'She's fourteen.'

'She was always on about it,' Rob said.

'I don't think she borrowed that money but whoever it belonged to was up to something.'

'You don't know that for sure.'

'I do know that, Robert Evans,' she said. 'I haven't lived this long not to know when something isn't right. I gave birth to you and your sister and I've seen you grow up. You're my children and I know you better than you know yourself. This isn't a game or a childish secret that you must keep; Rachel has been hurt and taken away. There's a reason for that and I'm convinced that money is something to do with it.' She paused to take a deep breath. 'If that money was legit, why hide it in a box?'

'So that the rest of the family don't ask to borrow some or so you didn't think she was up to something dodgy like selling drugs.'

'Don't be facetious, Robert.' Pauline pointed her finger at him. 'The police will be asking you about that money; you and her friends at school and I'll be telling them about Louise too, so if you know anything, now is the time to tell me.'

'The police can talk to Louise, not me. I don't know anything about the money, Mum. I'm going home,' he said, trying to keep his temper. 'Are you coming?'

'No,' Pauline said. She started walking towards the path which led deeper into the woods. The path her daughter's attacker had taken. 'I'm going for a walk. You go back and tell everyone not to worry. I'll be back when I'm ready. And when I get back, I want some straight answers from you.'

'I don't know anything. Okay,' Rob said. 'See you later.' Their eyes locked for a second. Pauline didn't believe her son. Rob was lying and she knew it and Rob knew that she knew.

CHAPTER 18

Alan called Kim and Richard and asked them to meet him in Emily's office. He shared their updates with the rest of the squad and checked if any new information had come in on the phones but there was nothing of any value. There were a few random sightings which had no substance to them. Everything had to be considered and then prioritised. The already cloudy waters surrounding the case were becoming murkier. He explained that the techs had pulled some vital information from Rachel's laptop which they needed to see for themselves rather than hear it second hand. They gathered in Emily's office to listen to the findings.

There were two large screens attached to her computer, both showed images of Rachel Evans pouting and posing for selfies. The filters made her eyes look bigger and her complexion flawless, like a model. They also made her look older. She could have been one of millions of teen girls doing the same thing online, every minute of the day. One of the screens showed images that she'd posted on Instagram, the other showed images uploaded to Facebook. In the bottom right-hand corner of each picture, Alan could see the dates that the images were posted. Most of them were uploaded around eighteen months prior. Emily clicked on the screen and the formation changed to columns of photographic tiles. Each column showed hundreds of images laid out in chronological order. There were thousands of selfies taken from every conceivable angle. All of them featured Rachel.

'As you can see, Rachel was prolific on social media,' Emily pointed out the obvious. 'She certainly liked to share her pictures and she had an audience who interacted with them.'

'That's a lot of selfies. How many are there, roughly?' Kim asked.

'We're not sure of the total number but this sample selection is taken from over the last eighteen months or so and equates to her posting about twenty images a day. Sometimes many more especially at a weekend when there was no school.'

'Why have you focused specifically on this eighteen-month period?' Alan asked.

'Because prior to that, her images are just innocent selfies and the odd group photo with her friends. As time goes by, things turn a bit darker to say the least.'

'That doesn't sound good,' Alan said.

'It isn't good at all,' Emily said. She appeared to be rattled by the evidence, which was unusual for her. 'You can see the images run from the top left of the screen being the oldest, bottom right, the most recent,' Emily explained, pointing to the dates. 'The pictures range from perfectly innocent selfies of herself and her friends eighteen months ago to something much more provocative as the months go by.' The images on the screens changed. 'As time goes by the interaction from her fans snowballs and becomes more suggestive, to say the least. There are more likes and more comments which could have attracted the attention of her parents or siblings or maybe even her teachers but she kept a lid on things by unfriending them all and she cleverly disabled the share option.'

'Why would she do that,' Alan asked. 'Facebook isn't my forte.'

'Probably to stop her family from seeing them inadvertently if an image was shared by a mutual friend.' Emily pointed to the images taken in the June prior. 'She then goes one step further. You can see from June last year, she set up fake profiles, using the pseudonym Caz Marino, probably to throw her family off the scent even further. None of the images on these platforms include her friends or family. The pictures she uploaded to the fake profiles are of her alone and they take a turn for the worse as regards the tone. She becomes much more daring. I'd go so far as to say she became reckless, probably without realising it. Most of her images are of her in her school uniform, which attracts a certain type of pervert and look at the interaction she's receiving on her fake platforms. She's become very provocative and the reactions to her pictures take a turn for the worse.'

'They've jumped from dozens of interactions in June to thousands of likes and comments in recent weeks,' Kim said. 'And from the comments I'm reading, most of them are quite lewd.'

'Some of them are downright disgusting,' Alan added, taking off his glasses. 'She was putting herself out there for the wrong type of men to see.'

'Shocking. Who talks to a young girl like that?' Richard said.

'Men like them. Men who trawl the web looking for this kind of entertainment,' Emily said. 'She has over twenty-five thousand followers on Twitter, thirty thousand on Instagram, and she's reached the limit on Facebook. June, July, and August took her from being a popular girl on social media to an internet sex symbol.' Emily opened up YouTube on one of the screens. 'She started a vlog in August and already has a huge following. The high numbers of interactions make her profile valuable advertising space and she'll probably have been in receipt of royalties. That is what attracted the internet sharks like blood in the water.'

'Internet sharks?' Alan asked.

'I'll explain,' Emily said.

'That might explain the money in her room,' Kim said.

'It might do,' Alan agreed. 'Sorry. Carry on.'

'The software used to unravel her social media pictures traces one image at a time to its original source.'

'Which would be her phone, I presume?' Alan asked.

'Or her laptop or tablet. It identifies an IP address and the user device so we can identify the difference between the devices.'

'I see. So, if more than one person is using the IP address, we can identify who has uploaded what?'

'Exactly. It was developed for hotels to distinguish which room and device content is posted from or downloaded to,' Emily said. 'In this case, the evolution software tracked thousands upon thousands of communications on her posts from all over the planet. It would take months and months to track them all so we're narrowing it down to users and IP addresses in the locality. I'm assuming you're not interested in anyone living abroad?'

'Not for now,' Alan said. 'We can share the information with Interpol once we've sieved through it.'

'Okay. There are some very concerning messages sent directly to her inboxes so, we're concentrating on them, especially the profiles she blocked, which are numerous. Some of the messages are aggressive. If she didn't reply, some became threatening and very abusive. We're running through the more frequent offenders to pinpoint where they are and we're focusing on IP addresses in North Wales for now.'

'Jesus.' Alan sighed. 'She was putting herself in front of the wolves.'

'That is incredible. She made quite a transformation over eighteen months,' Kim said, looking at the more recent pictures.

'The selfies are just the tip of the iceberg. Things get much worse,' Emily said. She clicked on a link to a different website. When the images changed, there was a sharp intake of breath from the detectives.

'Well, I didn't expect that,' Alan said. 'What the hell was going through her mind?'

'Bloody hell,' Richard said, nearly spitting his coffee everywhere.

The images of Rachel were pornographic and there were dozens of them. Alan, Kim, and Richard were sitting in stunned silence.

'There are hundreds of images and over ten pornographic films featuring Rachel.'

'Ten pornographic films?' Alan asked, incredulous. 'How the hell has she managed to do that, she's fourteen?'

'Everything is not what it seems. I'll explain why. There are ten on this site alone. We're trawling others as we speak and the films featuring Rachel are system-wide across the Dark Web.' She clicked on one of the photographs and the pixels were magnified. 'This is where things get complicated. You can see the slight blur here at the neck?' The detectives nodded. 'If you watched these films, you wouldn't notice the pixels merge, you would just see the normal definition of Rachel, not a closeup like this. It would have taken a lot of time and a professional photographer to produce all these images of Rachel, except the woman in these pictures and films is not Rachel Evans.'

'What?' Alan said, confused. 'That is clearly Rachel,' he said looking closer. He put his glasses on and shook his head. 'That is Rachel. I don't understand.'

'It's a picture of Rachel's face but the rest of the body isn't hers. The images of her face have been grafted on to the pornographic images of other women. They've used Photoshop or similar software to put Rachel's face onto already available images.'

'Why on earth would anyone do that?' Alan asked.

'Money,' Emily said. 'Rachel had inadvertently turned her profile Caz Marino into a valuable asset which organised crime has taken advantage of. See here,' Emily said pointing to the image. 'Someone has taken hundreds of Rachel's selfies and merged them into these images. They have ready access to pictures of her from the dozens of angles that she uploaded, and they've digitally manufactured these pornographic pictures and films and uploaded them to the Dark Web. Closeup, it's easy to see where the grafts are but on normal resolution, they look real. On this one she has tattoos on her leg and hands and in this film she has them on her back and the leg tattoos have gone. Rachel doesn't have any tattoos…she's fourteen. It isn't Rachel.'

'We're going to have to go back to the drawing board here,' Alan said, sighing. 'I wasn't expecting this. This shines a completely different light on the case.'

'The films they've manufactured are graphic, very graphic indeed. Two of them depict Rachel being tied up and abused, raped, and beaten. They're violent in the extreme. In one of them, she's eventually killed.' Emily paused.

'Someone made a snuff movie using her images?' Alan asked.

'They made several. The more graphic films are particularly popular. Rachel's image has become popular on the Dark Web and her fans are not what I would call *normal* human beings. Their tastes are somewhat warped. The messages her fans have left on the films are not men looking for romantic engagement with her, they're disturbed. Very disturbed indeed.'

'Does Rachel know about these films?' Alan asked.

'We don't think so. The evolution software pinpoints the source of the images and films being uploaded on the dark web. They are being uploaded from Ukraine.'

'Ukraine?' Kim said. 'Are you kidding? How the hell have they targeted Rachel from there?'

'Facebook would be my guess. They trawl the site looking for who is getting the most interaction then hack into their other social media platforms. It didn't take much to mimic her profile on the Dark Web. Rachel's images are out there for anyone to see and download. She inadvertently gave them everything they needed, and they had a readymade audience. They added links to her most popular pictures, which took her admirers directly to the Dark Web images, where they had to pay to reveal the content. She had no idea what was being done. She is a cash cow without even knowing it.'

'This is a massive problem as far as our investigation goes,' Alan said.

'Her poor mother will be traumatised. Someone took her daughter's pictures from her social media platforms and turned her into a porn star.' Kim added, shaking her head. 'Who would have suspected that?'

'Not me for sure,' Richard said. 'I've never seen anything like it in all my days policing.'

'We're sure she wasn't aware of the films?' Alan asked.

'As sure as we can be. Unless she trawled the dark web on another device, there would be no way she would know about them. They've found no evidence on her computer that she visited these sites.' Emily flicked her hair from her face. She looked relieved to have shared the burden of knowledge. 'Only individuals with certain tastes would frequent these sites. They're about the degradation of other humans, male and female, old and young; there're no boundaries.' She shook her head. 'They're about violence and they generate a lot of money. It's very clever. People subscribe with credit cards and the service appears as something innocent on their statements. It's a multi-million-pound business.'

'How many people have viewed those videos?' Alan asked.

'They have had tens of thousands of views and they've only been up there a few months; some of them only a few weeks,' Emily said.

'We've just found a lot more suspects and a possible motive to abduct her. It might not have been random,' Kim said. 'This really puts the cat among the pigeons.'

'What if somebody who viewed one of those images or films, recognised Rachel as the schoolgirl from the village and decided to act out their fantasy?' Alan asked. 'It's not beyond the realm of possibility. It's more likely to be someone who knows her or knows of her than a random attack.'

'I agree. I don't believe there was a nutcase waiting in the woods in the hope a young girl would inadvertently stumble into his grasp. I'm with you on this Alan. People become obsessed with internet porn,' Richard said. 'It's a real possibility one of her internet fans has snapped and decided to snatch her.'

'It's opened a can of worms,' Kim said. 'That's what it has done. From a public perspective, if this gets out, and at some point, it will, she's no longer the sweet innocent girl next door. This has taken us ten steps backwards.'

'What the hell are we going to tell the family?' Richard said.

'Nothing for now,' Alan said. 'We keep this quiet for as long as we can. They're going through enough trauma as it is.' Alan paused. 'Is there any way we can have these images and films taken down?'

'From the Dark Web?' Emily asked.

'Yes.' Alan nodded.

'Not a chance.' Emily shook her head. 'The only positive in this is that these films are aimed at a certain group of society who are driven by control. Subdue, restraint, imprisoning their victims.'

'Forgive me but I'm not seeing the positive here,' Richard said, frowning.

'Emily is saying that if she has been abducted by one of these nutters, they'll probably keep her alive for a while at least,' Kim said. Emily nodded her agreement.

'Is there anyway of tracing these perverts through their credit cards?'

'Once you catch them, possibly, otherwise not a chance.'

'I thought you'd say that,' Alan said.

'What do you want to do next?' Richard asked.

'I'm assuming we're going to have wait for more information from the evolution searches?' Alan asked.

'Yes,' Emily said, nodding. 'It could take a few days to narrow down anyone with an IP address in the locality. Then again, it could take just hours. If we get anything on the island, I'll contact you straightaway.'

'Thank you, Emily. In the meantime, we need to work on what we already have, starting with Ricky White. I want everyone close to Rachel eliminated from the investigation before we widen it,' Alan said. 'Let's ask him why he didn't go to the dentist appointment. Ask him to come in voluntarily first; if he refuses, arrest him.'

CHAPTER 19

Pauline Evans answered her mobile. The number calling was stored in her phone under the name Gwenda, her second cousin. Her phone hadn't stopped ringing since the news of Rachel's disappearance had spread. She didn't really feel like talking but answered the call to be polite. Members of the family who she hadn't talked to for years had been calling to express their concerns. They all meant well, so being polite was the least she could do, even if it was difficult. The last thing that she wanted to do was answer the same banal questions about Rachels' disappearance again and again. Everyone seemed to have an opinion and didn't mind sharing it and they automatically assumed the police weren't doing enough. Pauline wanted them to do more, she wanted them to call out the army, navy, and airforce but they didn't have a magic wand.

'Hello, Gwenda,' Pauline said, answering the phone.

'Hello, Pauline,' Gwenda said. 'How are you?'

'As well as can be expected,' Pauline said, closing her eyes. *How the fucking hell do you think I am?* she thought.

'I've been thinking of you,' Gwenda said.

First time for ten years, Pauline thought.

'I can't believe what's happened.'

'I'm going out of my mind, Gwenda, to be honest. I feel like I'm in a bad dream.'

'I can only imagine what you're going through. I'm so sorry for you.'

'Thank you.'

'Is there any news about what might have happened to Rachel?'

'No. Nothing new.'

'What are the police saying?'

'Not a lot. They're doing their best, but they can only work with what evidence they have.'

'Which is what?'

'A text message to a friend saying she had to see the headmistress, which was a lie. They searched the woods behind the school and found some blood and one of her boots. The blood type matches hers, but the DNA results haven't come back yet. She's missing and the evidence points to her disappearance not being voluntary; that's all they know. They can't actually say one way or the other.'

'Oh, Pauline, how awful. Do they think she's been kidnapped?'

'They're not saying that exactly yet, but it looks that way.' Pauline choked back a tear. Talking about it was very difficult. Her nerves were raw. 'She hasn't just disappeared into a puff of smoke. Someone must have taken her. I can't see anything else that makes sense.'

'Nothing does make sense,' Gwenda agreed. 'She wouldn't run away, would she?'

'No, Gwenda. She hasn't run away. Someone has taken her, and I'm frightened to death. I just want her back home.'

'I can't imagine what you're going through, Pauline. It's a nightmare. Why on earth would anyone take her?'

'The only reasons I can think of aren't worth thinking about. When I do, it drives me demented. She's a pretty young girl and there're a lot of perverts out there. I don't want to think about it.'

'It doesn't bear thinking about, Pauline. Don't torture yourself. The world is full of looneys nowadays.'

'It feels like that at the moment. I keep racking my brains thinking someone local has got my daughter and I'm thinking of who I know who's capable of taking her. If I said what I was thinking aloud, they'd lock me up.'

'That's only natural. You're bound to look at people and be suspicious. I don't know why the police aren't more upfront. They must think she's been kidnapped, so why don't they just say so?' Gwenda said.

'Because they're exploring all the other possibilities first.'

'They should be honest. They haven't mentioned any suspects to you?'

'Suspects?'

'Yes. If they think she might have been taken, then they must be investigating potential suspects. Surely, they should be talking to you about it.'

'No. They haven't officially said it's an abduction yet so why would they mention anything like that,' Pauline said. She thought it sounded like it was a loaded question. Gwenda was fishing for information. The hairs on her neck stood on end. 'Have you got something you want to say, Gwenda?'

'I'm not sure if I should. I don't want to talk out of turn, but I've heard a whisper from a very good source,' Gwenda said.

'A whisper about what exactly?' Pauline snapped. She knew the gossip mongers would be having a ball, but she didn't have time for it. Gossip and whispers were the last thing she needed. 'I haven't got time for tittle-tattle, Gwenda. My daughter is missing and I'm struggling to cope as it is. So, if you know something, tell me.'

'I'm not sure how to say this without dropping Amber in it,' Gwenda said, dropping Amber in it without thinking.

'Amber who?'

'My niece, Mia's daughter. She works in Valley at the dentist,' Gwenda said.

'I know her although I haven't seen her since she was a little girl. How would she know anything about Rachel?'

'Because of what a female detective said.'

'Kim?' Pauline asked. 'She's working the case. What has she said?'

'Well, she was working on reception when a detective went into the surgery asking questions.'

'Asking questions about what?'

'If anyone finds out about this, she could lose her job. You can't repeat this, okay?'

'Just spit it out, Gwenda, for god's sake.'

'Okay, okay. I'm just worried because she shouldn't be giving out information without permission because of the data protection stuff,' Gwenda said. 'She could get the sack.'

'Gwenda, just tell me what she said.'

'Sorry, I'm all a fluster.' Gwenda took a deep breath. 'Amber phoned me because the police went into the surgery yesterday asking questions about a patient called Ricky White. I didn't click when she first said the name but then the lights came on and I thought about you straightaway.'

'Are you sure it was Ricky White they were asking about?'

'Yes. I'm positive.'

'*Our* Ricky White?' Pauline felt her stomach knot. Her heart started beating faster. Anger bubbled deep inside her, building slowly.

'Yes. It's definitely him.'

'Is she sure?'

'Yes. Amber recognised your address.'

'What was Kim asking about him?'

'To cut a long story short, he had an appointment the day Rachel went missing, but he didn't show up. The detective was asking Amber to tell her if he attended or not. She's not supposed to give out information about patients, so she had to tell her that he didn't attend by just nodding her head. Technically she hasn't actually told her anything, but she actually did. If you know what I mean?'

'But she didn't say why they were asking about him?' Pauline said. Her mind started to spin out of control.

'No. Amber said she just nodded her head that he hadn't attended, and the detective asked her if she was sure and then she left.' Pauline couldn't speak for a moment. 'I don't know if it's significant, but I thought you'd want to know,' Gwenda said. 'I would want you to tell me if it was the other way around. Are you still there?'

'Yes. I'm here. I don't know what to say.'

'What do you think?'

'I don't know what to think.'

'I had to tell you. I'd want to know,'

'Of course. I understand. Thanks, Gwenda,' Pauline said. She couldn't think straight. 'I need to go. I'll talk to you soon. Bye.' Pauline looked at the blank screen and decided what to do. She could feel her blood boiling as she scrolled through her contacts to find Norman's number.

***

Ricky White was biting his nails when Alan and Kim walked into the interview room. He looked pale and nervous. His eyes were darting nervously around the room. He seemed to be looking anywhere but at the detectives. It was obvious that his previous encounters with the police had not gone well, hence he appeared to be feeling vulnerable.

'Hello Ricky. Thanks for coming in,' Alan said, sitting down opposite him. 'We need to ask you a few questions.'

'It wasn't through choice,' Ricky said.

'I beg your pardon,' Alan asked.

'I said, I'm not here through choice,' Ricky said, anger in his voice.

'Sorry. What's the problem?'

'Your lot made me look like a right knob at work. Everyone was looking at me like I'm Jack the Ripper or something.'

'I'm under the impression you were called and asked to come in to answer some questions, but you refused because your motorbike is in the garage.'

'It is in the garage. I'm not lying. It's in for an MOT.'

'No one is saying you're lying. You said you had no transport so, we said we'd get you here, conduct the interview, and take you back to work and that plain clothed officers would give you a lift?' Alan said.

'Yes, but I had to leave work in the middle of a shift. That looks suspicious itself and then I was driven away by men in suits. It doesn't look very good, does it?' Ricky protested.

'The officers had been to a funeral at the crematorium in Bangor, I believe.'

'They look like a couple of FBI agents.'

'We don't have an FBI here.'

'Funny man. It's obvious I've been taken away by the police and everyone knows Rachel is missing. It's out of order. Everyone will think I've done something to her.'

'The alternative would have been acquiring an arrest warrant and escorting you from the building in handcuffs. I'd count yourself lucky if I were you.' Ricky snorted his discontent. 'You're here voluntarily but if you feel uncomfortable or if you think you're being treated unfairly, we can make things official and get you a brief if you prefer that?' Ricky thought for a second. He knew once the process started, it was difficult to stop it. 'I don't want you feeling under any pressure. There's a duty solicitor in the building. Would you like him to sit in with you?'

'Yes, please,' Ricky said, nodding. 'I don't trust you lot.'

Kim stood up and left the room, returning a few minutes later with a confused looking brief in a creased grey suit.

'This is Mr McDonald,' Kim said. 'He'll sit in on your behalf.' The solicitor sat down and smiled. Ricky didn't return his smile; he shifted in his seat, uncomfortable with the situation. 'We'll step out for a few minutes while you have a quick chat.' Alan got up and followed Kim out of the room. He punched some coins into a vending machine and purchased two cups of brownish hot water, pertaining to be coffee. He handed one to Kim.

'That boy has got a chip on his shoulder,' Alan said.

'Most paedophiles do when they get caught and put on the register. It's not a club that most people want to be a part of.'

'He's being evasive already and we haven't asked him a question yet,' Alan said, checking his watch. 'That's long enough. Shall we go back in?'

'Let's go for the throat. If he's got anything to hide, he'll crack. He looks very nervous,' Kim said.

'He always does,' Alan said. 'Ricky White is an oddball.'

'Don't call him that to his face.'

'I'll try not to.' They walked back into the interview room. 'Okay. Are you done with introductions, ready to answer a few questions?' Alan asked. Ricky nodded his head. 'I see you have a bottle of water there in case you're thirsty, so we'll crack on, shall we?' Ricky shrugged and twisted the top off. He sipped from the bottle, noisily. 'We need to ask you a few questions about Rachel Evans, if that's okay.'

'You're wasting your time. I don't know anything about what happened to her.'

'What do you think happened to her?' Alan asked.

'What do you mean?'

'You said, you don't know anything about what happened to Rachel.'

'I don't.'

'What makes you think something has happened to her?'

'She hasn't come home, Sherlock,' Ricky said, pulling a face. 'Don't try to twist me up; that's what you lot do. It's obvious something has happened to her otherwise she'd be at home taking photographs of herself.'

'The official line is that she's missing,' Alan said. 'We don't know that something has happened to her yet although between us, it isn't looking good.'

'Whatever. I don't know anything, whatever you lot say.'

'You said Rachel takes a lot of pictures of herself.' Ricky shrugged. 'Does that annoy you?' Kim asked.

'Does what annoy me?'

'Rachel taking selfies?'

'No. It's just what she does. I see them on Facebook.'

'Do you look at her pictures?'

'Some of them. I don't have any choice,' Ricky said. 'They're all over Facebook. They come up in my news feed.'

'She's very pretty, isn't she?' Kim asked.

'Can't say I've noticed. She's my stepsister.'

'Do you look at her pictures on any other platforms?' Kim asked.

'No. I don't. I don't use any other platforms except Facebook and I only go on there because work has a page. They post extra shifts and overtime on there if people call in sick. It's first come, first served so, I check it when I need extra money. Apart from that, I hardly go online at all.'

'We'll need to look at your phone and any other devices you have to verify that,' Kim said.

'You'll need a warrant to do that,' Ricky said, glancing at his brief. His brief nodded to the affirmative. 'I'm not handing my phone over to you. I'll never see it again.'

'No problem. We can get a warrant if you like?' Kim said. 'Or you could cooperate with our investigation and save us the trouble.'

'Not a chance. I'm doing everything by the book. The last time I cooperated with you lot, I got bummed and I never got my phone or my tablet back. I'm still waiting for them. You're not getting my stuff without a warrant. Not after last time.'

'I assume you're referring to the underage sex investigation in Manchester?' Alan said.

'Of course, I'm referring to that. I knew it wouldn't take long for you to latch onto that and twist it to your own benefit,' Ricky said, defensively.

'It's on your record. We were bound to see it at some point.'

'It should never have been there in the first place. It was blown out of all proportion. She was my girlfriend. We were in a relationship.'

'You were fourteen. She was twelve,' Kim said. 'Still a child.'

'We loved each other,' Ricky said.

'The law says she wasn't old enough to make up her mind about that and that she wasn't old enough to have the capacity to give her consent to have sex,' Kim said, glaring at him. 'The fact you don't acknowledge that worries me.'

'Whatever. You lot go for the easiest target every time. Just because I've made a mistake, I'm made a show of at work. You've tried to, embarrass me and now I'm sitting here being interrogated because I've got a record, not because I've done anything wrong. You're all the same, you lot.'

'That's not the case, Ricky. We have to run a check on everyone who had contact with Rachel, starting with the immediate family. That's standard procedure,' Alan said. 'You committed a sexual crime, so there's a record of it but that isn't why you're here. We would have interviewed you regardless of the conviction. It's just standard practice.' Ricky shrugged and shook his head. 'This isn't a witch hunt by any stretch of the imagination, so maybe you should drop the attitude and just answer the questions. Being awkward isn't helpful.' Ricky shrugged again and blushed. The solicitor looked embarrassed.

'Let's get on, shall we? The day Rachel went missing, you were scheduled to work from eight o'clock in the morning until eight that night. Is that correct?' Kim asked.

'Yes, but you already know that. I know you've spoken to my shift manager. He couldn't wait to tell me you'd been on the phone asking questions. He's a twat and he doesn't like me, anyway. You should have seen the look on his face today when I was picked up. Over the moon he was.'

'Just answer the question please, Ricky.'

'Yes, I was on an eight-eight that day, so what?'

'Did you complete that shift?'

'Most of it,' Ricky said, blushing red. 'I had a dentist appointment.'

'What time was your appointment?'

'Half three.'

'What time did you leave work?'

'About three.'

'You ride a motorbike, don't you?' Alan asked.

'Yes.'

'What type?'

'It's a Honda 250.'

'Is it fast?'

'Fast enough.'

'How long did it take you to get to Valley?'

'Twenty-minutes or so.'

'So, you were at the dentist intime for your appointment?' Kim asked.

'No.'

'You didn't go to the appointment?'

'No.'

'Why not?'

'I don't want to say. It's a bit embarrassing,' Ricky said.

'I'm sure we can handle it,' Kim said.

'I was driving across the island and I needed the toilet. I had a bad stomach, if you know what I mean.' The detectives watched him but didn't react. 'I'll spell it out. I had a dicky stomach and needed a shit.'

'Okay. We get it and what?'

'I thought I could make it home in time, have a crap, and still get to my appointment but things didn't work out that way.'

'Carry on,' Kim said. 'Explain it to us. Don't stop now.'

'Are you being funny?' Ricky asked. His lips narrowed. The corners of his mouth twitched.

'What is funny about it?' Kim said. 'We need to know where you were when you should have been at an appointment. It's not a trick question.'

'All right.'

'Good. Just answer the question.'

'I was desperate for the toilet and got caught short on the bike. By the time I got home, I had to strip off my clothes, shower, and change. It was a right mess, shit everywhere. I missed the dentist and had to get back to work to finish my shift. My manager is a dick and he was on my case all last week, so I didn't want to get back late.'

'Was anyone else at home who can confirm that story?'

'No. They were at school or at work and it's not a story. Stories are made up. I haven't made that up. That is what happened.'

'Great. It should be easy enough to verify the facts.'

'What do you mean?'

'What did you do with your clothes?' Kim asked.

'I put them into bin bags. They were ruined and I didn't want to put them in the washing basket when they were covered in crap. I binned them.' Kim made a note. Ricky shifted uncomfortably in his seat.

'Okay. So, if you're telling the truth, your clothes will still be in the bin and we can verify your story?' Kim asked. 'The council don't empty the bins until Tuesday, do they?'

'I didn't put them in the house bins.' Ricky twiddled his fingers and looked at his nails.

'You said you binned them, now you're saying you didn't?' Kim asked, frowning. 'Which one is it?'

'Simple. You're not the brightest bulb on the Christmas tree, are you?' Ricky said, smirking. 'I didn't put them in the house bins because they were covered in shit.'

'So, you said. Where are they?'

'I put them in a bin bag and dumped them in the council bins at the pub, so they didn't stink the place out. The bin wagon was there at the time,' Ricky said. His expression was stone. 'I didn't want Pauline finding them and kicking off. She's always whining about how my clothes make the washing basket stink of the kitchens. She's not my biggest fan at the best of times. Any excuse to moan at me or my dad.'

'So, we can't verify what you're saying?'

'Nope. Sorry about that.'

'We can ask the council to search through the skips,' Kim said. Ricky looked surprised. 'There's always a lag time from them being picked up to being emptied at landfill.' Kim lied. She didn't have a clue when they were emptied. 'I'm going to ask one our detectives to make the call now. Excuse me a minute,' she said, leaving the room. Alan knew it was a ruse but waited patiently until she came back in. 'We're in luck. They haven't been emptied.' Ricky shrugged but didn't look overly concerned. 'Tell me, do you get on with Pauline?' Kim asked.

'She's all right. I don't think I'll be calling her mum anytime soon. We put up with each other. I'll be getting my own place soon. I just need a deposit, hence the extra shifts.'

'What about her other children?'

'What about them?'

'Do you get on?'

'I don't have much to do with them, to be honest. I work long hours and they're in bed early on school nights and I tend to work weekends, especially through the summer. We don't see much of each other.' Kim tapped her pen on her fingers and stayed quiet. 'If I didn't live with them, I don't think I would be missed, let's put it that way.'

'She has two young daughters, which begs the question, does Pauline know about your conviction?' Kim asked.

'What has that got to do with you?' Ricky snapped, turning and angry shade of red. 'That's nothing to do with you.'

'Oh, but it is everything to do with us. You're on the sex offenders register, Ricky,' Kim said. 'Everything you do is our business. That's why it's there, so we know what offenders are up to and where they are and who might be in danger.'

'Like Rachel,' Alan added.

'Fuck you,' Ricky said. 'I'm not a danger to anyone. I'm not a nonce or a paedo. I had sex with my girlfriend.'

'Who was twelve,' Kim said. 'So, technically you are a paedophile.'

'You bastards,' Ricky hissed. His frustration was clear. His expression was pained.

'Bastards, are we?' Kim said, half smiling. 'You look very angry, Ricky.'

'Is it any wonder?'

'Do you get angry often?'

'I know what you're trying to do,' Ricky said, folding his arms.

'And what is it we're trying to do?'

'You're trying to make me mad, so I say something stupid, so you can blame me for Rachel being missing.'

'We're not looking for someone to blame,' Alan said. 'We're trying to find out the truth about what happened to her. We don't arrest the first person who comes along. It's traditional in the police force to conduct an investigation to identify what the facts are.'

'Fucking hell. That would be a first.'

'Look, Ricky. There's no benefit in blaming you for anything unless we think you're guilty of a crime.'

'Bullshit. You haven't got a scooby-doo what happened to her, so you're trying to get someone to confess or stitch themselves up.' He shook his head. 'I'm not that stupid. You can go and fuck yourself with your questions and your register. I'm not answering anymore questions without a solicitor. And I don't mean this waste of space. I want a proper solicitor; one that speaks.'

The detectives waited until he'd simmered down a little before speaking. Kim tapped her pen against the table leg and Alan steepled his fingers and sat forward.

'Okay, listen to me,' Alan said. 'We'll get you another solicitor or better still, get your own. Then we can sit back down and start again. When we do that, the conversation is on the record and the process begins properly. At the moment, we're just having an informal chat, trying to give you the opportunity to explain where you were when Rachel went missing. I'm sure that makes sense because you should have been at work, but you weren't because of an appointment at the dentist which you didn't attend. Work or the dentist would be what we call, an alibi.'

'I know what it's called. I'm not stupid,' Ricky muttered.

'If you had been at the dentist, we wouldn't be having this conversation, but you didn't attend, so you have no alibi and here we are.'

'I've told you what happened.'

'In truth, you've given us nothing, Ricky. All we're getting from you is abuse because you're feeling sorry for yourself because you were quite rightly prosecuted for sex with a minor. You're not helping us or yourself,' Alan explained calmly. He leaned further forward and lowered his voice. 'I want you to listen to where we are, at the moment, just so you're clear. What we know for a fact is that you left work at three o'clock and then reappeared at work two-and-a-half hours later wearing different clothes. The clothes you were wearing were discarded in the bins on a public car park and put into a bin wagon right there and then, which is convenient at best.'

'It wasn't convenient. That's what happened.'

'So, you say but in effect, you disposed of your clothing at the time a young girl went missing.' He paused and then raised a hand. 'Hold on a minute, there's another thing. There were no witnesses at home. You didn't see or speak to anyone who can verify your story. So, you have no alibi but as you said, you know that anyway.' He looked at Ricky and nodded. 'You're right about one thing. You do need a solicitor and you need a bloody good one. We'll talk again tomorrow. Shall we say ten o'clock?'

***

Pauline felt sick to the core. She wanted to phone the detectives working on Rachel's case and ask them why Kim had been asking questions about Ricky. They should have told her. She was furious that they might be keeping her in the dark about the direction the investigation was moving in. Her daughter was missing, and the police were asking questions about her stepson. That couldn't be right. They needed to explain themselves. When she called Norman to tell him what had happened, he'd been very evasive. He said he would come home from work to discuss it face to face. He never discussed anything, so that was strange in itself. She was beginning to suspect something wasn't as it seemed.

Norman never came home from work early. He was fastidious about his building work and he was good at it. His reputation on the island was good. He was reliable and produced a high-quality finish to whatever he was working on. He wasn't the cheapest builder on the island, but he was one of the best. He also had a likeable manner with his clients. He could turn on the charm when it suited him. Apart from her children, no one had a bad word to say about him, which in a small community was vital as a tradesman. He always had plenty of work on but he often reminisced about how much more money he earned when he lived in Manchester, which had made her wonder why he'd left there to start again on Anglesey. Something had always mithered her about it and she had a sneaking suspicion that it was something to do with his son. She'd never really warmed to him and she thought she was a good judge of character. The conversation with Gwenda was echoing around her mind and her imagination was running riot.

If Ricky had done anything to her daughter, she would kill him and then she would kill Norman. She heard the key in the front door and Norman walked in. He looked like a builder should, dusty combat pants, faded checked shirt, high-viz gilet, and steel toecap boots. His yellow hard hat stayed in the van.

'Are you all right?' Norman asked. He struggled to meet her gaze. She knew straightaway he had something to hide. 'I came as soon as I could. I was doing that conservatory job in town. The one in Wian Street. It's nearly finished. The customer is made up.'

'I don't care about the conservatory. I want to know why the police are asking questions about Ricky,' Pauline said, trying to maintain her calm.

'Who told you that they are asking questions about Ricky?'

'My cousin, Gwenda,' she said. 'They are asking where your son was when Rachel went missing. Now, why would they be doing that?'

'I don't know.'

'You must have some idea. I can tell by the look on you face that you know something.'

'Okay, calm down. Tell me what your cousin said, exactly,' Norman said.

'She said that Kim, the female detective who came here, went into the dentist surgery to ask them if Ricky turned up for an appointment at half-three on the day Rachel went missing,' Pauline said. 'He didn't go to his appointment. That is when school lets out, so where was he?'

'I think you're jumping to conclusions.'

'I'm not jumping to conclusions. I'm looking at the facts I've been given and asking the question. Where was he if he wasn't at the dentist?'

'How would the police know he had a dentist appointment?' Norman asked, shaking his head. 'It doesn't make sense.'

'It makes perfect sense to me,' Pauline said. She gritted her teeth. Her nerves were jangling and she felt like she was going to burst with anger. 'They must have asked the hotel if he was working when Rachel went missing. The hotel must have said no because he told them he had a dentist appointment. But he didn't turn up so, where was he?'

'We'll have to ask him when he gets in from work,' Norman said. 'I'm sure he has a perfectly reasonable explanation. He's got nothing to hide, I'm sure of it.'

'Why are the police asking where he was, anyway?'

'When someone goes missing, they have to check everyone out,' Norman said.

'There's something not adding up here, Norman,' Pauline said, shaking her head. 'Why are they sending detectives to the dentist? Why not phone or email or ask him, if all they were doing was a routine follow up on a family member?' Pauline walked closer to him and stared into his eyes. 'The detective asked the receptionist for information protected by the data protection act. She asked her to break the law just so they would know if Ricky was there or not and she didn't have a warrant. There's a reason why they're cutting corners.' Norman looked away. 'Something made that enquiry urgent. Urgent enough to break the rules. They know something I don't and so do you. I can see it in your eyes.'

Norman walked into the kitchen and filled a glass with water; his hands were trembling a little. He gulped from it. His Adam's apple bobbed up and down. Pauline followed him and glared at him, waiting for an answer.

'I'm going to call the detectives and ask them why they're asking about your son. Or you can tell me what the hell is going on,' Pauline demanded. 'Why are they so keen to know where Ricky was?'

'Okay. Sit down. It's going to come out anyway,' Norman said, looking defeated. Pauline shook her head and folded her arms; she wasn't going to sit down.

'You can say whatever you need to say to me while I'm standing up, thank you. What's going to come out?'

'I should have told you before. Ricky got into a bit of trouble a few years back.'

'What kind of trouble?'

'He was fourteen and he'd been seeing a girl for a few months. They had sex and her mother found out. She found her contraceptive pills in her room,' Norman explained. Pauline looked like she was in a trance. She could feel her knees shaking. 'Ricky was arrested and charged with having underage sex. It's on his record. That's why the police are looking into his whereabouts, but they've got it all wrong. He didn't hurt anyone. The sex was consensual, but I know how it looks.'

Pauline didn't speak. She looked like she was going to cry.

'I was going to tell you but I was worried what you would think of him and the longer we were together, the harder it was to bring up. Once we decided to move in together, I didn't think it mattered anymore.'

'I have two young daughters.'

'Ricky is a good lad. He's no harm to them.'

'How old was she?'

'They'd been together for months,' Norman said. 'It was consensual.'

'I didn't ask you that,' Pauline said, almost in a whisper. 'How old was she?'

'It sounds bad, but she was older than her years.'

'Stop bullshitting me and tell me how old she was.'

'She was twelve.'

'Oh my God.'

'This has nothing to do with Rachel going missing. Ricky wouldn't hurt a fly; you know he wouldn't.'

'Twelve years of age?' Pauline said. 'I was still dressing up dolls and playing house at that age.'

'They grow up quicker nowadays,' Norman said. 'I blame the internet.'

'I'm not having a debate about the age of consent, you idiot.'

'I'm not trying to belittle what happened. I'm just putting it into perspective.'

'You don't see it, do you?' Pauline was shellshocked. 'Get out of my house,' she said.

'What?'

'Get your stuff and get out of my house and you'd better tell that pervert not to come back here.' Norman tried to touch her shoulders. 'Get your hands off me. You knew I had two teenage daughters and you let that thing into my home?'

'Ricky hasn't hurt anyone, Pauline,' Norman said. 'You're just upset. Let's have a cup of tea and talk this through calmly.'

'If you're not out of my house in ten minutes, I'll stab you with a carving knife right between the eyes,' Pauline said. 'I'm going for a shower and I want you gone when I'm done.'

'There's no need for this,' Norman said. 'I know how it looks but you're overreacting.'

'If Ricky has done anything to my Rachel, I'll kill him with my bare hands. I swear to God I will. Get out and don't ever contact me again.' Pauline walked out of the kitchen and climbed the stairs; she paused halfway up. 'He's on the sex offenders register, isn't he?' she asked. 'That's why the police are focusing on him.' Norman looked at the floor. 'Answer me. Is Ricky on the sex offender list?'

Norman didn't answer. He left through the kitchen door. She heard him on the phone to Ricky as he climbed into the van and drove away.

CHAPTER 20

The Following Day

Meredith Robson was walking through the fields as she did every day. She was sixty-six and retired from nursing. It had been her career from leaving school and she'd loved it until austerity began to choke the NHS to death. There was no longer enough time to be a nurse. Not a proper nurse like she used to be in the early days. They had time to care for patients back then not patch them up and kick them out like they did nowadays. So many staff had resigned year on year that every shift she worked was short-handed; in the later years, the pressure was immense, and the job became intolerable. Treating patients on trolleys in corridors because of a lack of beds was not her idea of being a nurse. Successive governments promised the world and delivered nothing. It was a massive sense of relief when she finally hung up her matron's uniform but if she was honest with herself, she missed it. She missed the people, the daily contact with colleagues and the relationship with patients. Her friends messaged online and kept in touch, but it wasn't the same. She'd always had a sense of purpose to life but now that was gone. Now all she had to do was care for her husband Trevor.

What Happened to Rachel?

Once upon a time, spending all her time with him would have been wonderful but Trevor was no longer the man she married. They had spent most of their lives together and were very much in love. It was almost perfect until he became ill. He was an empty shell now; the old Trevor was gone. Parkinson's had ravaged his mind and body and there wasn't much of him left that was recognisable. She had some support. The carers came every day at the same time to turn him, wash him, and feed him and it gave her the one-hour respite that she needed to stay sane. She cared for him the other twenty-three hours of the day and it was a terrible burden. Feeling it was a burden swamped her with guilt and emotionally, she was on an escalator down. It was a no-win situation. Eventually death would release him, and her sense of guilt would increase and would be compounded with the sense of loss. She knew it was coming and she wondered how she would cope.

Her daily walk to the lake became a ritual. It gave her the space she needed to put things into perspective, just for a short while. The Trevor she married was no longer there and she had to be strong while the blood still circulated around his body and his brain further disintegrated into something resembling a sponge; until nothing of him remained. Earlier in the disease, he'd asked her to leave him enough tablets to kill himself but of course, she never did. Sometimes, she wished she had. Recently, she had thought about smothering him with a pillow or injecting him with insulin but deep inside she believed in the sanctity of life and the importance of allowing death to happen naturally. The terrible indignity of wasting away was painful to watch, but that was life. Death would come when the time was right for him to let go and she couldn't interfere in the process. God would decide, not her. She would have enough of her own life left to rethink her priorities and make a plan to enjoy the rest of what little time she had left.

It all seemed to be so unfair. They had worked hard all their lives and brought up their family together. They'd paid off their mortgage early and planned for their retirement. They saved so they could afford to spend their twilight years together comfortably in the sunshine somewhere, probably Lanzarote, but the disease had taken that option from them. Trevor had required fulltime attention a year before she retired, and the cost of care was crippling. It had been a terrible struggle to stay at work while he deteriorated but their financial plan revolved around her working until sixty-five, so she could claim a full pension. They hadn't planned on the cost of care workers coming every day. It had drained the coffers and moving abroad was no longer possible.

Life had taken her down a cruel path and it was compounded six months ago when her daughter and her two grandchildren were killed in a car accident while on holiday in Spain. Her son-in-law was left on a ventilator for a month before he followed them over the rainbow bridge to wherever beautiful people go when they die. Trevor would join them when he passed, and they would all wait for her on the other side until it was her turn to die. She wasn't ready to go yet, not by any means, but it gave her comfort that she would see them again one day. Her faith gave her hope when there was nothing else left.

Meredith heard scurrying in the undergrowth to her left. She'd reached the edge of the lake at Llyn Llwenan. The water rippled, blown by the breeze, and lapped against the pebble shore, which was dotted with trees and bushes. She was startled as a crow flew from the bushes, flapping its wings frantically; it squawked, and the sound echoed across the lake. There was a rotten smell tainting the air. She stopped and watched as four magpies followed the crow skyward, disturbed by her approach. They'd been feeding on something at the water's edge. Her father used to say crows and magpies were carrion and that they fed on the dead. A shiver ran through her as she walked towards the water. There was something floating on the surface. The smell of decaying flesh was overpowering. She crept closer and could make out long dark hair floating around a bloated face; it was discoloured with purple bruising. The eyes were swollen shut and deep blue, almost black. Some of the flesh had been pecked from the cheeks. She couldn't help but stare at the swollen corpse while her brain computed the scene and translated what she was seeing into the obvious conclusion. It was the naked body of a young girl. A deep rent around the neck told her the throat had been cut almost to the bone. She knew a schoolgirl had gone missing from Bodedern and she put two and two together. The news had been full of it. She took out her phone to call the police.

'I didn't weight the body enough, for fuck's sake,' she heard a voice say. A lump hammer struck her from behind, cracking her skull like an egg. Her legs folded and she could see the sun shimmering from the surface of the lake as she knelt. A second blow to the top of her head collapsed her crown and sent shards of bone into her brain. She thought she could see her daughter across the lake smiling and waving at her, which was confusing as she was dead. Then another blow severed her spine and switched the lights off.

CHAPTER 21

Louise looked through the curtains to check who was knocking. She was still very jittery about the threats Amie Muir had made, despite the assurances Smithy had given her. She didn't trust her, and she certainly didn't trust Smithy. She smiled, pleased to see Rob standing there; apart from Rachel, he was her favourite cousin. He looked tired and his eyes were puffy from crying. It was to be expected considering what was happening. She hugged him tightly and pulled him inside. He clung to her for a while, taking comfort in the warmth of her arms. She felt good. He kissed her cheek and pulled away.

'Are you okay?' he asked.

'I'm fine. You look like you've been crying,' she said.

'You look like you're going to Newry Beach to dig bait,' Rob replied. Louise was wearing ripped jeans and faded sweatshirt that could have fit both of them in comfortably.

'Come in, funny guy.' She grinned, closing the door. 'Is there any news about Rachel?' Louise asked. She walked down the hall into the living room. Rob followed her. The house smelled of cigarettes and curry, but it was clean and tidy.

'Nope but I need to talk to you. I've been texting you.'

'Why, what's up?'

'Didn't you see my texts?'

'My phone is charging. What's the matter?'

'Is your mum in?'

'No, stupid. The pub is open.'

'How long will she be?'

'Chill. She'll be there until closing time. It's darts tonight,' Louise said. 'Not that it matters what night it is. She lives in the place.'

'Nothing new there, eh?' Rob said.

'Nope. Same old Mum.' She could see how anxious he was. 'What's got you so shaken up?'

'Apart from my sister being kidnapped, you mean?'

'You haven't come to see me to talk about Rachel,' Louise said. 'Seriously, what's up?'

'The police found the money in her room.'

'No way.'

'They took it.'

'What, all of it?' Louise said. Rob nodded. 'Shit. I owe that to Walter.'

'They took everything.'

'How did they find it?'

'Mum said she was going to clean my room and I had it hidden under the mattress. I couldn't leave it there and I couldn't take it to school, so I hid it in a handbag Rachel never used. It was in an old shoe box in her wardrobe. I thought it would be safe but when she didn't come home, the police searched through her things and they found it. Obviously, they asked Mum where Rachel got the money from and she had no idea.'

'So, they don't know it's ours?'

'No. I couldn't tell them that. Mum would have a hissy fit. She's bending her head about it as it is. If she thought you were involved, she would be losing her marbles.'

'What did she say?'

'She's convinced Rachel was up to something dodgy.'

'Why?'

'Because Rachel is shit with money. She spends her money as soon as she has it. She never saves anything.'

'Oh, no. I can't believe the police found it. We're in big trouble.'

'Mum even asked me if she was involved with you, selling drugs.'

'OMG.'

'That's exactly what I thought. I didn't know where to put myself.'

'No way,' Louise said. 'How does she know about that?'

'This is Anglesey, Lou,' Rob said. 'Everyone knows everything about everyone. She's heard the rumours about what you were up to and then when they found the money, she put two and two together.'

'Shit. It will get back to my mum, eventually. She might be a piss-head but she hates dealers. If she thought I'd been selling, she'd boot me out.'

'You're not wrong,' Rob said. 'Mum knows I'm lying. I can't exactly tell her the money was mine and I've been selling weed to my mates that I was buying from you. If she starts digging, it's only a matter of time before someone opens their mouth and points a finger at me and then she'll know we've been in it together.'

'Well, it's not going to be a problem anymore. Smithy has put paid to our little venture. He took everything I had for Walter and gave me a couple of hundred to shut me up. Walter will be going ape-shit with me. He'll think it was my idea to set him up. I wish I'd never said yes to him.'

'Walter messaged me the other day. It must have been the day he got arrested.'

'What did he want?'

'He was asking me if I wanted to sell for him like you. Did you give him my number?'

'No. Honestly I didn't.'

'I reckon he's gone through your friends list on Facebook and got it off my profile, I've deleted the messages now, just in case the police see them.'

'Did you reply to him?'

'Yes.'

'What did you say?'

'Well, when you told me how much you were making, of course I said yes. We chatted for a bit by text and he wanted to meet, then it went quiet.'

'You might have deleted them from your phone, but they'll still be on his. The police will go through his phone and check his messages. You need to get rid of your phone.'

'It's new. I'm not throwing my phone away. He was quite clever not to actually mention what I would be selling for him. It will be okay. They can't prove I was going to do anything wrong.'

'He's a dealer. He's just been arrested with a shitload of coke and cash on him. It will be obvious what he was messaging you about, stupid.'

'I haven't actually done anything wrong yet. I don't think I have, anyway.'

'What about the weed you sold to your friends?'

'Only me and you know about that.'

'Yes, and the people you sold it to, stupid.'

'Apart from them,' Rob conceded. 'I don't think any of them will grass me up. The point is, Mum is going to tell the police about you selling drugs because she thinks the money could be the reason why someone has taken her.'

'What?' Louise asked. 'Are you saying Aunty Pauline thinks Rachel was kidnapped because of that money?'

'She doesn't know what to think but she can't explain where the money came from, so she's looking for a reason. She needs a reason why Rachel was taken to try to make sense of it all. I can't tell her she's barking up the wrong tree, can I?'

'Not without dropping us in it. Oh shit,' Louise said. 'If the police come here asking me about drugs or Rachel going missing, my mum will go ape-shit.'

'That's why I came to see you. I didn't know what to do.'

'Don't worry. I won't say anything to them. I'll deny everything. Telling them the truth isn't going to help them find Rachel, anyway, is it?'

'I don't see how it can. If I thought it would, that would be different.'

'I can't believe she hasn't turned up yet. We know it has nothing to do with the money, so what do you think happened to her?'

'I really don't know but when we found the blood and her phone in the woods, I knew she wasn't lost or hanging with her friends. Something bad has happened to her.' Rob shrugged and sat down on a bean bag. He hugged his knees. 'You know what she was like with her selfies. She's always being mithered by blokes on Facebook. A lot of them were much older. I told her to stop posting so many pictures, but she told me to mind my own business and blocked me. We never spoke about it again, but it makes me wonder if it has something to do with her social media.'

'I know what you mean. I thought the same. I messaged her on Instagram and warned her about the school uniform pics. She was getting some really disgusting comments from dirty old men. She told me to wind my neck in and blocked me. I hope one of those perverts hasn't done something to her.'

'That is what worries me.'

'Me too.'

'I know that prick David Laws was sending her dick-pics. He's going to get a smack in the mouth from someone. One guy threatened to kill him.'

'I saw that on the internet. I know he was sending her gross pics, but do you think he's done anything to hurt her?'

'I don't know but I'm going to ask him the next time I see him.'

'Dirty perv. I hate boys like him.'

'Me too. Anyway, let's talk about something else.' He put his chin on his knees. 'Tell me about what happened with Smithy?'

'I don't want to think about it. It makes me shiver inside. He's so scary.'

'He's a big guy and from what my friends say, he's got an evil streak in him.'

'He has. When he found out I was selling, he came to the skateboard park with his goons and they pulled me into a van. I was crapping myself. He knew I was selling stuff and said he'd known for a week and had been waiting and watching to see where I was getting it from and who was supplying me. Once he'd worked out it wasn't anyone in Holyhead, he knew it was someone from away. Then he made me carry on as normal so he could set him up. I said no, but he flipped out. I thought he was going to kill me.'

'He was bound to work out it wasn't anyone in town giving you the weed. He's not stupid and no one would dare. What did he say?'

'He said if I was older, they would tie me up and throw me off the mountain into the sea with weights strapped to me. He said the only way I could get out of it was to set up Walter, arrange to meet him in the park and that they would be there. I felt really bad for Walter. He was an okay guy but what else could I do?'

'You didn't have any choice, Lou. Smithy is a loon. No one messes with him.'

'I know. It's been a nightmare,' Louise said, lighting a cigarette; she puffed smoke into the air. 'Do you want one?'

'No thanks.'

'Anyway, he made me set up Walter. I had to get him into the toilet block, which was easy enough and then they jumped him and robbed him.'

'Where you there?'

'At the beginning. But then Smithy told me to piss off. He took all my cash and slapped me around the head. I felt like a dickhead. I walked back up the hill to the skateboard park and watched what happened from the top of the half-pipe.'

'You didn't stay there, did you?'

'I did.'

'What if they'd seen you?'

'It was dark.'

'You're mad. Then what happened.'

'They must have stripped him and tied him up in the bogs and called the police because he didn't come out and the next thing was, the police were everywhere.'

'This is madness. What happened then?' Rob said, laughing.

'I'm not kidding. I watched Smithy and his goons leaving. They were laughing and joking when they left the park. I bet they were only gone about twenty-minutes when armed police turned up and pulled Walter's minder out of his car.'

'No way.'

'You should have seen his face. He shit his pants. I'm not kidding. Then they went into the toilets and came out with Walter in handcuffs.

He was half naked and wrapped in tinfoil like a chicken in the oven, so he's going to be well pissed off with me.'

'That's crazy.'

'Tell me about it,' Louise said. 'I knew I was in trouble but I didn't realise how much. Later that night, I had the psycho bitch that he works for texting me that she was going to have my legs cut off with a chainsaw.'

'A chainsaw?' Rob said, shaking his head. 'Walter works for a woman?'

'Yes. She's called Amie something or other, and she's the big boss apparently and she's a full-blown nutcase.'

'What do you mean?'

'Smithy told me she had some rival guy put through a tree shredder.'

'Oh, man. That's proper sick. I told you not to get involved, Lou,' Rob said, half smiling. She could see he was becoming unsettled.

'I didn't see you saying no to him, smartarse.'

'True. What are we going to do about the money we owe him?'

'It's Amie I'm more worried about. If I could do it all again, I would have told Walter to fuck off in the first place but I thought it was going to be easy and no one would know. I was thinking about the money.'

'But we did what we did. We can't change it now. What are you going to do about the crazy woman?'

'Smithy said he'll speak to her and smooth things over. I don't know how you smooth over something like that. He tied Walter up and then called the police. They arrested him and his minder and took the drugs and the money. He'll be proper pissed off with me. I can't see him settling for an apology,' Louise said. 'I keep looking at my phone to see if he's messaged me. He hasn't, so I'm wondering if he's still in the cells.'

'Block his number and his Facebook. It's Facebook that got us into this shit in the first place.' Rob stood up and put his hands in his pockets. 'Better stay low and keep off the internet. We're agreed that we say nothing about the money?'

'Definitely,' Louise said, nodding. 'We'll stay quiet, deny everything, and fingers crossed Amie and Walter don't blame me and Rachel turns up soon.'

***

Netty Owen checked her watch again. Meredith was fifty-minutes late, which was very unusual. She was always back on the hour without fail. There had never been a day when she was even five minutes late. It was totally unheard of. Meredith knew how hectic their workload as care workers was. It was literally a race between clients from the moment they clocked on until the last visit of the day. Netty had to send her colleague Sharon to look after the next client alone, while she waited for Meredith to come home. She couldn't leave Trevor on his own, not for more than five minutes. She tried to ring Meredith again but her mobile was going straight to voicemail. She looked in on Trevor. He was lying on his back, mouth open. A gentle snoring sound came from the back of his throat. He was in a deep sleep.

Netty had a real dilemma. She was becoming increasingly concerned that something had happened to Meredith. She contemplated following the path which she took every day to see if she'd fallen and banged her head or twisted an ankle or something worse, like a stroke or heart attack. The only other option was calling 999 and reporting it to the police but was it really an emergency? She couldn't do that and explain that a fit and healthy lady had gone for a walk and not come home. They would ask if she'd looked for Meredith and she hadn't. Trevor was sleeping and would be okay for a short while as long as he didn't wake up. Sometimes he got very confused and upset when he first awoke. Netty tucked Trevor in and headed through the kitchen for the back door. She fastened her coat. It was only ten minutes to the fields which bordered the lake. Netty tried to think positively. Meredith was probably enjoying the sunset. She closed the backdoor behind her and headed down the path towards the lake.

***

'I told you there wasn't enough weight on her. You don't listen. Now there's another one dead.'

'Why didn't you do it yourself, if you're so smart?'

'Now we've got twice the work, stupid. If I had done it, we wouldn't need to be doing this, would we?'

'You're always clever after the fact. What did you kill the old one for?'

'Because she saw the girl, idiot.'

'Twice the work and twice the chance of someone seeing us. Sometimes, I wonder what goes through your head.'

'Stop whining and put her in the water. The quicker we get her in, the better it is for you. You worry too much.'

'I need to worry when you're around. I need to have eyes in the back of my head just to keep an eye on you. It's like having a child to look after.'

'Give it a rest, will you? I can't hear myself think. All I can hear is your whinging, day and night. You're driving me around the bend.' There was a dull splash as Meredith landed in the water. 'There we go. That wasn't so hard was it?'

'Shit.'

'What?'

'There's a woman coming down the path.'

'Where?'

'At the top of the field over there.'

'Did she see us putting her in the lake?'

'I don't know.'

'She's heading this way, but she's in the dip now, so she can't see us from there.'

'What shall we do?'

'Let's go. We need to get out of sight. I'll sort it out.'

CHAPTER 22

Netty looked across the meadow towards the lake. Dusk was settling on the island, turning the water slate grey. Three RAF training jets roared overhead in an arrow formation. She could feel the vibration in her chest. As they flew out of earshot over Snowdonia, she thought she'd heard an engine but wasn't sure if it was nearby or if it had been carried on the breeze from the expressway a few miles away to the west.

The path narrowed and she had to concentrate where she placed her feet. She checked her watch again, worried about how long Trevor had been alone. It wasn't very long, but it was already too long. She picked up the pace as she came out of the dip and the path rolled gently down to the water's edge. The meadow appeared to be empty. There was no obvious sign of Meredith on the path. She decided to walk as far as a small copse of trees at the far end of the lake. The path took a turn there and then threaded through a dense wood for miles. It would be dark soon and she wasn't comfortable going any further than that. If she hadn't found Meredith by then, she would turn around and head back and call 999. She had done everything she could to find her.

Meredith may have had a breakdown of some kind and carried on walking. She wouldn't be surprised, and she wouldn't blame her, if she had. Many people in her position had mental health problems. Full-time carers were under an immense amount of pressure mentally; especially when caring for loved ones. Watching a parent or spouse waste away was soul destroying and it tested their resolve to the limits. Some struggled on, but some snapped. Meredith was deteriorating. Netty had noticed her decline and mentioned it to the social care unit. She needed some support, mentally and physically.

As she walked, her head full of thoughts, a dark patch caught her attention. It was on the grass to her right. She noticed there was a rotten smell in the air, thick and lingering. It was an odour she'd encountered too many times not to recognise it immediately. She'd found dozens of elderly people dead in their homes, some had been there for a while. A shiver ran down her spine. It was the stench of death and decay. She leaned closer to the stain so her eyes could focus on it properly. It was wet and sticky and dark red and there were pinkish globules of goo clinging to the undergrowth. It was clearly blood and it was obviously fresh and there was a lot of it. Why would there be so much blood on the ground?

The news of Rachel Evans disappearing from Bodedern flashed through her mind. It was the other side of the lake and they suspected foul play; as far as she knew, they hadn't caught anyone yet. Her disappearance had even overshadowed the blanket coverage of the virus. The situation Netty found herself in was dangerous. Meredith was missing and there was a large patch of blood on the path where she walked every day. It was time to escalate it to the emergency services. She took out her phone and dialled 999. The screen showed it was dialling but wasn't connecting. Some parts of the island had patchy network coverage and the rest of it was like being on the moon.

Netty heard an engine starting nearby. She felt relieved as headlights illuminated the scene. It would be the local farmer who owned the land around the lake. He was a nice man called Owain, and a friend of her late father. He would help her. The vehicle came from behind the copse of trees and hurtled towards her without slowing. Netty waved her arms in the air to slow it down, but it kept on accelerating. She realised too late that it wasn't going to stop. Her feet felt like lead as she turned and stumbled up the path, trying desperately to escape the oncoming truck. She slipped and fell to her knees. The engine grew louder. Her legs were shaking as she got to her feet and staggered on, gaining speed as she ran. Her feet slipped on the wet grass and trying to stay upright was impossible. She got another five yards when the truck ploughed into her. She was thrown forward violently; the breath knocked from her lungs; her pelvis shattered. She held onto the phone and heard a female voice saying, 'Hello, which service do you require?'

The truck ran over her, crushing the life from her. She felt nothing as the truck reversed over her several times to make sure she was dead.

CHAPTER 23

He watched through binoculars as the beam trawler weighed anchor and headed off south towards the Llyn peninsula, on its journey back to Spain. It had stopped fishing while it unloaded its cargo of Peruvian cocaine, just over a ton of it this time. It was loaded into three ribs, which belonged to Smithy. The ribs sped away in different directions at full speed, capable of outrunning anything the coast guard sailed. They would land at different points around the island. Splitting the load, lessened the risk, something the big city dealers seldom grasped. The importers who had lost their shipment in Holyhead harbour had left a huge gap in the market because of their greed and stupidity. The supply to Liverpool and Manchester would be severely disrupted. He scrolled through his phone and clicked on a contact.

'Smithy?' his contact answered.

'Yes. It's me. I would say the eagle has landed but it would be a bit corny, so I'll just say the coke has arrived.'

'How much have you got?'

'As much as you need.'

'I'll take the lot.'

'Sounds like things are bad?'

'That's a fucking understatement. This lockdown means users are stockpiling. They're spending every last penny to make sure they don't run out and with most people being told to work from home and the pubs closed, they're sat on their settee sniffing the stuff like it's going out of fashion.'

'It's the perfect storm,' Smithy said. 'The smart people will make a lot of money. The idiots will fade away and die.'

'Like the idiots who lost that truck you mean?'

'Exactly. You don't add risk to a multimillion-pound shipment by stuffing the vehicle full of skin trade; it's amateurish and reckless. If you're going to enter the shitty world of human trafficking, do it in isolation not in tandem with smuggling class-A's. The two don't mix.'

'I agree, one-hundred per cent. I like the way you operate and you're sure you can guarantee the supply?'

'Yes. Absolutely positive.'

'And the price will stay the same all the way through lockdown?'

'We agreed sixty-thousand a kilo. I'll stand by that, no matter how long it lasts.'

'Sound. Some people would take advantage of the situation and try to squeeze their customers.'

'I'm looking long term. When things return to normal, I'm hoping to continue our arrangement.'

'If the price stays the same and the quality isn't compromised, our arrangement stands.'

'Perfect.' The ribs disappeared from sight behind South Stack and he sighed with relief and got back into his Capri. It was getting cold.

'The lockdown is going to cause distribution issues. What about the transportation from your end getting it off the island?'

'The police are busy trying to enforce the lockdown here. They're overwhelmed trying to close the caravan parks and chasing the tourists across the island. The virus is sapping manpower,' Smithy said, confidently. They were also busy with the disappearance of Rachel Evans from Bodedern. They were looking the other way while he made the most of the situation. 'Don't worry about my end. I'll get it to you. I'll call you tomorrow and let you know where and when it will be delivered.'

'Excellent.'

The call ended and Smithy smiled to himself. He was ready to plug the gap left in the supply chain by the seizure at the port. He was set to receive over five tons of high-quality cocaine over the next ten weeks. If he could do the same again before the Liverpool and Manchester outfits sourced a different supplier and got their acts together, he could shift ten tons of quality product. He would put the money in the offshore banking void and take a step down; it was time to get out and walk away. He wouldn't need to work again for the rest of his life.

Smithy drove along the coast road towards his flat. The road snaked along the headlands in a series of tight bends, too narrow to pass another vehicle. There was no one on the roads. The lockdown was beginning to bite. He parked up at the rear of his building, which was in darkness. All the other flats were owned by tourists and used as holiday lets. The holidaymakers drove him insane. During school breaks, tourists descended on the island in their shorts and flipflops despite it being freezing. They parked in his spot regardless of the sign, which clearly stated it was for the owner of flat number 1. He had let a few tyres down over the years as a punishment for not adhering to the parking rules. Not that the idiots realised it was a punishment. They just assumed it was bad luck. Families were the worst offenders. Their multiple devices drained the broadband strength, which was crap to begin with, to the point where he couldn't watch a football match live or enjoy a film without buffering. He didn't want to move, instead he intended to buy every flat in the building, whether they were for sale or not. There were plenty of ways to convince people to sell.

The sound of the waves on the rocks drifted to him as he crossed the courtyard to the communal door. He put his key in the lock and the door opened before he'd turned it. It creaked open slowly. Smithy reached inside and turned on the lights. The hallway and stairwell were empty. He didn't recall locking the door, yet he was sure he had. The exchange had been on his mind when he left home earlier. Maybe he had been absent-minded and not locked it properly. Maybe but it was unlikely. It was more likely one of the other owners had been into their flat to change the bedding before the next plague of tourists arrived although when that would be depended on how long Boris enforced the non-essential travel ban. It was more likely they had left it open than him. They didn't care about the building or its upkeep. To them, they were cash-cows, milked to death. To him, it was his home. Some of the flats hadn't been refurbed since the seventies. The bathrooms and kitchens were like something from an old sitcom where the residents sat in worn armchairs chain smoking and being casually racist. Walking into them was like going back in time, although the views from the windows were incredible, which kept the visitors coming back.

He shut the door and headed upstairs, unlocking his apartment door. The cleaner had been in. It smelled of bleach and kitchen degreaser. She was a diamond. There was never anything out of date in his fridge and whenever he was running low on something, she would stock it up and leave the receipts on the kitchen worktop. She would make someone a lovely wife one day. He had thought about fucking her, but she was from town and he didn't want a partner from there. It was a small port and the residents were diamonds with a real sense of community, but they all knew each other's business and in his line of work, that wasn't acceptable. Even the most casual of comments could attract the wrong type of gossip, which would spread like wildfire through the pubs and eventually it would land in the wrong ears. The police were ultra-aware of him already, hence the need to make a quick killing and get out from under the spotlight before they built a case they could prosecute. It was only a matter of time before they caught him and locked him up. Everyone who had been in his position before had ended up in jail. Of course, they all thought they wouldn't get caught and that they were cleverer and more careful than their rivals and predecessors and of course, they were none of those things. Sometimes, blind luck made the difference between getting caught and not getting caught. He was sharp and he knew it, but he was intelligent enough to know that once the police started looking at you, they would never look away.

Cases took time to build; infiltration by undercover officers was virtually impossible because it was a tight community but sometimes, they found leverage from within an outfit. Sometimes, the smiling friend was a Judas. Other times, regular customers would be arrested for an unrelated crime and could be coerced into becoming informers. It was like walking through a minefield blindfolded. Sooner or later it would all end in tears. Being under investigation meant being subject to observation and surveillance, which was par for the course. It could take years to gather enough evidence to convict an entire outfit and roundup those on the periphery but it had happened to others on the island and it would happen again if he wasn't careful. He could trust only a few and then only so far. Heavy is the head that wears the crown.

Smithy walked down his hallway into his kitchen and switched on the lights. He saw a very attractive woman sitting on one of the stools at his breakfast bar. She was small and slim, and her exposed arms were tattooed and defined. She smiled at him but there was no affection in it. It was reptilian.

'Hello, Smithy, I'm Amie Muir.' He didn't have time to react before he was grabbed by three sets of strong arms and restrained. There was a sharp scratch on the back of his neck, and he felt a needle going in. A warm sensation flooded through his veins as he lost consciousness.

'And you will be very sorry you crossed me.'

CHAPTER 24

April Byfelt was having a bad night. Knocking on caravans and holiday homes and telling visitors they had to pack up and go back to their primary residence was not her idea of police work. They were mostly met with a reasonable response but there had been some resentment and anger too. Caravans can rent for a thousand pounds a week and not everyone was happy to forfeit their money and go home. The fact the local pubs and restaurants were all going into lockdown had helped. There was nowhere to go to eat or drink and the local Tesco looked like it was weathering the apocalypse. The shelves were empty. It made some people's decision easier to bear. She looked at her phone and had a message to contact Bob Dewhurst at the station.

'Hello, April,' he said. 'I didn't put this out over the comms, but we've had a call from a nurse, Cerris Parry, who's working at a house in Pen-llyn.'

'That's the other side of Bodedern, isn't it?'

'That's the one.'

'By the lake,' April said. 'What's the call about?'

'There's an elderly couple who live there, Trevor and Meredith Robson. Trevor is very poorly and has carers going into the house for an hour every day. Cerris is one of them. When they go in, Meredith

Robson goes for a walk down to the lake to stretch her legs and get some fresh air. Today she didn't come back.'

'Okay.'

'One of the nurses, Netty Owen, stayed with the husband to wait for Meredith to return, while the other nurse, Cerris carried on with the round.'

'Okay,' April said, trying to follow where this was going.

'To cut a long story short, Cerris hasn't heard anything from Netty or Meredith, so she went back to the property and there's no sign of either of them there. Trevor has been left alone for hours and he's very distressed but she's obviously very concerned that the two women are missing.'

'Oh dear. Pen-llyn is the other side of the woods from where Rachel Evans went missing, right?'

'Yes. My thoughts exactly.'

'That can't be a coincidence, can it?' April said.

'I don't think so. That's why I'm not putting it over the comms. I've alerted the DI and he's asked for uniformed backup.'

'I'll take two units and head over there now.'

***

Louise zigzagged down Porth-y-felin hill on her board. Halfway down, she noticed the Vic pub was closed. Her mum had drunk in there for years until she got barred for being too pissed. It was like a ghost town. There was no traffic on the road as social distancing was beginning to take a grip on society. She leaned forward and pointed the front of the board down the hill, picking up speed as she reached the bottom and went under the sandstone arch, which supported the quarry road where it crossed above Porth-y-felin. The incline had given her more speed than she would usually dare risk as she passed beneath the bridge onto the Newry Beach. It was a blind bend but there was nothing on the road. It was such a rush. She steered the board in a wide arc and eventually stopped opposite the sailing club. The marina was quiet, but the sea was still rough as the storm dissipated. She could hear the distant roar of waves crashing over the breakwater.

She decided to ride down the path onto the promenade and then head up the hill home. Not that there was any great rush to go home. Her mum was there, sulking and being moody because the pubs were closed. She hoped it would only be a short lockdown. Listening to her mum moaning about what the government should be doing would drive her insane, hence the ride on her board to kill the boredom and give her ears a rest. Her mum had been chattering on the phone for an hour, trying to find drinking partners, who were willing to risk the lockdown and come to the house. Obviously, they would have to bring alcohol. She didn't seem to grasp the concept of the lockdown, replacing one gathering place for another. Sometimes, she wondered who the adult was and who was the teenager.

A police car trundled along the Newry, its occupants eyeing her suspiciously. They looked like they were going to stop and speak to her but suddenly, the blue lights went on and it sped away towards the town centre. A van drove through the archway and climbed the hill towards her. She ducked into one of the shelters and waited for it to pass. The sole occupant barely looked in her direction. She was still a little on edge. Her phone had stayed quiet and there had been no contact from Walter or his boss. Maybe Smithy had smoothed things over, just like he promised.

A motorcycle roared down Walthew Avenue, making the most of the quiet roads. He barely slowed down to take the roundabout, dropping his knee and tilting the machine, before accelerating off towards the harbour. It was time to head home. Her nerves couldn't cope. Listening to her mother moaning would be less stressful. She turned the board and headed into the alleyways, which ran between the big houses and linked the beach roads to the housing estates. They used to be cobbled and were impossible to ride but the council had covered them in asphalt. She'd travelled a hundred yards or so, when headlights appeared at the end of the alleyway. They blinded her momentarily. She blinked to clear her vision and tried to focus on the vehicle. The silhouette was that of a van. It blocked her path and approached slowly. She suddenly felt scared. Louise stopped and picked the board up and turned to run back the way she'd come. A single headlight turned off the road into the alleyway, blocking her exit. Her heart was beating faster than it had ever beaten before. She felt cold sweat forming on her forehead, neck, and lower back. The walls around her were too high to climb and topped with broken bottles fixed into cement. She tried the handle of a wooden door which led into a back garden, but it was locked. The door opposite had no handle to turn, it was fitted with a mortice lock. There was nowhere to run.

CHAPTER 25

Alan arrived at the house in Pen-Llyn and parked up on a narrow lane which led to a farmhouse about a mile away to the west, where the road terminated. A lot of the narrow roads in that area were access only and were dead ends. The Robson property had a driveway but there were already several cars and a police van parked on it. He climbed out and walked to the front door. It was open. He stepped inside and shouted hello. Inside, April Byfelt was talking to a woman in her fifties, who was dressed in a green nurses' tunic. They stopped talking and turned to greet him.

'This is DI Williams,' April said. 'And this is Cerris Owen. Cerris called this in when she realised Meredith Robson and her colleague Netty Owen were missing.'

'Hello Cerris,' Alan said. 'I'm aware Mrs Robson takes a stroll every day towards the lake, while you see to Mr Robson.'

'Yes. She walks the same path every day. She's always back before we leave, without fail. Something bad must have happened.'

'When you left here, your colleague Netty stayed to wait for Meredith to return?' Alan said.

'Yes. She must have gone to look for her.'

'What time did you leave?'

'Four o'clock. I had to be in Bodedern for four-fifteen.'

'And what time did you call us?'

'Nine-thirty,' Cerris said. She looked embarrassed. 'I would have called it in sooner but I couldn't get hold of them on their mobiles and I didn't want to bother you when this lockdown is happening and you have a missing teenager to deal with. I came back here when I'd finished my round but there was no sign of them, so I called you. I didn't know what else to do.'

'Okay. You did the right thing, Cerris. So, they've been missing for about five hours,' Alan said to April.

'Yes.'

'Has anyone been down to the lake yet?' Alan asked April.

'No. I wanted to wait for you before I sent anyone out there,' April said. The concern in her eyes told him she thought it was possibly connected to Rachel Evans. 'It's unlikely that two grown women have sprained an ankle or become lost.'

'Agreed,' Alan said. 'How many officers do we have here?'

'Five and myself.'

'You look after things here. I'll take the others and have a skirt around the paths. Once we know what we're dealing with, we'll decide what to do.'

'Okay,' April said.

Alan and the four uniformed officers set off from the back gate and followed the path to the meadow. The land dipped and then sloped down towards the water. They spread out over twenty yards or so and searched the area with their torches. The clouds had gone now, and the sky was glistening with a million stars. He could see Venus hovering above the North star somewhere over Holyhead mountain. They walked on for about ten minutes.

'I've got something here,' a constable said. Alan walked over to him and they crouched over a pale pink object, which was nestling in the grass.

'That looks like a top set of false teeth,' he said. 'And they don't just fall out on their own.' They looked around and saw a trail of blood running for about ten yards. There were tyre tracks on the grass, deeper in some places than others.

'I think someone has been run over,' the officer said.

'I think you could be right,' Alan said.

'There's more blood over here,' another officer shouted. Alan began to fear the worst.

'Okay, mark anything you find,' Alan said. 'I'll call for backup and get CSI in. We need to work out what's happened here.'

'Over here, sir,' a young officer called in a panic. 'There's a body in the water. Quick, come and see. Over here!'

'Calm down, son,' Alan said, approaching. 'What's your name?'

'Eddie, sir.'

'Okay, Eddie sir,' Alan said. 'Don't panic. Have you seen a dead body before?' The smell of decomposition tainted the air. He shone the torch onto corpse.

'No, sir.'

'This is your first. It's never a pleasant experience, Eddie but we have to deal with it more than most people do. Rule number one, don't panic because they're already dead and there's nothing we can do except manage the processing and removal and accord them as much dignity as we can.'

'Yes, sir.'

'Good lad. Now, tell me what you see,' Alan said.

'From here, it's a young girl. She's been in there a while,' he said.

'Correct. There's nothing we can do for her now except get her out of there in one piece and find out how she got there. Then we need to decide whether someone else had a hand in putting her in there. In the meantime, we don't want to contaminate the body or the scene. We're going to need CSI and the divers.'

'Shall I call it in, sir?'

'Yes. And ask Bob Dewhurst to organise a team of dogs. We need to find the two women who are missing. I can't see them from where we're standing.'

'Do you think that's Rachel Evans, sir?' the constable asked. He looked like he was about to vomit. Alan shook his head and shrugged.

'I don't know for certain. It's a young female with long brown hair. She fits the description, but we can't be sure until we lift her out. We'll soon find out.'

CHAPTER 26

Louise felt travel sick. She'd been bundled into the back of a van, her hands fastened behind her back with zip ties. Duct tape was stuck over her mouth and wrapped painfully around her head to blindfold her. She'd never been so frightened in her life. The images of people being fed into tree shredders kept running through her mind. She could hear Smithy's voice in her head. 'She's a proper nutcase,' over and over.

The men who had taken her didn't say much, but they did say Walter was looking forward to seeing her. She was in real trouble and she knew it. This was the real world of dealers and class-A drug wars and she was stuck right in the middle of it. She was fourteen and spent most of her spare time riding her skateboard. It was a different universe to the one she was in now. Her life was in the balance and she wanted to see her mum. She had no idea if she would live or die. All she could do was wait and pray.

The drive hadn't taken all that long in reality, although it felt much longer than it actually was. Her arms and legs were numb and were starting to cramp. The cold metal floor had dug into her muscles and bruised her where the corrugated ridges touched her limbs. Her head had rattled off the side of the van every time it went over a pothole. The driver seemed to be aiming for them purposely and all the time she was immersed in complete blackness. She wondered where they were taking her. Was she destined for the tree shredder or was Amie going to watch while her legs were amputated with a chainsaw? Louise wanted to be home with her mum. She was way out of her depth in this world.

She felt the van going through a series of tight bends before it eventually slowed down and came to a stop. The engine was turned off and she was left in the van for about ten minutes before she heard the side door sliding open. The cold night air rushed in. She was dragged roughly from the van and stood up on shaking legs; pins and needles spread down her thighs and into her calves. A strong wind tugged at her clothes and she could hear the surf hitting the rocks; she could smell the sea close by. They were still on the island and near the coast. Maybe they were going to throw her in and let her drown. She tried to move her legs as slowly as possible to delay the inevitable, but they dragged her along at a pace. Suddenly, the wind was gone. They took her into a building and then dragged her up two flights of stairs. Being out of the biting wind was nice and it meant they weren't going to toss her off the headlands but it did nothing to convince her she wasn't going to be hurt in another way. She heard a door opening and voices talking in gruff scouse accents. It had to be Walter and his outfit. This was payback time. She could hardly breathe.

Louise was strapped to a chair with duct tape. Her arms and legs bound to the metal at the wrists and ankles. She heard the click of a switchblade next to her ear and she waited for the blade to slice her flesh. Adrenaline pumped through her veins and she felt like she was verging on the edge of a panic attack. The tape was cut from her face and ripped away, tearing the hair from her skin. She cried out in pain as they cut the tape from her head and ripped the hair from her scalp. She blinked to see clearly. The face of Walter Dallow leered at her. He was released on bail as the drugs weren't on his person.

'Here she is,' he said, cheerily. 'My little mate, Loulou. I've been looking forward to seeing you again. I haven't seen you since you fed me to the wolves and got me banged up. Scheming little bitch.'

'I'm sorry for what happened, Walter,' Louise said, her bottom lip quivered. She could hardly speak. 'Smithy made me do it. He said he would throw me off a cliff if I didn't. I told him I didn't want to do it. Smithy forced me.'

'I know he did, Loulou,' Walter said, stroking her hair. She could smell sweat beneath his aftershave. It turned her stomach. 'But you could have warned me.'

'What do you mean?'

'You could have sent me a text or a message and told me not to turn up. Smithy wouldn't have known any difference.'

'They took my phone and sent you the messages. I was scared,' Louise said. She started crying. 'I'm frightened of him.'

'They're crocodile tears,' Amie said, stepping into view. 'You're crying because you got caught out. Has she sent you a message saying sorry, Walter?'

'Nope. Not a whisper of an apology.'

'I was scared the police would read it If I sent a message.'

'You've got an excuse for everything, haven't you?'

'I'm just scared,' Louise said. 'I'm really sorry. I just want to go home. I'm scared.'

'Oh, my dear girl,' Amie said, smiling. She pointed to the corner of the room behind her. Walter dragged the chair around so that Louise could see. A man was hanging naked from a wooden beam, fastened at the wrists by a chain. His face was a bloody mess and his torso was a crisscrossed with deep cuts and contusions. A series of large polythene sheets covered the floor underneath him and the walls around him. She couldn't be a hundred per cent sure but she thought it was Smithy. Her heart stopped in her chest. Her mouth opened and she vomited into her lap.

'I know you're scared. You need to be very scared, my love. You need to be more than scared. You need to be fucking terrified,' she said; the smile turned into a grin. 'We offered you an opportunity. We were good to you. We even shared the profits with you and what did you do?' Amie shook her head. 'You fucked us over.'

'I'm so sorry,' Louise cried. 'Please don't hurt me.'

'You didn't just turn us over to the locals, you involved the police.'

'I didn't do that,' she sobbed. 'Smithy did that. I didn't know he was going to do that. Honestly, I didn't know what he was going to do. I swear I didn't know.'

'Well, we'll never know. Poor old Smithy didn't last as long as I was hoping. He was a tough cookie though, fair play to him,' Amie said, smiling.

'Oh my god,' Louise muttered. She looked at Walter. 'Is he dead?'

What Happened to Rachel?

'He doesn't look very good, does he?' Walter said. He walked over to the corner of the room and poked Smithy in the chest. 'Loulou wants to know if you're dead or not,' he said, to the bloody victim. Smithy didn't respond. Walter smacked his face, but he didn't wake up. He shook his head. 'We can't leave him here. Sort him out,' he ordered.

Three men in forensic suits approached the hanging corpse. They took Smithy down and placed him on the polythene sheets. One of the men covered the furniture with more plastic sheeting. Amie and Walter shared a cigarette while they watched. Louise was trembling in her seat; she felt like she was going to piss her pants when one of the men picked up a chainsaw. It had been hidden from view behind an armchair. He pulled the ripcord and the saw growled into life. Louise watched in absolute terror as they dismembered Smithy limbs first. He was dismantled into ten pieces in under five minutes. When they took the head, Louise couldn't hold herself together any longer, urine ran between her legs and onto the floor. A puddle formed beneath her stool. Each piece of him was wrapped individually in plastic and his head was placed into a plastic storage box. The polythene sheets were peeled from the walls and taken up from the floor and stuffed into bin bags and the chain was removed. The men took them away one at a time and ten minutes later, that corner of the room looked like nothing had ever happened there.

'There we go, Loulou,' Walter said, grinning. 'To answer your question, I think we can safely say he is dead. He won't be setting anyone up again. Your mate stitched up the wrong man this time. He's dead as a dodo.'

'Dead and gone like he'd never been here at all,' Amie added. 'My team are very good and incredibly efficient. It's an absolute pleasure to watch such professionalism at work. It's impressive, wouldn't you agree, Louise?' Louise broke down into a dribbling wreck. She could hardly bring herself to look up. 'I want to know who his lieutenants are,' Amie said. She approached Louise and picked up a glass of water from the table. 'Are you thirsty?' she asked. Louise nodded that she was. Her throat was so dry, she could hardly swallow. She put the glass to her lips and let her drink. Louise emptied the glass and then licked her lips. 'Is that better?'

'Yes. Thank you,' Louise said. Her eyes were bleary with tears. She wondered how they would kill her. Her mother's face drifted into her mind, drunk and smiling. She realised how much she loved her, maybe too late. 'Please don't hurt me. I just want to go home.'

'I'm not sure we can do that?' Amie said, shaking her head.

'Please. I'll never tell anyone. I promise I won't. I just want to go home.'

'How can I trust you after everything you've done?'

'You can. You can trust me. I'll do anything just let me go home.'

'I knew Smithy was planning something big. There were rumours flying around the city about a rockstar on Anglesey, who was going to be supplying the entire north of the country with cocaine. The same person who stitched me up and got Walter arrested. That can only be one person. Michael Smith. Smithy.'

'I don't know anything about that. How could I?'

'Maybe you do and maybe you don't. But you do know the people who do. I want to know what he was up to. And I need to know who his sidekicks are.'

'What do you mean?' Louise mumbled, frightened and confused.

'I asked Smithy for the names of his lieutenants, but he didn't want to tell me. He was loyal, unlike some I can mention, eh, Louise,' Amie said. 'You're from the town and you've been around. You know who he hangs around with. I want to know who his main men are.'

'His goons,' Louise said, almost in a whisper.

'Pardon?' Amie said, frowning.

'That's what we call them in town,' Louise said. 'All the kids say here's Smithy and his goons.'

'Goons. I like that. And you know their names and where they live, don't you?'

'Yes. I know some of them but not all of them,' Louise said, nodding. 'But I can find out about the ones I don't. I'll do anything I can. Please just don't hurt me.'

'What car does he drive?' Amie asked.

'It's an old one. A Capri, I think. He had it restored.'

'There's one outside, parked at the back,' Walter said.

'Get rid of it,' Amie said. 'Make sure it can't be found.' Walter and another man left the room.

'Who was his closest friend?' Amie asked.

'He was always with a guy they call Ghoul.'

'Ghoul?'

'Yes. He has long hair and a ring through his nose and his tongue has been split like a snake,' Louise said. 'And he has tattoos everywhere, arms, hands, even on his neck.'

'He shouldn't be difficult to find. Good girl. I thought bringing you here might persuade you to help. You can tell me who else he hangs around with…'

CHAPTER 27

The Next Day

The daylight brought a different aspect to the crime scene at the lake. Despite the sunlight, it had taken a much darker tone. The enormity of the situation was becoming clear. It was no longer about missing persons. Pamela Stone and her team had sectioned the area into three different incidents. Alan and Kim were focused on the body in the water. The lifeboat station at Trearddur Bay had loaned the use of an inflatable raft which could be positioned underneath the corpse, deflated. The body would be fragile and could literally fall apart if it was tugged. The raft could be inflated underneath the corpse and then removed without causing any damage. A team of divers arrived in a police minibus and began unloading their tanks and equipment. The lake was nearly a kilometre long and deep in places. It was Anglesey's largest natural body of fresh water, Llyn Cefni and Llyn Alaw were bigger but they were manmade. The edge of the lake was a hive of activity. Pamela Stone approached.

'The blood belongs to two people,' she said. 'One is type O and the other is type A. I'm struggling to get hold of medical records for your missing persons because of the lockdown. What I can tell you is the false teeth are fitted with a dental palate which is more akin to the wearer having had a traumatic injury rather than the natural loss of teeth over a period of time. If I had their records, I could tell you if they belong to one of your victims.' Alan raised his eyebrows at the word victim. Pamela noticed his concern. 'There is brain matter on the grass over there. You're not looking for live ones in my opinion.'

'I thought as much.'

'The tyre tracks have come from behind the copse over there and then the vehicle goes back and too a few times before heading off to the gate at the far side of the meadow. The gate leads onto the road where the tracks turn left towards Bodedern or right towards the farms over there.'

'What type of vehicle are we looking for?' Kim asked.

'Something big like a truck or people carrier, maybe a van. Once we've identified the tread, I'll be more specific to the make and model.' She looked at the recovery team as they removed the body from the water. 'Any opinions yet?'

'I think the blood patterns are close to the water's edge where we have a dead girl floating in the water. The smell of decomp is very strong, so she's been in there a while. The smell is too strong to miss, so I think Meredith noticed the smell then spotted the body and someone else spotted her. He stopped her from alerting the police about the body in the lake, so he could remove it and then Netty comes along, looking for Meredith and disturbs them. Whoever was driving the vehicle had to shut them up. The absence of their bodies tells me the killer probably took them away.'

'Why not take the girl out of the lake too?' Kim asked.

'Too much trouble. She smells and he was in a panic,' Alan said. 'I'm guessing he put her in there in the first place and he has a good idea how decomposed her body is. It wouldn't be easy to get her out of there in one piece.'

'That makes sense to me,' Pamela said. 'Shall we have a look at her?'

They approached the body and the recovery team placed the raft onto the grass. The girl was lying face up. Alan went to the other side to see if he could see her face close up. Despite the fact, she was facing him, he couldn't identify her as Rachel Evans. Kim was behind him.

'What do you think?' she asked. 'Is it Rachel?'

'The facial damage is too bad to recognise any features, but she has long brown hair, similar height and weight,' Alan said, shrugging. 'I'm pretty sure it's Rachel but until Pamela confirms it, we keep an open mind.'

'Her throat has been cut from front to back, ear to ear. The spine is the only thing holding the head to the body.' She paused. 'Take a look at her wrists,' Pamela said. She pointed with a gloved hand. 'And her ankles.'

'She's been restrained,' Alan said, looking at deep sets of indentations to the skin. The surrounding tissue was bruised and coloured by hues of purple and deep blue. 'The wounds are deep, probably made by metal handcuffs. Just like on the fake videos we saw of her online,' he added. Kim took a deep breath and nodded in agreement. 'We need to chase up Emily on those IP addresses.'

CHAPTER 28

Louise was sitting in the back seat of a Mercedes at the end of a cul-de-sac, which overlooked Salt Island, where the Irish ferries docked. Amie had made her sit on a towel because of her wetting herself. They were looking for the address of another of Smithy's associates. She didn't know the house number where he lived but one her friends had reliably told her which street Sam's house was on.

'This is Sam's street?' Amie asked.

'Everyone calls him Monkey,' Louise said. 'No one calls him Sam. That's his car there,' she added, pointing to an old Mustang which was parked on a driveway. 'That must be his house. According to my friend, he's one of the main goons. You know who they all are now.'

'You're sure there are only five of them?' Amie asked.

'Yes. They were always together. Whenever I saw Smithy and his goons, it was them.' Louise had spent all night explaining to Amie who was who and where they lived. Amie didn't take a single word for granted. They drove to every address and made her point out the exact house and which car they drove. She didn't know them all exactly, but she had a good idea. The information was good enough for Amie to be sure.

'And this guy, Ghoul,' Amie said. 'He's Smithy's righthand man?'

'That's what the people in town say,' Louise said. 'Anyone who messes with them, Ghoul hammers them. He's a hardcase.'

'I'm sure he is,' Amie said. 'Just like Smithy was.'

'I won't to go home,' Louise said. 'I've done what you asked. I won't tell anyone what happened. I promise I won't.'

'Take her to Gwelfor Avenue,' Amie said. 'It's the blue house on the right. The one with an old campervan on the driveway.' Louise looked shocked. 'Yes, Loulou. I know where you live and I know where your mum drinks and where she shops and who she fucks and if you want her to remain in one piece, you'll keep your sweet little mouth shut tight. Do you understand me?'

'Yes,' Louise said. A tear ran from the corner of her eye. 'I promise I won't say anything and I'm really sorry for what happened to Walter,' she added. 'You can let me out here. I'll walk home.'

'Are you sure?' Amie said. 'I was going to come and have a little chat with your mum. I'm sure she's been worried sick about you, wondering where you've been all night. I could explain things to her for you if you like?'

'Please don't,' Louise said. 'Just let me out and I'll never say a word to anyone. I promise.'

'Let her out,' Amie said. The back door was opened and Louise climbed out. 'Bye-bye Loulou. Remember what I said. Not a word to anyone.'

Louise didn't say goodbye and she didn't look back. She ran as fast as she could, and she didn't stop running until she was home. Sweat poured from her brow and her hair was sticking to her head. Her lungs were burning, and she was gasping for air. The horror she had seen that night was fresh in her mind. The enigma that had been Smithy was in pieces in bin bags and she'd watched his dismemberment. They were images that she would never forget, burnt into her brain. If that wasn't bad enough, her mother was now a target if she ever said anything about what had happened. She couldn't let that happen to her mum. Louise went down the side of the campervan and through the side gate. She climbed up onto the garage roof and then opened her bedroom window, climbing in with practiced ease. Her bedroom was as she'd left it. She undressed and washed herself. She went into her bedroom and slid under the covers and pulled them over her head. Her mum wouldn't be up for a while. She usually slept until about dinnertime. Louise closed her eyes. She was exhausted. When she did finally go to sleep, her dreams were those of the haunted.

CHAPTER 29

The divers went into the lake with thirty yards between them to minimise disturbing the silt at the bottom. The water was clean and rubbish free and the visibility was good. It didn't take them long to identify what they were dealing with. The dogs had identified that there were multiple victims in the vicinity and the situation was going from bad to worse. Alan watched a spaniel sniffing the grass along the shore. It became excited and sat down for the fourth time in twenty-minutes. The handler marked the spot and waved to Alan. Alan nodded that he understood. The dog, Rolo was having the time of his life identifying graves.

'That's the fourth,' Kim said. The spaniel, who was called Rolo because of his chocolate and caramel coloured fur, was eager to carry on the search. 'That dog is never wrong. I've seen him working a few times. If he indicates that there's a body buried in a particular spot, you can bet your mortgage on it he's right.'

'I know. We could do without him being right anymore,' Alan said, sighing. 'The divers have marked three victims in the water, which brings our total to seven. This place is a graveyard. We're going to have to scale this investigation up,' he said. 'Get on the phone to Caernarfon and tell them we need officers and we need them today. Anyone who is knocking on caravans and pissing off the tourists needs to be in the operations room at Holyhead by three o'clock. Call Gareth and tell him I want detectives from St Asaph and Caernarfon. Call the chief and bring him up to speed too. Once we've looked at these bodies, I'll ring him myself. It looks like Rachel Evans is just the tip of the iceberg.'

'I'll call him now,' Kim said. She walked away to make the calls.

Alan walked to the water's edge. The first body that the divers had found was being lifted onto the shore. Pamela approached to inspect the victim. The corpse was placed onto a body bag and dragged onto the grass. Pond weed was wrapped in her hair and water trickled from her nose and mouth.

'She's fully clothed and very fresh. This is one of your missing women, I think. Her skull has been crushed at the crown, massive blunt trauma to the head with a square shaped instrument. Probably a hammer of some kind,' Pamela said.

'That is Meredith Robson,' Alan said. He prodded a bulge in her clothing. 'She's been weighted down with big pieces of stone stuffed into her clothing. This has been done in a hurry, probably with the intention of coming back to do the job properly if we hadn't turned up.'

A second body was lifted and put onto a tarp next to Meredith. 'This is Netty Owen,' Alan said. A tyre mark ran down the centre of her face. 'She's been run over.'

'The mandible is completely dislocated from the skull. The maxillary and nasal bones are crushed, and her teeth are missing, which would explain the set you found.' Pamela studied the lower body. 'I'm guessing from the angle of her legs that her pelvis is shattered, and her knees have been dislocated. I agree she's been run over. Probably a few times by the look of her injuries, they're too severe to be caused by anything else. She's been weighted down with stone too. This looks like it's from a drystone wall. There are plenty of them around here.'

'There're miles of them. It shouldn't be too difficult to find a section with bits missing from the top. I'll get someone to check around the local area. It might help us identify where the killer has been. He clearly comes here often, and he's been a busy boy. There are seven bodies that we know about. This guy needs taking down and we need to stop him quickly.'

'This has to be connected to Rachel Evans,' Pamela asked herself aloud. Alan looked at her and shook his head. 'I know it is, but I can't for the life of me work out how.' The third body was brought onshore. 'This one has been in the water much longer,' Pamela said. 'The victim has been wrapped in a blue tarpaulin, similar to what you might see covering a trailer or a patio set. It is green with algae indicating it has been underwater for a considerable time. Elastic bungees have been used to fasten the tarp around the body and heavy chains have been wrapped around the legs to weight the body down. The chain is corroded with rust and encrusted with algae.'

'This one has had a lot more time spent on the disposal,' Alan said.

'The killer had more time to make sure the body didn't surface,' Pamela said. 'Which is likely.'

'He's familiar with this area, so he's local to the island. Which means we might be looking for someone who lives nearby. We need to identify who the victims are to have a hope of finding the killer.' Alan looked tired as he spoke. The case was draining him. His mobile rang. 'It's the pathologist,' he said to Pamela. It was the initial results of the post-mortem on the body from the lake. He listened; his expression pained. His eyes closed, waiting for the news.

'You're absolutely certain?' he asked. He listened for a few minutes. 'Okay. Thank you.' The call ended and he looked at Pamela and Kim.

'What did they say?' Kim asked.

'The pathologist doesn't know who our victim is, but she does know for certain that it isn't Rachel Evans. Her dental records don't match the victim.'

CHAPTER 30

The operations room at Holyhead police station was packed. Uniformed officers and detectives had been drafted in from all over North Wales. Alan was ready to start the briefing when the ACC appeared at the back of the room. He gestured to Alan that he needed to speak to him in private. Alan made his way to the door. The room was full of chatter as the detectives new to the case were being brought up to speed. Kim followed Alan through the throng. They stepped into the corridor and Alan closed the door behind him.

'Hello Alan,' the ACC said. 'Apologies for the interruption.'

'No problem, Gareth,' Alan said, shaking his hand. 'Sorry. We shouldn't be doing that, should we?'

'I keep forgetting too,' Gareth said, smiling. He was a tall man in his fifties with a ruddy complexion and white hair. His uniform was pristine; the silver buttons gleaming. 'The commissioner has asked me to find out what the hell is going on. He's seen the number of men seconded to this case and he's having a panic attack about the budgets.'

'We're running a very complicated murder investigation. We have multiple victims and Rachel Evans still missing. I need every man and his dog to work on this until we put this psycho away.'

'I understand that. The press were giving him a hard time last week for sending all the tourists home and now it appears we've got a serial killer on the island. He said his ears are bleeding from all the enquiries. Is there any light at the end of the tunnel?'

'What can I say?' Alan said. 'It is what it is. I'm about to hold the first briefing. Tell him we haven't dug up the bodies for fun. Someone put them there and we're trying to discover who it was before he buries another one.'

'I understand that,' Gareth said. 'Can't we give him something to placate the paparazzi?'

'I don't know if there's anything that would placate that bunch. They're like sharks circling a sinking ship,' Alan said. 'My priority is to this investigation not the Daily Post or the accountants.'

'Come on, Alan. Covid-19 has drained the entire year's budget for the traffic division already. This is going to be a fifty-detective investigation, isn't it?'

'At least.' Alan thought about his next words carefully. 'We're convinced that the location of the bodies indicates that the killer is a local. He lives on the island.'

'What makes you so sure?'

'Have you ever been to Llyn Llwenan?'

'No. I can't say I know where it is, to be honest.'

'That's my point. Most of the people who live on this island haven't been to that lake. The killer has intimate knowledge of the area, which should make it easier to find him.'

'Okay. Give me some idea of the timescale,' Gareth looked deflated. The commissioner was a tough taskmaster. He could be like a dog with a bone over some issues, especially budgets.

'Do you want me to pick a figure out of the air?'

'Of course not.'

'We're just getting started, Gareth. You're welcome to sit in on the briefing if you like and you can gauge where we're at. Then it's up to you what you feed back to him?'

'Fair enough. I suppose that will have to do,' Gareth said, nodding. 'My apologies for the delay but I have to ask the question. Please carry on with your briefing.'

Alan went back into the operations room and the noise died down. He looked around the room and recognised some of the faces. They had sent good detectives, which was a bonus. He needed the finest investigative brains on this one.

'Thank you,' he said. Silencing the room. The image of the young girl recovered from the lake appeared. 'We can confirm the female we pulled from Llyn Llwenan is not Rachel Evans.' A ripple of comments ran through the room. 'The pathologist estimates she's been in the water for about a week but we don't know who she is. The cause of death is exsanguination caused by a single cut to the throat which very nearly decapitated her. She has injuries to the wrists and ankles, which indicate that she was restrained for a substantial period of time. We have to assume the killer has a property where he can hold his victims without fear of being disturbed and I think he lives in the vicinity of Llyn Llwenan.' Another ripple of sound travelled among the detectives. 'I'm going to send an ordinance survey map to each one of you, either to your phones or to your laptops. Starting at the lake, we're going to be knocking on doors and searching every barn, garage, farmhouse, outhouse, lockup, absolutely everywhere that the killer could hold a victim or multiple victims. There are eight bodies recovered so far, three from the water and four buried along the bank plus victim one, who was floating.' The image changed. 'This is Meredith Robson. She lived near the lake and walked along this path here every day,' Alan said, pointing to a map on a second screen. 'She was found in the water here, no more than fifty yards from where we found the first victim. Meredith was weighted down with stones, which tells me the killer panicked and rushed the disposal. Blood and brain matter were found on the grass here, so it's likely Meredith had been for a walk and seen the body in the water and the killer was in the vicinity. He had to stop her from reporting it.' Another photograph appeared. 'Netty Owen was a nurse, working at the Robson home, who went to the lake looking for Meredith when she didn't return home. She was found in the water here. Again, she was weighted down with stones. Her injuries and tyre tracks at the scene suggest she was run over by a large vehicle, possibly a truck or a people carrier or a van. Forensics are checking the tread pattern to try to narrow down the possible vehicles.' The images changed to the graves found near the lake. 'We brought in the dogs and they identified four sets of remains. They're in varying states of decomposition ranging from months to years. Initial reports confirm they're all female. They're all young and they all have long brown hair.' A murmur spread around the room. 'All the victims are showing signs of restraint at the wrists and ankles.' He waited for the chatter to fade. 'We are dealing with a serial killer who holds his victims captive for a long time. He has very specific tastes, but he has become erratic. He has been operating in the area for years undetected, we have to ask what has changed? The disposal of this victim,' Alan pointed to victim number one, 'was very sloppy. I think the storm disturbed the body. Detailed analysis of the body show rope marks in the flesh here. They're faint but they're there. She was weighted down using rope around the waist, but the job was shoddy and the body resurfaced during the storm causing a domino effect. We think Meredith stumbled across the body in the water, so she was silenced and likewise Netty Owen. They do not fit the profile of the other victims. They're incidental.'

'If Meredith was just taking a walk when she saw the body, what was the killer doing at the lake?' Richard asked.

'He might visit his victims,' Kim said. 'Maybe he frequents the graves.'

'Or he might have been checking to see if the storm had disturbed his victims,' Alan added. 'He wasn't waiting there for Meredith to take her walk. I'm convinced of that.' Alan pointed to the younger victim again. 'She doesn't fit into this group. Six victims with long brown hair, similar build. He is very specific. Rachel Evans fits the profile, but she isn't there. My question for you is where did these victims come from?'

'They can't be from the island,' Kim said. 'They would have been missed.'

'Like Rachel,' Richard said.

'My point exactly. If there were six young women missing from communities on the island, we'd be more than aware of it. We need to know who these women are, where they're from, and more to the point, where is the killer keeping them?'

'Have we interviewed any suspects, guv?' a detective from Caernarfon asked.

'We interviewed one of Rachel's schoolfriends, David Laws,' Alan said. 'He'd been harassing her on social media, and he sent her a series of dick-picks from his phone. On the day she went missing, she sent him a message threatening to have her brother beat him up. He's a testosterone filled idiot, but he's not our man. The second interview we did was with Ricky White. Ricky lived in the family home. He's the son of Norman, Pauline Evan's partner, and he's on the sex offenders register.' A murmur passed through the crowd. 'He had sex with his twelve-year-old girlfriend when he was fourteen. He's very unlikeable, but he's not capable of this,' Alan said pointing to the image of the graves by the lake. 'If Rachel is part of this and we don't know that she is, then we may have two killers on the loose. Ricky White has no alibi at the time Rachel left school,' he added. 'We need to conduct a follow up with him today and either rule him in or rule him out.'

'I can do that,' Kim said. 'I'll call him and get him in.'

'Good. Thank you. I want five teams reporting directly back to me. We're going to dissect the properties around the lake and work outward. We'll meet back here at 10 p.m. for a debrief.'

CHAPTER 31

Rob Evans dialled Louise for the third time. She wasn't picking up. His anxiety levels were off the scale. He needed to know if the police had been to see her to ask if she knew anything about the money found in Rachel's room. No news was good news. He thought about going into Holyhead to see her, but the buses had stopped running and he had no money for a taxi. He tried to calm himself down by thinking there was no massive emergency, but it was easier said than done. If she had heard anything from the police, she would have contacted him. The atmosphere in the house was one of sheer desolation. He heard the front doorbell ring and his mum going to answer it. She was climbing the walls waiting for news about Rachel. He went downstairs to earwig what was being said and get a drink. There was a female detective in the living room, accompanied by a male uniformed officer. His mum was sitting on the settee, breaking her heart, again. He feared she'd been given the news everyone was dreading.

'What's happened?' he asked.

'We're here to give your mum an update,' the detective said. 'We pulled a body out of the lake at Llyn Llwenan this morning but it's not Rachel. We didn't want you hearing the news and making assumptions that it is Rachel.'

'Why would we think that?' Rob asked, confused.

'Because the victim is similar in age to Rachel,' the detective said.

'Who is she?'

'We don't know yet. It would be easy to put two and two together and come up with five. We don't want you to worry unduly.'

'It isn't Rachel. That is good news, Mum,' Rob said. He sat down next to her and held her hand. 'It's good news, Mum. What's upset you?'

'I'm on pins all the time. Every time the doorbell rings, I think they're going to tell me Rachel is dead,' Pauline said.

'But she isn't.'

'She must be. Where else can she be?'

'We're looking for her, Pauline,' the detective said. 'Don't give up hope just yet.'

'Are you still looking for Rachel or are you looking for a body?'

'We're looking for Rachel, Pauline.'

'I've been told that Kim Davies was asking questions at the dentist about the whereabouts of someone. That makes me think Rachel is dead,' Pauline said. The detective looked uncomfortable, but she didn't reply. 'Have they interviewed Ricky yet?' Pauline asked. Rob frowned and looked surprised and confused. The detective looked embarrassed.

'He's been interviewed, but it was suspended. As far as I'm aware, he's been told to attend the station for a follow up.'

'What did he have to say for himself?' Pauline asked.

'Ricky?' Rob said. 'Ricky White. Our Ricky?'

'Shut up for a minute,' Pauline said. Rob looked shocked. 'Did he say where he was when Rachel went missing?'

'What?' Rob said. 'Do they think Ricky has got something to do with this?' he asked, looking at the detective. 'Where is he, anyway? He can't be at work. All the pubs are shut.' Rob stood up and ran up the stairs. He opened the door to Ricky's bedroom and looked inside. The bed had been stripped. There were four bin bags full of clothes lined up against the wall. Rob opened the wardrobe. It was empty. He ran into his mother's bedroom and opened Norman's wardrobe. That was empty too. There were three bin bags stacked behind the door. His mother had packed up all their clothes. Rob ran back downstairs into the living room. 'You've packed up all their things,' he said. Pauline nodded. 'Have you split up with Norman? What's going on?'

'We are trying to verify where Ricky was at the time Rachel went missing,' the detective said, trying to calm the situation.

'Why are you looking at Ricky?' Rob asked.

'It's standard procedure to rule out family members first.'

'That's not the truth,' Pauline said. 'It's because he's on the sex offenders register,' she said, bitterly.

'What?'

'That's the real reason.'

'Ricky is on the sex offender register?'

'Yes.'

'Why?'

'He had sex with a twelve-year-old girl.'

'Ricky is a paedo?' Rob said. 'That doesn't surprise me. I never liked him. Did you know?'

'Of course, I didn't know,' Pauline snapped. 'Do you think I would have let him into this house for one second, if I'd known?'

'Did the police know?' he asked the detective.

'Not until we ran a check on his record,' she said. 'He was charged by Greater Manchester Police, not us. Once we started investigating Rachel's disappearance, his record came to our attention. So, we questioned him.'

'Do you think he's done something to Rachel?' Rob asked, his hand started to tremble. 'If he has hurt my sister, I'll fucking kill him!'

'Calm down, son,' Pauline said. 'And don't swear.'

'Where has he gone?' Rob asked.

'I don't know,' Pauline said.

'Do you know where they are?' he asked the police.

'No. We don't know where he is staying. And if we did, we wouldn't tell you,' she said.

'What do you mean?'

'You're very angry and I understand why but you can't jump to conclusions. He may be perfectly innocent, and we don't want you to do anything stupid that might endanger him or yourself.'

'Do you know where he was when Rachel went missing, or not?' Pauline asked.

'Yes. He said he was here,' the detective said.

'What, in this house?' Pauline said.

'Yes. That's what he's said to us.'

'And there was no one here to prove he's telling the truth,' Pauline said.

'Apparently not.'

'So, he hasn't got an alibi?'

'No. But we're still investigating that. Please don't read anything into that. Let us do our job.'

'I've let you do your job, but nothing has happened. My daughter is still missing.'

'We're doing our best. There have been significant findings in the last twenty-four hours but we're not in the position to say if they're related,' the detective said. She turned for the door. 'If anything changes or there is some news, we'll be in touch.'

'I won't hold my breath,' Pauline said as she closed the door. She put her forehead against the wood and closed her eyes. Rachel's face drifted in her mind, but she could no longer remember her voice.

CHAPTER 32

The Matrix Unit, Liverpool

Paul Pulson was sitting at his desk, catching up on where the Matrix cases were up to. Many of them involved undercover officers working the streets and bars of Liverpool city centre and the surrounding areas. The country was going into lockdown and the pubs and clubs had been told to close their doors. The government guidelines were that undercover officers were to remain in post, despite the lockdown, wherever possible. For most undercover officers, catching Covid-19 was the least of their worries. They had taken weeks, months, and sometimes years living in bedsits, squats, and crack dens to infiltrate organised criminal gangs. The infiltration period was a delicate and dangerous process. Disappearing for a few weeks to self-isolate was not an option. Everything had to appear to be normal. Any behaviour out of the ordinary could start alarm bells ringing and put their position in jeopardy. If they were suspected of being an informer, they would be tortured and killed. If they were suspected of being an undercover police officer, they would be subjected to similar treatment but a hundred times worse. It would be better to take their own life than allow themselves to be captured. There was about to be a huge paradigm shift in the way society behaved. They would have to adapt to survive. Paul couldn't help them from behind a desk, but he still needed to know where they were and what they were up to.

The lockdown would bring immense challenges for the drug enforcement agencies. From the evidence Paul had heard so far, it appeared that it wasn't only toilet rolls and pasta that were being stockpiled by the public. Drug consumption was going through the roof as people prepared to isolate. Even casual users wanted a stockpile in their home, so they didn't have to venture out to find their dealer. Working from home meant people were going to bed later and the use of alcohol and class-A's had rocketed. Some dealers had sold a month's worth of product in three days. The increase in demand was driving prices up at an alarming rate and putting huge pressure on the supply chain. The capture of a shipment in a North Wales port, which was destined for the north-west region, had thrown another spanner in the works for suppliers and users alike. The city was almost dry of decent product and that would bring a whole new set of problems. The underworld was creaking at the seams and that made it more dangerous than ever.

Paul opened an email from the Drug Squad in the Greater Manchester Police. It was a request to call their Detective Superintendent, a woman called Casey Barrow. Paul had followed her career. She was a shooting star who had climbed the ranks like a firework. The fact she was female and black, hadn't hurt her progress one bit. She was the same rank as Paul, achieving the position in half the time. That stuck in his gullet a little. He wondered if any of her promotions had been acquired on her back. It was a cynical and misogynistic point of view, but he couldn't help the way his mind worked. He wasn't stupid enough to air his question in public; he kept his opinions to himself. The days of sexual discrimination and racial prejudice being accepted in the force were long gone. He clicked on her extension number and called her.

'Hello, DS Barrow speaking.'

'Casey, this is Paul Pulson from Matrix, Liverpool,' he said. 'I got your email asking me to give you a call. How can I help?'

'Hello Paul. Thank you for coming back so quickly. I know you must be up the wall preparing for this lockdown. They will be challenging times.'

'Things are going to get a bit mental on the streets,' Paul said. 'Our undercovers are reporting supplies are drying up and the prices are skyrocketing. I can see the dealers knocking each other over just to maintain supply.'

'I agree totally and that's the reason for the call. We've been looking into the seizure in North Wales last week. Apparently, it was headed here,' Casey said. 'The shipment being intercepted at Holyhead has left a hole in supplies.'

'It was a fluke that they found it but it was a big one.'

'A lot of the big ones are flukes. This one will choke the flow and destabilise things.'

'Yes, it couldn't have come at a worse time. How can I help?'

'The reason for the call is that a detective from Holyhead got very creative tracking the vehicle back to its owners. To cut a long story short, the crime scene photographs showed some of the vehicle parts were newer than others. Some of the engine parts were adapted to hold product but using the serial numbers, he traced the individual parts back to the wholesale supplier which was Europarts.'

'Smart guy,' Paul said. 'And they sold them to who?'

'A haulage company by the name of Manchester Logistics. The last registered address was in Salford but it's from the nineties. We checked it out and there's a multistorey car park on it now. The company went into administration in two-thousand and sixteen and none of the directors are traceable.'

'So, it's a dead end?'

'I thought so, initially but we stumbled across something,' Casey said. 'We did a little digging into the land registry and discovered that the piece of land was once registered to another company along with some dockside properties in Salford and a plot on the Mersey. The company who owned them was based in Liverpool, hence the call. I'm hoping you might have heard of them. The company was called Liverpool Shipping Co and they were based at the Queens Dock.' She paused. 'Does that mean anything to you?'

'Nope. I haven't heard of it. How old is the information?'

'Twelve years.'

'I was in the MIT back then,' Paul said. 'It doesn't ring any bells. Have you found any names?'

'Yes. Two directors by the name of Young. Andrew and Wendy from Woolton?'

'Nope. That means nothing to me. I can do some digging and ask some of the old-timers who are still working if the name means anything to them. You never know.'

'Thanks, it's worth a try, I suppose. The last one is the company secretary, who was registered as William Muir?'

'Woah,' Paul said. 'Muir spelled how?'

'M-U-I-R.'

'That has to be Billy. I think you might be on to something, Casey,' Paul said. 'William Muir or Billy as he was known to everyone, was a major player in Liverpool in the late nineties and early two-thousands. He was right up there with the big boys. His crew was into everything, drugs, prostitution, protection, firearms, you name it, Billy Muir ran it.'

'That sounds like you're talking in the past tense.'

'I am. His first wife divorced him when she found out he was having an affair with an employee. That was about fifteen years ago. She was a much younger woman, called Amie. Rumour had it she was a stripper from one of his clubs, although she denies that nowadays,' Paul explained. 'Amie is a real piece of work. She's a total psychopath. Her husband, Billy disappeared without trace about five years ago. Local opinion is that he was murdered and disposed of and that Amie ordered it. She says he's in the Far East shagging lady boys.'

'She sounds like a diamond.'

'Far from it. Rumour has it she put one of her rivals, a guy called Harris, through a tree shredder. Harris is missing but of course, we have no witnesses.'

'Very creative.'

'Normally, the removal of a force like Billy Muir would trigger a powershift between the other outfits in the city, vying for his territory but that didn't happen. Amie stepped into his shoes and didn't just hold her ground, she expanded. I remember talking to one of the main players a few years ago. I was interviewing him about a historic case. He'd walked away from the business a few years before. I asked him why he walked away, and he said, Amie Muir. He said he had money in the bank and preferred to have his legs attached.'

'You're kidding,' Casey said.

'Nope. We've been trying to get someone into her ranks for years but every time we turn an informer or send an undercover in her direction, they clam up or vanish. Everyone is terrified of the woman. We've got her linked to at least a dozen murders, but we have nothing of substance to make an arrest. No one will say a word against her. We can't touch her. Her rivals tend to vanish. She's a very smart lady. Dangerous but smart.'

'I think she's responsible for that lorry in Holyhead,' Casey said. 'From what you've just told me, that shipment belonged to her.'

'I wouldn't put it past her to be trafficking into the sex industry. She's ruthless. No wonder the natives are getting tetchy,' Paul said. 'If Amie Muir owned that lorry, she has lost millions and a lot of cocaine. It explains why supplies are drying up. Have the NCA got the information about the haulage company?'

'They have it but they're unlikely to see the link back to Billy Muir without having local knowledge.'

'I doubt they'll connect it. Not for a while,' Paul said. 'If it's okay with you, I'm going to give it twenty-four hours before I point them in the right direction.'

'Why the delay?'

'I need to get our UC's off the streets before it kicks off. If the NCA start poking their nose into her operation, people in Liverpool will start getting killed. She will silence as many people as she possibly can.'

CHAPTER 33

Monkey drove into the car park at Port-y-post. The Mustang growled as he pulled up next to Ghoul's Harley; the chrome on the bike glinted in the weak sunlight. Ghoul was sitting on a low wall outside the flats where Smithy lived, smoking and watching the waves roll in. Seagulls were squawking noisily overhead, battling against the wind. He pulled deeply on his cigarette and waited for Monkey to park the Mustang.

'Have you heard anything from him?' Monkey asked, climbing out of the car. His black hair was cut into a combover and shaved at the sides. He scratched at four days of stubble on his chin.

'No. Nothing at all. His phone is off, and his car isn't here,' Ghoul said. He toyed with the silver horseshoe bar, which pierced his septum. 'I've been knocking on the door for twenty-minutes. I thought he might be pissed and in bed but he's not answering the door. Where do you think he is?'

'Fuck knows,' Monkey said. 'The last time I heard from him was yesterday. I called him from the rib when we unloaded the gear and he was up at South Stack watching the transfer. He said he was going home. I called him about twelve last night, but it went straight to voicemail. The last thing he said to me was don't be late tomorrow.

You know what he's like when we have gear to move. He's a proper pain in the arse.'

'He has picked a shit time to go walkabouts. We've got a ton of coke to move,' Ghoul said. 'How was he going to transport it?'

'He said he had a plan, but he didn't tell me what it was. He said it could change at any minute because he still had people to talk to.'

'People like who?'

'Buyers. Everyone's flapping because of this virus shit. He said the prices keep going up. He was fishing for the best deal. It doesn't matter where it's going, it still needs to be moved.'

'We're going to struggle to get it off the island. There are police all over the bridges and all along the A55. What are we going to do?'

'He wasn't going to use the roads, I'm sure. I think he was going to use the ribs and sail them across Liverpool Bay at night.'

'That makes sense. But where is he?'

'Let's have a look in the flat. He might be on the floor passed out. It won't be the first time he's gone on a session after an exchange,' Monkey said. He opened the boot of the Mustang and took out a leather case, which was the size of a paperback. It unzipped to reveal two sets of skeleton lock picks laid neatly in two lines. They approached the main door. 'It won't take me long to get in. His locks are shit. I told him when he bought them, but he didn't listen.'

Monkey looked at the barrel and selected the correct lockpick. He put it into the keyhole and the door creaked open slowly.

'That was quick,' Ghoul said, impressed.

'Too quick,' Monkey said. 'I didn't do anything.'

'What do you mean?'

'The door was open,' Monkey said. He looked closely at the stainless lock. There were uneven striations on the metal around the keyhole. 'This lock has been picked. The scratches are fresh. Twenty-four hours or less.'

'How do you know?'

'I used to do this for a living, remember. The scratches are shiny. You can tell they're recent because they dull quickly. Especially in the salt air,' Monkey said. 'Someone broke in here. I'm getting seriously concerned about where he is.'

'Me too,' Ghoul said. 'There's only one way to find out. Let's go up and have a look.' They climbed the stairs and motion sensors flicked the lights on. Their footsteps echoed up the stairwell. 'Do you think he's in there?'

'I really don't have a clue.'

The flat door was locked, but it didn't take Monkey long to open it. It had the same telltale striations on the barrel as he'd seen on the front door, confirming someone had picked it recently. He opened the door and they walked into the hallway. The flat was dark and gloomy and had a sour odour.

'Put the lights on and open the blinds,' Monkey said. Ghoul walked around the flat switching all the lights on. With the blinds open, the weak sunlight seeped in. He checked every bedroom, the bathroom, and the kitchen. The flat looked normal at first glance. They looked at each room again, taking each one in turn. The main bedroom was empty, and the bed was made. 'He didn't sleep here last night.'

'Is he still seeing that Nia girl?' Ghoul asked. 'He could be at hers.'

'He hasn't been seeing her for months,' Monkey said, shaking his head. 'She's up the duff from someone else now.'

'No way. Who?'

'I don't know and neither did Smithy, but he won't be with her.' They went back into the living room. The ceiling was vaulted, and the roof joists were exposed and varnished. 'Can you smell that?' Monkey asked.

'I can smell something off.'

'It's not off, it's shit,' Monkey said. 'I can smell blood and I can smell shit but I'm not seeing either.'

'I don't like this one bit.'

Monkey walked around the living room. He stopped at the bay window to look at the view. There were cigarettes crushed in an ashtray on the sill.

'Look here,' Monkey said. 'Smithy smokes Stirling menthol. The tips are white. The cigarettes in the ashtray are brown.'

'He never smokes normal cigarettes.'

'That's my point. This isn't looking good.'

'He could have had a date we don't know about,' Ghoul said. 'Or he might have had a friend around.'

'He hasn't got any friends except us and when was the last time you were invited here?' Monkey said.

Monkey sat in the deep window seat and looked around the living room. One of the chairs at the breakfast bar was in an odd position. He crossed the room and looked at it and touched the chrome arms.

'What are you looking at?'

'Look here.' There was a sticky residue on the metal. The same residue was on the front legs. 'I think someone was taped to this chair,' Monkey said.

'What happened here?'

'He had a hanging chair in that corner. It was bolted to that beam above the window so he could sit in it and watch the waves.'

'The chair is in the spare bedroom,' Ghoul said. 'I noticed it when I put the light on. He loved that chair.'

'Is the chain still attached to it?' Monkey asked. Ghoul went to bedroom and checked. He came back and shook his head. 'Why would he take it down and where is the chain?' Monkey stood beneath the beam and looked around. There was sticky residue on the carpet and on the walls. 'See these lines here and here. Feel them.'

'They're sticky like glue. The same as on the chair.'

'Not glue. Duct tape.'

'What are you thinking?'

'I think they taped plastic sheets to the floor and to the walls,' Monkey said.

'Who did?' Ghoul asked, confused.

'Whoever strung him up and killed him.'

'Do you really think he's dead?'

'Something bad happened here.'

'You're fucking kidding me?' Ghoul said, staring at the beam with his mouth open.

'I wish I was, mate,' Monkey said. 'Look there, you can see the residue where the tape has been.'

'I can't get my head around this. Is Smithy really dead?'

'It looks that way.'

'What are we going to do?'

'We're going to get out of here and tip off the police,' Monkey said.

'The police?' Ghoul said. 'Smithy won't want the police involved.'

'Are you stupid,' Monkey said. 'Smithy is probably in the sea.'

'Fuck. I can't get my head around this,' Ghoul said. He sat down on the settee. 'Let me think this through, mate.' He held his head in his hands and took a deep breath. 'Smithy is missing and you're telling me, someone broke into his flat and somehow managed to tie Smithy up, tape plastic sheets down so there's no blood, hung him from the beam and then killed him?'

'Yes. That's exactly what I'm saying. I can't see any other explanation.' Monkey shrugged and ran his fingers through his hair, nervously. 'Can you think of any because if you can, I'm all ears?'

'Why would they hang him up?' Ghoul asked. 'To torture him?'

'Probably,' Monkey said.

'Why though?'

'Look at the timing. We get the biggest shipment we've ever had and Smithy goes missing. There are signs of a break in and signs that someone other than Smithy was in here. Someone might want to know where the coke is.'

'Only three of us know that and we're both here. He's not here. His car isn't here.' Ghoul walked to the fridge and opened it. He took out a beer. 'Do you want one?' Monkey nodded and took one. They opened them and swigged from the bottles and an uneasy silence fell over them while each gathered their thoughts.

'The only way to know if you're right, is to go to the container. We need to go and check the gear is where it's supposed to be.'

'Are we making too much of this? He might be in Tesco for all we know or banging some bird from town.'

'Look at the facts. We've just landed a ton of coke. You know what he's like as well as I do. He's like the Duracell bunny when we get a delivery; he's hyper until it's offloaded,' Monkey said, shaking his head. 'In all the time we've known him, when have you ever known Smithy not to answer his phone?'

'Never. I know you're right but I'm trying to think of alternative explanations,' Ghoul said. 'I'm trying to think clearly. Who would want to hurt him?'

'Fucking hell, Ghoul. That's a long list,' Monkey said, shaking his head. 'How long have you got?'

'Okay, silly question. Let me put it another way. Who would be able to carry out what you said happened to him?' Ghoul asked. 'Breaking in with all the stuff they would need would take a lot of organising. Smithy is a big man and he can handle himself. He wouldn't go down without a fight.'

'Maybe you're right but if a professional wants you out of the way, there are ways and means of taking people down. He might be a tough nut, one to one but if someone points a gun in your face or hits you over the head with a bat, it's all over.'

'Okay. Let's think who would go after him?'

'No one from the island. Not a chance.'

'I agree. It wouldn't be a local.'

'I'm thinking it's someone from away and someone he's pissed off recently.'

'Like who?'

'Like that outfit from Liverpool,' Monkey said. 'Smithy stitched that Walter bloke up good and proper and made a fool of him in the process and from what Smithy told me, his boss, Amie something, she's called, is a nutcase. She threatened to cut Louise Lee up with a chainsaw.'

'How do you know that?'

'Smithy told me,' Monkey said. 'He picked her up outside school the day after Walter was lifted, to put her straight. Louise was shitting a brick because Amie had sent a text message to her the night Walter was busted.'

'So, what happened?'

'Smithy said he was going to sort it.'

'Did he speak to her?'

'Yes. He told me she wasn't pleased, but he'd smoothed it over.'

'Maybe it wasn't as smooth as he thought it was.'

'That's what I'm thinking.'

'If Amie threatened Louise, she'll have a mobile number for Amie. We could ask her, if she's still in one piece, that is. Lets' go and check on the coke and then we'll go and ask her if she's heard any more from Amie.'

CHAPTER 34

Kim sat down in the interview room. Richard followed her in and closed the door. She set up the recorder and formally introduced the people in the room.

'Present are detective sergeants Kim Davies and Richard Lewis,' she said. 'Can you state your names for the tape please?'

'Ricky White.'

'Ffion Roberts, solicitor.'

'Thank you,' Kim said. 'For the tape, this is to recap our first interview and to formally establish your whereabouts last Wednesday at three-thirty.' Ricky stared at the wall behind her head, uninterested. He appeared not to be focused on or bothered by what Kim was saying. 'Are you okay, Ricky?' Ricky ignored her. A thin smile touched his lips. 'Are you okay to answer some questions?'

'Are they the same questions I answered the first time around?'

'Some of them will be,' Kim said.

'Then the answers will be the same because I was telling the truth,' Ricky said.

'Okay, that's fine,' Kim said. 'Let's get on with it, shall we?'

'Great. I can't wait.'

'You were working on an eight until eight shift at the Liverpool Arms in Beaumaris?'

'Yes.'

'Can you tell me what time you took your break that day?' Kim asked.

'I left the hotel at about three o'clock.'

'Why did you leave the hotel?'

'I had a dentist appointment.'

'And your appointment at the dentist was scheduled for three-thirty?'

'Yes.'

'But you didn't attend your appointment, did you?'

'No. I told you last time.'

'Can you explain why you couldn't attend, please?'

'You know why,' Ricky said, rolling his eyes. 'I'm sick of this already. I explained it to you last time.'

'Yes, you did. It's for the tape,' Kim said. Her expression hardened. 'Can you advise your client it would be better to cooperate?'

'It would be beneficial to you if you just answer their questions,' Ffion said.

'Okay, okay. I had bad guts that week and I got caught short on the way to the dentist. I had an accident and had to go home to change my clothes.'

'Because?'

'Because they were covered in shit,' Ricky said. He smiled.

'And what did you do with the clothes you took off?'

'I put them into two bin bags and dropped them in the council bins behind the George.'

'On London Road in Bodedern,' she prompted. 'Just to be certain as there are other pubs on the island call the George.'

'Whatever.'

'It is the pub in Bodedern you're talking about?'

'Yes.'

'What would you say if I told you we had those skips searched thoroughly and there was no trace of your bin bags or your clothes?' Kim asked. She sat back to watch his reaction. His eyes focused on hers. She could almost see the cogs turning in his mind. He was worried.

'I wouldn't say anything because it's bullshit. They could have fallen out on the way to the tip or they could have been taken somewhere else. How do you know what happened to all that rubbish after it was moved?'

'The skips are covered in transit to stop waste falling off the wagons and each skip has an identification plate nowadays. The environment protection act passed in the nineties stipulates every carrier has a duty of care to document what they pick up and where they drop it off,' Kim said. She looked at the solicitor who nodded her agreement. 'I think you're lying about disposing of your clothes.'

'I didn't dispose of my clothes. I threw them away,' Ricky said. 'They were covered in shit. There was shit in my jeans and shit on the back of my vest and sweatshirt. There was even shit in my socks. Pauline Evans is a cleaning freak and she doesn't like me. I took my dirty clothes away from the house and threw them in a skip so that she didn't see them.' He shrugged and looked at his brief. 'Can she search a skip for my clothes anyway?' he asked. 'Would it be admissible evidence?'

'If they thought they had reasonable grounds to connect them to a crime, they can look,' she said. 'Whether they would be admissible or not is another question.' She turned her attention to Kim. 'I understand the need to establish my client's whereabouts and I think he's answered your questions in a clear and honest fashion and unless you're going to charge him with an offence, I see no need to inconvenience him any longer, detective.'

'Okay,' Kim said, calmly. She knew Ffion was right, but she wanted to wind him up some more to provoke a reaction. The solicitor was too good at her job to allow that to happen. 'There's just one more thing. Would you be prepared to volunteer your mobile phone to us?'

'How does, not a fucking chance sound to you?' Ricky said, smiling and shaking his head.

'It sounds absolutely charming. We're aware you've had to change address?'

'Yes. Thanks to you lot.'

'We need to know where you'll be staying,' Kim said, handing him a pen and paper. Ricky wrote the address down and slid it back across the desk. 'Interview terminated.'

CHAPTER 35

Monkey and Ghoul travelled together in the Mustang. Ghoul left the Harley at the flat. The roads were quieter than usual. The atmosphere in the car was solemn. Smithy had gone missing and all the signs at his flat indicated he was dead. That was an earthshattering blow to them both. They had been friends since primary school and Smithy was more like a brother than a boss. None of them had ever signed on the dole or worked a real job in their lives. They left school with no qualifications and lived on their wits. Monkey became proficient at breaking and entering, mostly targeting businesses. Smithy went into selling cannabis straightaway and made more money in a year than most people made in ten. They were like the three musketeers; the rest of the outfit revolved around them. It had felt like they'd been blessed, as if they were untouchable and indestructible. Until now that is.

They approached the traffic lights at Valley and turned left along the Cemaes Bay road. A police car followed them for a few miles but turned off at the Bodedern road.

'There's still shit going on in Bodedern.'

'They'll be looking for that schoolgirl who's missing,' Monkey said.

'I've heard she's a bit of a selfie queen,' Ghoul said. 'You have to be careful what you post online nowadays. There are lots of lunatics out there.'

'There are too many. I don't know why they let them out of jail. Rapists and paedos need to be shot.'

'I heard on the news they had found bodies at the lake near Bodedern,' Ghoul said. 'Probably while they were looking for that girl.'

'More than one body?'

'Yes. Five or more, I heard. That'll be some psychopath on the rampage. It will keep the police busy for a while.'

'They won't be worried about a few kilos of coke here and there while that's going on.'

'Or about Smithy going missing,' Ghoul added. 'What are we going to do if doesn't turn up?'

'I don't know, Ghoul. I really don't know.'

The rest of the journey went quickly. There were only a few cars on the road and the odd dog walker in the villages. They reached Tregele and turned left towards the coast. The nuclear power station loomed on the headland to their right. A mile or so further on, Monkey turned onto a farm track and the car rocked violently as he navigated the potholes. It was a long and narrow lane which seemed to lead to nowhere. After ten uncomfortable minutes, they reached a metal gate which was half open. Monkey stopped and parked up. The metal chain which locked the gate to the post was hanging loose.

'That's not good.'

'I locked that myself,' Ghoul agreed.

They climbed out of the car and walked through the gate. The grass was knee high and swayed in the sea breeze. A hundred yards on was the spot where their shipping container was buried in the ground. It was invisible from the road and could only be seen from one aspect. They walked around to the doors.

'Fucking hell,' Ghoul said. The doors had been cut open. An acetylene tank and a lance had been discarded in the grass. They looked inside and then looked at each other.

'Only the three of us know about the container.'

'Smithy must have told them where the coke was; nobody else knew except us. You were right. He must be dead.'

'At least we don't have to worry about moving it. Someone has already done that,' Monkey said. 'Poor old Smithy. I was kind of hoping I was wrong. I don't want to think about what they did to him to make him talk. He wouldn't have given up this shipment easily.'

'Whoever did this, needs sorting out, Monkey,' Ghoul said. His eyes were full of tears. Monkey nodded. 'They killed our friend and took all our gear. I'm going to find out who it was and I'm going to tear them to pieces.'

CHAPTER 36

He watched the police coming and going; the anger inside him was growing, burning a hole in his black soul. All the activity down at the lake was making him uneasy. He thought they would never find them, but the storm put paid to that. They found them and they dug them up. One at a time. They wouldn't have found them but for that dog. That dog had some kind of special talent to be able to find them with its nose. He felt cheated. Not that it mattered. All that mattered was the fact they had found them, and they'd dug them up. They would be looking for the man who put them there and they would take him away and lock him behind bars for the rest of his life. It wasn't fair. They had no idea how much they'd meant to him. His girls meant all the world to him and he'd kept them together where they belonged. But they wouldn't appreciate that would they? How could they understand? No one did.

It had all fallen to pieces and he couldn't see any way back. Everything was his fault, but he wouldn't admit it. He could talk to him until he was blue in the face, but he wouldn't listen; he never had listened to anything he said. Not even when they were kids. If he said it was black, he would say it was white. He was forever getting him into trouble, telling lies, and stealing things but never taking the blame himself. Even though he always denied he was to blame, no one ever believed a word he said. They always believed anything but what he said. Things got worse after his mum died. Eventually, social services stepped in. When they took him away, he laughed at him. He thought everything bad that happened to him was funny. He could never admit to how much damage he'd done. Irreparable damage.

One day he would stop him laughing and shut him up for good. The axe in the woodpile was sharp enough to split his skull in half and one day, he would do it. He would cut his stupid head off his shoulders and that would keep him quiet forever. Things had come to an end because of him. He'd ruined everything again, just like he always did. This time, he couldn't fix it. This time, they would come for him and when they did, he wasn't going to get him out of trouble. He would tell the police what he'd done to his girls. There was no way he was going to walk away from this. Not this time.

***

Emily opened the PDF document and read the second update from Evolve. They had listed dozens of IP addresses linked to Rachel's photographs. The company had focused on profiles which commented on the dark web first, which was what she'd asked for but they were the profiles that had the most protection and were therefore harder to track. The users didn't want to be identified, so they disguised their identities. Revealing their browser history could be reason for divorce, dismissal from work, or even arrest and incarceration. She scanned the information, but it was useless. The closest user on the list was in Amsterdam. Even the most dedicated psychopath was unlikely to travel from Amsterdam to Anglesey. It was a huge disappointment. In hindsight, she'd asked for the information in the wrong order. If someone local had been stalking Rachel, it was more likely they would be doing it on her genuine profiles on Facebook and Instagram, not the dark web.

The pornographic images were fakes. The dark web posts had been uploaded from the Ukraine and appeared to be most popular in China, Thailand, and the Philippines, with a smaller number of followers in Eastern Europe. The likers were deviants and their comments and messages were deranged but none of them were based close enough to the island to be a danger to Rachel. To rationalise it, Rachel wasn't aware that those profiles existed, so they weren't the reason why she'd made her way home through the woods on the day she went missing. Something else had driven her into the trees that afternoon. Emily picked up the phone and called Evolve. She needed them to change their focus and concentrate on the genuine profiles.

***

Monkey pulled the Mustang onto the curb and turned the engine off. Ghoul got out of the car and walked up the path. Monkey saw Louise looking down at them from the bedroom window. She looked terrified. Monkey gave her a thumbs up and smiled. He gestured that she should come out to the car. Ghoul was already knocking at the door. After a few moments, Jen Lee opened it.

'What do you want?' Jen said, looking him up and down.

'Hello Mrs Lee. My name is Ghoul. I wanted to have a quick word with Louise if that's okay.'

'My name is not Mrs Lee and your name isn't Ghoul. It's Emeriss.'

'How do you know that?' Ghoul asked, surprised and a little embarrassed. No one had called him Emeriss for years.

'I knew your mam when she was alive. She was a nice lady,' Jen said. 'What do you want to talk to Lou about?'

'It's okay, mam,' Louise said, coming down the stairs. She was wrestling with a hoodie. 'I won't be long.' She squeezed past her and kissed Jen on the cheek, which she hadn't done for a long time. Jen looked surprised. 'I need to have a chat with them. There's nothing to worry about.'

'They're drug dealers,' Jen said.

'I know who they are and what they do,' Louise said. 'I'm not taking drugs and I won't be taking drugs anytime soon. I just need to talk to them for a minute.'

'I don't want you hanging around with the likes of them,' Jen said.

'I'm not hanging around with them,' Louise said. 'I'm going to have a chat with them and then they'll go away.' She pulled Ghoul by the sleeve. 'Come on.' They walked up the path and got into the Mustang. Louise waved at her mum from the back seat and smiled as they drove away. Jen thought her smile wasn't as bright as it used to be.

Monkey drove to the Newry Beach and stopped near the marina. He turned the radio off and looked at Louise in the mirror. She looked back at him. Monkey thought she was strangely confident for a girl of her age. Maybe that was why Walter Dallow had picked her as a protégé.

'We're not here to have a go at you,' Monkey said. 'I'm Monkey and this is Ghoul.'

'I know who you are,' Louise said. 'You were in the car with Smithy last week when he came to my school.'

'I was, yes.'

'Why are you here?' Louise asked.

'Have you seen Smithy?' Monkey asked. Louise didn't answer immediately. She looked out of the window at the yachts, thinking about her answer. 'We're worried about him.'

'Why?' Louise asked, without blinking. The sound of the chainsaw echoed at the back of her mind. Amie Muir's words had chilled her to the bone.

'We can't find him.'

'What makes you think I know where he is?'

'I don't think you know where he is,' Monkey said. 'But we wondered if you had heard anything.'

'Like what?'

'Smithy told me you had received threats from a woman in Liverpool and we think she might have something to do with him going missing.'

'Are you talking about Amie Muir?' Louise said. She thought about Smithy hanging from the ceiling, battered and bloody, his face unrecognisable. The sound of the chainsaw whirred in her brain.

'That's her. What do you know about her?'

'Not much. I know Walter works for her,' Louise said. 'I didn't know that until Smithy and you guys set Walter up and dropped me in the shit with her.'

'Sorry about that,' Monkey said, shrugging. 'I'm sure you understand what that was about. It was nothing personal, just business. Tell us what happened after he was arrested.'

'It was a few hours after the police took him from the park. She sent me a text message threatening to cut my legs off with a chainsaw. She must have thought I had something to do with arranging it. I had no choice in it. She's dangerous.'

'Nice lady by the sounds of it,' Monkey said.

'Like you said, nothing personal, just business,' Louise said. 'But you might get your legs sawn off in the process. Smithy said she was a psycho, a real fruit loop.'

'It sounds like he was right.'

'Smithy said he was going to sort her out and tell her to leave me alone.'

'We know he spoke to her, but we don't think he sorted her out,' Ghoul said. 'In fact, we think she might have sorted him out.'

'That doesn't sound good. Smithy said she was a psycho. He should have thought about that before he ripped her off and got the police involved,' Louise said, shaking her head. She was trying to maintain her calm, but she was struggling. She didn't want them to see how shaken she was. Louise kept eye contact with them. 'This is all very interesting but what has any of this got to do with me?'

'You got a text message from Amie Muir,' Monkey said. 'We want her number.'

'No problem,' Louise said, scrolling through her phone. She found the text and showed them the number. Ghoul put it in his mobile.

'What are you going to do, send her a nasty text message?' Louise said. Monkey laughed. Ghoul joined in when he got the joke. 'I can't see her being too bothered.'

'No. I don't think she would be.'

'Seriously, what are you going to do with her number?' Louise asked.

'I don't know,' Monkey said. He turned around in his seat to face her. 'You haven't heard anything from her since that text?'

'Nope. Not directly,' Louise lied. 'But I'll tell you something you need to think about.'

'What is that?'

'I heard on the grapevine that there was a man and a woman in town asking questions about you two,' Louise said.

'In town?' Monkey said. 'Where?'

'Gleesons and the Stanley,' Louise said. 'The bloke fits Walter's description.'

'What the fuck are they doing in Holyhead?' Ghoul asked.

'Walter had a property on the island,' Louise said. 'I remember him talking about it. It's somewhere near Pentraeth.'

'When were they in town?' Monkey asked, concerned.

'Yesterday and the day before. That's what I heard.'

'You heard from who?'

'Just friends in town. Everyone has been talking about it on Facebook. From what they said, the woman looks like Amie Muir,' Louise added.

'How do you know what she looks like?' Ghoul asked.

'I Googled her when Smithy told me her name. I was scared so, when I got home, I looked her up,' Louise said. Ghoul typed her name into his search bar. 'A-M-I-E M-U-I-R,' Louise spelled it for him. 'She's about my height with a gym body and tattoos on her arms.' Ghoul found a picture of her walking from a court. 'That's her.' The men looked at a few news articles about her.

'Tell me what you heard?' Monkey said. 'Don't leave anything out.'

'They were asking about you and Smithy,' Louise lied.

'Asking what, exactly?'

'They were asking where you lived, what cars you drive, who you live with, and how many kids you have. And they were waving a lot of cash about. You can guarantee they found out what they wanted to know. There's always someone who will talk. If you think she's gone after Smithy, you need to watch your backs.'

'Don't you worry about us,' Ghoul said. 'We can look after ourselves.'

'Whatever,' Louise said. 'Are we done?'

'Do you have Walter's number in your phone?' Ghoul asked.

'Why, are you going to send him a nasty text too?'

'Just give me the number, smart arse.'

Louise found the last text from him and showed them the number.

'I hope you don't mind if I go now but I don't want anyone to see me talking to you two. If that woman is after you, I don't want her to see me with you. I'm out of here.' She opened the back door and climbed out. Monkey wound the window down. 'If I was you, I'd find her and kill her before she kills you.' Louise closed the door and ran across the road. Monkey watched her disappear into an alleyway.

'She's a clever kid, that one,' he said. 'And do you know what?'

'What?'

'She's right.'

CHAPTER 37

He watched a car driving down the track towards the farm. It was a silver Mercedes. There were two men inside. He knew they were policemen before they arrived. He wasn't surprised. It was only a matter of time before they widened the search for Rachel Evans and came knocking on the door. It was inevitable. No one had knocked on the door for months and the last man who did was lost. It was a parcel delivery driver looking for another farm on the other side of the lake. His satnav told him to follow a path around the lake which was actually a footpath. That didn't happen when you used a map, he told him. The driver had looked at him as if he was from another planet. Maybe he was nowadays. Maybe he always had been.

The policemen in the approaching vehicle weren't lost. They knew exactly where they were going. They were looking for a killer and they wouldn't stop looking until they found one. The net was closing in. He went into the kitchen and took the shotgun from the wall. He broke it and loaded two cartridges into the barrels, snapping it shut, ready to fire. The car pulled into the farmyard and stopped near the barn. He stuffed a dozen cartridges into his pockets. There were plenty more if he needed them. He walked to the front door and hid the gun in the corner behind the hinges. If push came to shove, they would get both barrels. The policemen got out of the vehicle and ambled towards the farmhouse, chatting and looking around at the barns and outbuildings. They looked serious and brooding. He opened the door before they knocked.

'Good afternoon,' he said. 'How can I help?'

'Good afternoon,' Alan said. 'Dewi Pugh, is it?'

'Yes. That's right,' Dewi said, nodding. 'Do I know you?'

'No. I don't think so. We check the registered owners of properties before we start knocking on doors. Sometimes, the information is wrong but most of the time, we're right. It saves us a bit of time when we're canvassing for information.'

'I see. You caught me off guard for a minute. I thought my name was on one of your naughty lists,' Dewi said.

'Why would your name be on a list?' Alan asked, smiling.

'I don't know. You tell me.'

'Don't worry. Your name isn't on any lists that we have, naughty or otherwise. We check those records before we come out too,' Alan said, smiling. 'I'm DI Williams and this is DC Gaskell. We won't take up much of your time.'

'Very good, that's reassuring. I'm a busy man. I have a farm to run. What can I do for you?'

'Are you aware we've found some bodies at the lake?'

'No.' Dewi shrugged. 'I've seen people coming and going and cars on the meadow, but I wasn't sure what was going on. I mind my own business.'

'You haven't heard anything about it?'

'No. Nothing.'

'It's been on the local news and all over the internet.'

'I don't have a television or the internet. I've no time to listen to the news,' Dewi said, grumpily. 'I have a farm to run.'

'It must be hard work keeping a place like this going,' Alan said.

'It's nonstop. Five o'clock in the morning until nine at night, seven days a week. There're no weekends on a farm. The animals need feeding, even on a Sunday.'

'I can hear pigs and chickens. What else do you keep here?' Todd Gaskell asked. The farmer eyed him suspiciously.

'I have a small beef herd and a few dozen sheep, although I'm whitling the numbers down now,' Dewi said.

'Why is that?' Alan asked.

'It's time to wind the business up and sell it on,' Dewi said. 'My brother used to help run the place with me, but he's not been well for a while. It's getting too much for me to run on my own, at my age.'

'I'm sorry to hear about your brother,' Alan said. He gauged the farmer was in his sixties. His face was gaunt, the cheekbones prominent with a sallow complexion. He looked underweight. 'Where does he live?'

'My brother?'

'Yes.'

'In the cottage.'

'What cottage?' Alan asked, looking around.

'We have a cottage on the top field about half a mile further down the track. He's lived there all his life, but he's not there at the moment.'

'We'll need to speak to him at some point,' Alan said. There was a twitch at the corner of the farmer's left eye. 'Is he on holiday?'

'Hospital.'

'Oh dear. Sorry to hear that.' Alan pointed towards the lake in the distance. 'Look, Dewi, the reason we're here is we've found several young girls buried down by the lake and recovered a couple more from the water,' Alan said. Dewi didn't flinch. 'We think they were held somewhere for a while before they were murdered.'

'Really?' Dewi asked, disinterested. 'That's a terrible business. I'm shocked.'

'Yes, it is terrible,' Alan agreed.

'What makes you think they were held somewhere?' Dewi asked, frowning.

'They have scars on their wrists and ankles which tells us they were shackled for a long period of time.'

'Oh, I see. Very clever. I never thought of that. That's why you're detectives and I look after livestock.'

'Yes. I suppose it is,' Alan said. 'The killer would need an isolated place to keep the victims until they were murdered.'

'Isolated like a farmhouse?' Dewi said, looking Alan in the eye.

'Exactly. Hence, we're here, knocking on your door to ask if you've seen anything suspicious.'

'No. I can't say I have. You're more than welcome to have a look around the farm if you need to,' Dewi said. He looked distracted for a moment. Then he looked confused. His lips moved, but no words came out.

'Are you okay, Dewi?' Alan asked.

'What?'

'Are you okay?'

'Yes,' Dewi said. 'I'm fine. You want to look around. Hold on a minute and I'll get my keys and show you around. There's nothing here to hide. Give me a minute,' he said, turning for the door. Alan stepped nearer to the front door and listened. There was no sign of anything out of the ordinary. Dewi reappeared, stepped out of the farmhouse and closed the door behind him. 'We'll start in the barn, shall we?'

'That would be good thank you,' Alan said. He studied Dewi's face. He didn't look like a man with anything to worry about, yet there was something about him that made him uneasy. The barn was a huge wooden structure with a corrugated tin roof and metal pillars holding it up. It was piled high with bags of animal feed, bales of hay, and drums of diesel which were stacked next to a blue tractor. He could smell the fuel. 'Have a look around if you like,' Dewi said. 'You won't find any bodies in here.' Alan and Todd had a quick look around. Everything appeared to be in order.

'I'm happy with what I can see from here,' Alan said. 'Let's move on.' They walked towards the pigpens. The smell of faeces became stronger and the urine was making his eyes water. There were fifteen pens in a row, each one was full of healthy-looking animals. They were barging each other away from the feeding troughs and squealing as the men approached. The animals associated seeing Dewi with being fed. The volume became deafening.

'It's nearly feeding time. They get a bit loud when they're hungry.' He gestured that they should walk ahead along the path which separated the pens from each other. 'Go and have a look around the pens and I'll wait here for you. If they see me, they'll think they're being fed and stress.'

Alan walked along the concrete path until he reached an open stretch of grass, which led down towards the lake. He could see Snowdon on the horizon. Snow covered the upper slopes. Everything appeared to be normal. They retraced their steps to the farmyard. Dewi was across the yard unlocking the door to a single storey outhouse, which ran perpendicular to the farmhouse. It had tiny windows; the frames were cracked and peeling and there was moss growing on the roof. The door was splintered at the bottom and it looked like mice had chewed a way through it.

'Help yourself,' Dewi said, stepping back from the door. 'We used to use this as a workshop and a saddlery for the horses but it's just a place for the spiders to breed now.'

'Do you have horses?' Alan asked. He hadn't seen any stables. His ex-wife, Kath had kept horses. The first one was called Krisdan, using the Christian names of the eldest two boys. The memory came with a pang of sadness.

'Not anymore. My brother did a bit of teaching back in the day.'

'He ran a riding school from here?'

'Yes. A long time ago. We had a paddock on the top field.'

'I don't remember hearing about it,' Alan said.

'Why would you?' Dewi asked. He looked confused again.

'My wife used to keep horses down near the quarry at Holyhead. She used to teach kids at a couple of riding schools on the island. I never heard of this one,' Alan said.

'We didn't advertise on the island. It was all word of mouth between the tourists on the caravan parks and the like. It was more of a hobby than a business,' Dewi explained. 'There's still some tack in there somewhere. I meant to sell it on but never got around to it. Anyway, I need to crack on. Take a look around wherever you want to. I need to go and feed the pigs.' He handed Alan the bunch of keys. 'You know where I am when you've finished.'

'Are you sure you don't mind where we look?' Alan asked as he took the keys.

'No. Not at all. Do whatever you need to do.'

'Right you are,' Alan said. 'We won't be long. Your cooperation is much appreciated.' Dewi walked away, hands deep in his pockets, his shoulders stooped. He looked like the world had ground him down.

Alan went through the door into a workshop that was trapped in time. Long swathes of gossamer hung from the oak beams, which held up the slate roof. Tools of all types hung from hooks on the wall, covered in dust and webs. Some of them were agricultural tools and some were for joinery but one thing they had in common was their age. They heard the tractor fire up and through the window he saw Dewi drive it out of the barn. The trailer was loaded with feedbags. It trundled across the farmyard and went out of sight behind the pigpens.

'This place is like a museum,' Todd said, looking around. He turned the handle on an old vice. There was a piece of pine still held between the jaws. 'I don't know what most of these tools are for.'

'I bet there are a few of these old workshops on the island, locked up and unused,' Alan said. 'These tools would fetch a small fortune on the *Antiques Roadshow*.'

He went through the workshop and under an arched doorway which led to the saddlery. Leather bridles hung from wooden pegs, the bits and buckles long since rusted. Rows of saddles were straddled across a beam. The stirrups were pitted with rust spots. Most of them were made to fit smaller breeds, probably for children to ride. Everything was covered in a thick layer of cobwebs. Nothing had been touched for years.

'As interesting as this is, no one has been in here in a long time. Let's move on,' Alan said.

'Where now?' Todd asked.

Alan looked through the keys. An old Yale key was marked with a sticker. The biro ink was faded and almost unreadable. He held it up.

'This says, *cottage*,' Alan said. 'Let's go and take a look at his brother's place. He said we can look wherever we want to.' Todd looked unsure. 'Don't worry. If he's around, we'll ask him if he minds. If he's not, we'll have a quick look at the cottage ourselves.'

They left the outbuilding and Alan locked the door. He looked across the farmyard towards the pigpens. There was no sign of Dewi or the tractor, and the pigs were quieting down. They sounded like they were being fed. Alan thought of looking for him around the pigpens but decided to knock on the farmhouse door instead. He tried three times but got no reply. Dewi was behind the door, holding the shotgun to his chest. His eyes were closed, and his lips were moving as if he was talking to someone. Alan knocked again and then looked through the letter box. Dewi put his finger on the trigger. The door was unlocked and part of him wanted the detective to try the handle and step inside. In his mind's eye, the door opened. He pulled the trigger and Alan's head exploded, spraying the walls and ceiling with bone fragments and brain matter. Teeth were stuck in the doorframe and pink goo dribbled down the mirror on the hallstand. Another loud knock on the door brought him back to reality. Sweat ran from his brow. He heard footsteps leading away from the door.

'He must be busy somewhere on the farm,' Alan said, walking away from the farmhouse. He headed for the car. A gaggle of geese waddled from behind the farmhouse, noisily heading for the barn. 'Let's drive down the track and take a look at the cottage.'

'Okay. We might as well look now otherwise, we'll have to come back another time,' Todd said. 'Let's cross it off the list.'

Todd drove the Mercedes along the track. Hawthorne hedgerows lined either side and a strip of grass was growing at the centre. The potholes were deep and flooded with rainwater and the half-a-mile drive felt like ten. When the cottage came into view, the detectives exchanged glances. Dirty net curtains hung in the windows; heavy drapes behind them. The upper floor windows were boarded up with plywood sheets. The cottage was built from limestone rocks with a porch and a single chimneypot. It didn't look like it had been well maintained for a long time. Alan could see a stable block to the rear of the building. Some of the doors were missing, others hanging precariously from a single hinge. The roof had collapsed in several places. There was a small paddock to the right, penned in by a three-bar fence.

The hairs on the back of Alan's neck stood on end. His spider senses were tingling again. He looked through the bunch of keys. There were twenty or more, a variety of shapes and sizes. The age range spanned decades. Some of the mortice keys looked to be Victorian in age, others were shiny and new. Alan thought about what the farmer had said. He ran through it in his mind. Dewi had willingly given them access to his property, handing over the keys voluntarily. His behaviour was unusual, not suspicious but unusual, yet his instincts told him there was something wrong with Dewi Pugh.

'What did you make of Dewi Pugh?' Alan asked.

'He's a strange old bloke,' Todd said. 'Some of his generation are still stuck in the last century. It was good of him to hand over the keys. He can't have anything to hide. Why do you ask?'

'I think it's odd he gave us the keys and told us about the cottage, don't you?'

'I didn't think it was odd at the time but now you mention it, why would he?' Todd said. 'With hindsight, it does seem a little strange or he could just be an old man with nothing to hide who's socially awkward.' Alan didn't answer. 'What's wrong?'

'Nothing is wrong, but something isn't right,' Alan said.

'That's very profound. Was that something Sherlock Holmes said in a book?'

'No. It was something Bob Dewhurst said in a pub,' Alan said. Todd laughed. He parked the car at the side of the cottage and turned off the engine. 'Come on. Let's see what there is to see.'

CHAPTER 38

Rob was sitting in his bedroom typing on his laptop. He had spent the last forty-minutes online telling the world that Ricky White was a paedophile and that the police had interviewed him in connection with the disappearance of Rachel. The Facebook community was awash with reaction and within half an hour, a friend from Trearddur Bay had posted the address where Ricky and his dad were staying. He'd seen them carrying their belongings up the stairs of the building next door to where he lived.

Norman White had bought a six-month rental agreement on a flat in Trearddur Bay. Rob was stirring up a hornet's nest. Ricky's profile was being bombarded with abuse, which made Rob feel better. The fact he'd shared a house with the pervert for eighteen months made his blood boil; he'd never liked him from day one. He wondered if Ricky had been drooling over his sisters all the time he'd been there, sneaking a peek in their underwear drawer when no one was around. It made him want to puke. He wanted to punch his face in. Exposing his criminal record was the only way he could strike at him for now.

Making accusations was one thing, actually being on the register was another. Anyone could check if Rob was telling the truth. Ricky couldn't deny that he was a sex offender and his father couldn't hide it from anyone anymore, like he'd hidden it from his mother. Not only had she lost her daughter, she'd lost her partner, and Rob blamed Norman for lying and Ricky for being a nonce in the first place. The pair of them could fuck off and die as far as he was concerned. He was going to make sure everyone would know for future reference, that Ricky White had been convicted of having sex with a twelve-year-old.

***

Norman was standing in the window of his new abode, admiring the view. The flat overlooked the golf course and St Ffraids Church. If he stood on tiptoes, he could see the sea in the bay. Estate agents would call it a sea glimpse, not a sea view. It was a picturesque place to live, but he was devastated to be there; it was just him and Ricky again. Ricky's past had caught up with them. He thought back to when Ricky was a child.

His relationship with Ricky's mother had been tempestuous. They had met when they were young, and she got pregnant too soon. Their parents advised them to terminate the baby, but they decided to make it work and have the child. It was a disaster waiting to happen. She had anxiety issues, which he never really understood and if he was honest, he didn't really try to. He saw her mental health issues as her being a moody bitch and he couldn't tolerate her mood swings.

When he started working for himself, the hours were long, money was tight, and the situation worsened. They split when Ricky was five and it was very distressing for him. He loved his father and his mother was volatile and shouted at him a lot. Her ability to afford to bring up a child on her own was questionable. She would have her nails done before she would put food in the cupboard. For Ricky, the following few years were unstable at best. Norman struggled to balance his business with seeing his son but he made as much effort as he could and they ticked along for a few years until Ricky's mother became addicted to prescription drugs and had a complete meltdown. She was hospitalised and Ricky was identified as a vulnerable infant and placed in his father's custody by social services. Norman was an excellent father. He made sure Ricky was sent to school on time, was well nourished, clean, and well turned out. They spent their time together doing his homework and reading books in the evenings and at weekends, visiting museums and Ricky's favourite places, which were castles.

When his mother was well again, social services asked Ricky where he wanted to stay, and he didn't hesitate to say that he wanted to remain with his dad. Everyone appeared to be happy with the decision and access was given to his mother every other weekend. It appeared to be working well for all concerned until one weekend, she didn't bring him back. She hopped on a ferry from Holyhead and took Ricky to southern Ireland. No one knew where she'd taken the boy and it was seven months before they were traced and brought home.

Ricky was returned to the custody of his father and his mother was prosecuted and given a suspended sentence. The court insisted all future access was supervised. A few months later, approaching Christmas, she was found dead having swallowed a bottle of tramadol, sixteen paracetamol, and two strips of ibuprofen. There was no note but on reflection, her reasons for killing herself were clear. Ricky was destroyed. His mum was sometimes difficult to be with, but she was his mum and he loved her. Norman would lie in bed sometimes and hear Ricky crying. He knew only time would heal the pain; in the meantime, he would be the best father he could be.

Norman and Ricky became inseparable. It was them against the world. Norman built a lucrative building company and Ricky became a well-mannered, well-liked young boy, and everything was good until Sasha arrived on the scene. Ricky began to demonstrate attachment issues, which Norman associated with the loss of his mother. Months went by and the friendship grew. They were very young, and they fell in love. Norman warned his son that they were getting too involved, but he didn't listen to his dad. With hindsight, Norman wished he'd put his foot down. Sasha's mother discovered contraception in her room and called the police. That was when their world fell apart again.

Ricky was prosecuted. Norman did his best to protect him, but it was impossible. Manchester is a big city but the community they lived in was close knit and Ricky was vilified at school. His friends turned on him and he couldn't go out of the house. He was a pariah and he was in danger. Everybody wanted to beat him up or worse. One day on the way home from school, he was thrown into a hedgerow and urinated on by three older boys. One of them said his older friends were going to take him somewhere quiet and cut his balls off. The boy pulled a flick-knife while he was making the threat. That was the final straw.

Ricky had gone home distraught that night and Norman decided there and then, they were moving to somewhere remote, where there was less chance of Ricky being recognised. They had visited the castles of North Wales and fallen in love with the area. He started looking that night and put a deposit down on a house in Llangefni the next day. They moved from Manchester and started again. Ricky finished his schooling with no more dramas and reasonable results. He wanted to be a chef, so Norman encouraged him in that direction.

Life returned to a fragile normality. Norman met Pauline at a friend's barbeque and the rest was history. Everything was going okay, and Norman thought he and Pauline would watch the kids move out, one by one, and grow old together. They were attracted to each other and got on well. Things went so well, he'd almost forgotten Ricky's conviction existed. It was easier to pretend that it had never happened. He hadn't meant any harm when he failed to tell Pauline about his conviction. He genuinely believed his son was a nice young man with a good heart and was no danger to anyone, especially her daughters. The fact Pauline had daughters didn't strike him as a problem. Ricky was a normal kid, not a monster.

Norman was shaken from his thoughts when Ricky cried out.

'No, no, no. I don't fucking believe this!' Ricky moaned from the settee. He was looking at his tablet. His face was red with anger, his eyes full of tears. 'You horrible little bastard. I can't believe you've done that.'

'What's the matter?' Norman asked. He walked away from the window and went over to the settee where he could see what was bothering him.

'Rob Evans has put it all over the internet that I'm on the register,' Ricky said. 'He's ruined everything. The little shit. I'm going to kick his face in!'

'That won't solve anything,' Norman said. 'Calm down and we'll work something out. It's not the end of the world.'

'It is for me,' Ricky said. 'Work will never take me back when they reopen. We've been furloughed but the restaurant manager said some of us might be made redundant. He was looking right at me when he said it.'

'You don't know that for sure,' Norman said.

'I do. Especially after the police talked to him. He doesn't like me, anyway. I knew he meant me when he mentioned redundancy. This will make his mind up for him. I can't believe he's done that to me. Everyone will think I've done something to Rachel. I won't be able to go anywhere without people wanting to kill me.'

'It won't be as bad as you think it will. People react angrily and then a week later they've forgotten what they were mad about.'

'Like they did in Manchester?' Ricky said, sarcastically. 'They forgot it really quickly, didn't they?'

'Calm down. It'll be fine. We need to tell your side of the story.'

'What exactly is my side of the story?' Ricky asked. 'I can't deny what happened, can I?' he said, wiping a tear of frustration away. 'We were too young, and I get that but to other people it makes me a paedo.'

'People will calm down and see it for what it was,' Norman said, not believing what he was saying himself. He was actually thinking that they might have to move again.

'Listen to some of these comments, Dad,' Ricky said. '*You dirty paedo. If I see you in Holyhead, you're a dead man.*' He read. '*We know where you live, paedo.*' A second comment said. '*Sleep with one eye open, we're coming for you.*' Another local threatened. '*You had better hope the police get you before we do, you, vile paedophile.*' He looked at Norman and shook his head. 'Does that sound like it won't be as bad as I think it will be?'

'I'm going to call the police,' Norman said. 'They can't get away with making threats like that.'

'The police?' Ricky said. 'They're just as bad. That Sergeant Davies hates my guts. She looks at me like I'm something she's stood in. She wants to lock me up just for breathing. They're not going to help someone who came here from Manchester because he's on the sex offenders register.'

'They have a duty of care to protect the public, no matter what's on your record. Making threats like this is against the law. I'm going to ring them right now,' Norman said.

'Don't bother,' Ricky said. 'It will only make things ten times worse.'

Ricky stood up and stormed off to his bedroom. Norman heard the door slam. He sat back and closed his eyes. The lockdown would mean work would be on hold for a while. It would be difficult to carry on financially for more than a few months, especially with Ricky furloughed. He had lost Pauline and couldn't see a way back for them. Not with the way she felt about his son. Now the conviction was the talk of the town and Ricky was being vilified again. He was a good kid. Norman was proud of him but there was a dark cloud looming over him that he couldn't shake. People misunderstood him. Calling him a paedo was bad enough but the death threats made him sick to the stomach. Things couldn't possibly get any worse.

CHAPTER 39

They watched the lights go out one at a time. It was three o'clock in the morning and they'd been circling the streets around the property for hours. They couldn't park up. It would be too easy to spot a strange vehicle in such a quiet street. The police were busy trying to enforce the lockdown, but they were also pulling over vehicles to make sure their journey was essential. They couldn't afford to be searched. Monkey had a sawn-off shotgun under his seat and Ghoul had an old Colt revolver in his jacket. The property they were watching belonged to Amie Muir. She had a number of properties and they'd driven around three of them before they identified one which was occupied. There were two vehicles outside. A blue Porsche Boxster and a red Range Rover. Monkey spotted Amie in a window through a pair of binoculars. She was home.

'She's gone to bed,' Ghoul said. 'What are we going to do now?'

'We'll wait half an hour and then go in there and blow her head off,' Monkey said. He took out his lockpick case and smiled. 'Won't take me long to open up.'

Ghoul nodded. He was nervous. Killing Amie wasn't the problem. They had killed people before and laughed about it later. They were a long way from home. That bothered him. Once the job was done, they had to get back to the island, avoiding the police and traffic cameras. It was a long drive at the best of times. The roads were virtually deserted, which made them easier to spot. Ghoul planned to use the back roads out of the city towards Mold and then drive over the moors to Ruthin before dropping onto the A5. Then they could head through the mountains back to the island. Under normal circumstances, staying in a hotel and travelling home in daylight would be safer but there were none still open. It was a huge risk, but they'd both agreed that it needed to be done if they had any chance of recovering some of the shipment. Monkey had brought pliers and an electric power drill to persuade her to tell them where it was. It was obvious they must have hurt Smithy to make him disclose where the container was hidden. It was payback time and they needed to take her out of the equation once and for all. She wasn't the type to let something lie; they couldn't let her live. Smithy tried to negotiate with her, but it had failed. It had failed badly.

'Come on, it's showtime,' Monkey said. 'Let's go and square things up, shall we?'

'I'm ready when you are,' Ghoul said.

They stayed low and ran across the road, navigating a drystone wall to get into the neighbour's garden. Monkey led the way between the houses to the back of Amie's house, a small rucksack on his back. A high fence surrounded the property made from metal railings with spikes on top.

'How are we getting over that?' Ghoul asked. They crouched behind an oak tree. There were security lights fitted to the walls. Ghoul could see motion sensors beneath them. 'She's got the place wired up like Fort Knox.'

'We'll climb onto the garage over there and drop into the back garden on the other side and then go through those hedges over there. The sensors won't pick us up in the bushes.'

'Okay. But I don't like this. We're too exposed here, Monkey.'

'Stop moaning,' Monkey hissed. 'We've come this far. If we don't do this, she'll come for us. She won't walk away and just hope we don't retaliate. It's her or us. Let's get this done now.' Monkey squeezed his shoulder. 'Come on, mate. We need to do this for Smithy.'

'Okay. You're right.' Ghoul patted him on the back. 'Sorry, mate. Let's do this for Smithy.'

They stooped low as they ran from the tree to the neighbour's garage. Monkey clasped his hand together to give Ghoul a bunk-up. Ghoul scrambled up and then offered a hand to pull Monkey onto the roof. They crawled across the roof and dropped onto a well cultivated lawn. The bushes were thick and sculptured and the men kept close to them to avoid triggering the security lights. Within minutes they were at a set of patio doors and Monkey took out his housebreaking tools. Ghoul watched him twist the pick a few times and then he twisted the handle and the door opened. They went inside. Monkey crossed the room to an interior door, which was closed. He opened it and slipped through into the darkness. Ghoul was only a few seconds behind him but when he reached the door, Monkey was gone. He looked left and right. There was a wide hallway which appeared to lead to a kitchen one way and a stairwell the other. A chandelier hung from the ceiling. It was a big house. He reckoned there were at least six bedrooms on the upper floor. His heart was pounding in his chest as the seconds ticked by.

Monkey reappeared and beckoned him from a doorway beneath the stairs. Ghoul followed him. Monkey lit the way using his phone and they descended a flight of stairs, which led to the cellar. He put his finger to his lips to stop him asking questions and made his way across the concrete floor. Ghoul could see squares of light at the end of the vast cellar and figured it was coming from the street lights outside and filtering in through a gap under the doors. The cellar led into a double garage. He heard the sound of his own footsteps change. Each step made a crackling noise as if he was walking on polythene. He stood frozen to the spot, scared he might wake someone up. The lights came on and he was blinded at first. He put his hand over his eyes and blinked. There were people around the room, most of them holding Uzi's, which were pointed in his direction. He recognised two of the faces immediately; Amie Muir and Walter Dallow.

CHAPTER 40

Alan and Todd checked the stable block to the rear of the cottage. Inside, there were rotting bales of straw, which stank of molasses. Empty feed nets hung from the ceilings, where they were still intact. Beams of sunlight penetrated the gloom through the holes in the roof and particles of dust and pollen floated in the air. The structure was crawling with rats, woodworm, and earwigs but there was no sign of human activity. It would have housed eight horses and ponies when it was functional but that was a long time ago. They walked across the paddock which was overgrown with brambles and nettles. Alan studied the rear of the cottage as they approached. The backdoor and windows were boarded up with the same timber used on the upper floor. There was no exit or entry from the rear.

'It seems like a strange thing to do,' Alan said, pointing to the timber covering the upstairs windows.

'It is,' Todd agreed. 'But are they trying to keep people out or keep people in?'

'You've got a suspicious mind,' Alan said, nodding. 'I was thinking exactly the same thing.'

They made their way to the front door. Alan sorted through the keys and opened a Yale lock and a mortice lock. The door creaked open to reveal a narrow hallway with two doors going off, one each side. At the end of the hall was the stairs. The smell of damp drifted to them, tinged with the sour odour of decay. Alan stepped inside and opened the first door to his left. It was a tiny living room furnished with an old cloth settee, a television from the eighties and a red carpet. A soiled sheepskin rug had been placed in front of an open fireplace. The grate was still full of ashes and mould had grown through the wallpaper above the mantlepiece. There were no pictures or ornaments, which made the room look sparse.

Todd opened the second door and stepped into a small kitchen. There was a tub sink with a wooden draining board, a tall refrigerator with a stainless-steel handle and a table with two chairs. The table had been covered with floral sticky-back plastic in an attempt to make it look more modern. A blast from the past when people repaired things. Fungus was growing along the skirting boards but everywhere was neat and tidy.

'I feel like I've walked into the Twilight Zone,' Todd said. 'When did he say his brother had gone into hospital?'

'He didn't,' Alan said. 'But we need to ask that question.'

Todd took out his phone and switched on the torch. They climbed the stairs. There was an unwholesome smell of sweat and urine. At the top of the stairs was a landing, a tiny bathroom, and two bedrooms. He opened the door on the left and shone the light inside. A shaft of sunlight pierced the darkness through a crack in the shuttering. There was a single bed against the far wall. The frame was metal with a wire base and a thin mattress on top. Dangling from the headboard were handcuffs. The mattress was badly stained. Dark patches spotted the material, some much bigger than others.

'That looks like blood to me,' Todd said. He looked closer. 'Some of it historic but this patch looks quite recent.'

'Now I am in the Twilight Zone too,' Alan said. He stepped into the room and looked around. There was a tin bucket half full of liquid. 'That explains the stink of urine. I don't think Dewi Pugh has been completely honest with us, do you?'

The only piece of furniture in the room was a single wardrobe. Alan opened it. Half a dozen dresses hung on wire hangers. They were clean and pressed. Some of them were protected in plastic as if they'd been picked up from the drycleaners. He noted four pairs of high heels on the bottom shelf, all red.

'Forensics will be busy in here,' Alan said.

He closed the wardrobe door and left the room. Todd followed close behind him. Alan opened the second bedroom. The torchlight lit the room. A double bed took up most of the floorspace. The bed was made. Four pillows leaned against the headboard and a blue quilt covered the mattress. Six teddy bears were sitting in a line, propped up against the pillows. Their beady eyes glinted in the light. The middle bear was bigger than the rest and held a love heart. Its left ear was missing. Metal rings were fitted to the wall above the headboard. They stepped into the room and Alan saw a dark wood dressing table. There were photographs stuck on the mirror with sticky pads. Each picture was of a young girl riding a horse; they were smiling and happy. Every girl had long brown hair fastened in a ponytail. Each photograph had a lock of brown hair hanging below them, fastened with a black ribbon. There were fourteen.

'Trophies?' Todd asked.

'No doubt. They're all pretty girls with long brown hair,' Alan said. He opened the top drawer. 'Passports,' he said, using his pen to lift the documents. 'Bulgaria, Hungary, Latvia, Estonia. They explain where our victims came from and why no one noticed they're missing.'

'How would he convince them to come here?'

'I don't know but I can hazard a guess the horses were involved,' Alan said. 'Young girls love horses. A job abroad at a riding school on a beautiful island would be a powerful lure. Once they were here, they would have been easily overpowered and the farm is in the middle of nowhere.' He opened the second drawer. There were purses, keys, jewellery, and mobile phones. 'We should be able to identify them from these. At least we can contact their families and tell them what happened to their daughters.'

'That's not a phone call I want to listen to,' Todd said. 'How do you want to play this out?'

'We'll call it in, request armed backup, seal off the access road and then it's up to Dewi Pugh. He's a farmer, so there will be shotguns in the farmhouse.'

'Are we assuming he knows what his brother was doing?'

'I think we have to for now,' Alan said. 'If Dewi's brother is in hospital, he didn't kill Netty Owen and Meredith Robson. Whoever killed them knew about the body in the lake.'

'If he's involved, why give us the keys?'

'Maybe he knew what was going on and wants it to stop,' Alan said.

'Another question we have to ask is if he's involved in this, where is Rachel Evans?'

'Probably in the farmhouse,' Alan said. 'Hopefully, we can ask him at the station. Let's make some calls and bring him in.'

CHAPTER 41

Ghoul thought about reaching for his weapon, but it would be suicide. They were surrounded and outgunned. He looked at Monkey, but something was wrong. He was smiling. That confused him. Monkey stepped off the plastic sheet and walked towards Amie.

'What took you so long?' she asked.

'We had to go the long way around,' Monkey said. 'My friend Ghoul didn't like the look of your security lights.'

'I told you they would be off,' she said.

'You did, but he's not stupid,' Monkey said. 'Well, not that stupid.'

'What the fuck is going on, Monkey?' Ghoul asked frowning. He felt a sickening sense of fear in his guts.

'There's been a change in management, Ghoul,' Monkey said. 'I'm taking over from Smithy.'

'Did you plan this all along?'

'No. I saw an opportunity to step up, but I needed a little help from my new friends. Smithy saw the lockdown coming and he knew what it would do to the prices. He was smart, but he was going to take the money and cut and run. We would have been left high and dry with our dicks hanging out.'

'What are you talking about?' Ghoul asked, shaking his head.

'Smithy was going to walk away. I couldn't let that happen.'

'Did you have something to do with killing him?'

'I thought you said he wasn't stupid,' Amie said.

'Did you set Smithy up?' Ghoul asked, horrified.

'Yes. But I knew what you would do if you found out. You've always been so loyal to him. I had to make sure there was a clear run to the top,' Monkey said. 'Don't take it personally. Take it as a compliment. With you and Smithy gone, the natural progression is for me to step up. Business is business at the end of the day.'

Ghoul was speechless. He couldn't believe his old friend had stabbed him in the back.

'That's how you knew what had gone on at Smithy's flat,' Ghoul said. 'There I was thinking how smart you were, looking at the clues and telling me what you thought they meant.'

'I bet you thought I was CSI Anglesey, didn't you?' Monkey chuckled.

'No. I think you're a fucking spineless worm,' Ghoul said. 'Put your sawn-off down and fight me fair and square, you shithouse.'

'I don't think so,' Monkey said, raising the gun. He fired both barrels and Ghoul took the blast in the chest. It knocked him off his feet. He staggered backwards and collapsed, his eyes wide open, blood and saliva running from his mouth. His eyelids flickered and he tried to stand up. Monkey reloaded and fired again. This time, Ghoul stayed still.

CHAPTER 42

The farmhouse was surrounded by armed police. The track which led to the Bodedern road was sealed off and the road to the cottage was blocked by Alan's vehicle. Dewi Pugh had refused to open the door but had been seen in the upper windows carrying a shotgun. The armed unit had been ordered to hold off in case Rachel Evans was in there alive. Alan had asked for a negotiator but was told the area negotiator had tested positive for Covid-19 and been admitted to Ysbyty Gwynedd. It would be up to Alan to talk him out.

'We've got a number for the landline,' Kim said. 'There's an iPhone registered to the address too, under the name Alwyn Pugh.'

'That must be the brother,' Alan said. 'Have we got any details about the brother yet?'

'Nothing,' Kim said. 'We're running an online search on both of them. Births deaths and marriages are closed. Emily is checking the internet archives. I'll ring her now to see what she's got.'

'Check all the local hospitals to see if they have a patient by that name. Dewi said his brother had been sick and went to hospital.'

'Okay. I'll ask them to call around now,' Kim said.

Alan dialled the landline. It rang out for over a minute before Dewi picked up.

'Hello,' Dewi said, as if nothing was wrong.

'Dewi, this is Alan. We met earlier.'

'Yes. I can remember that far back. I can see you've invited some of your friends over.'

'We need you to come out and talk to us, Dewi.'

'I don't think so. There seems to be a lot of guns about.'

'They're a precaution, Dewi. No one is going to hurt you, but we need to ask you some questions.'

'What about?'

'You know what about, Dewi, your brother Alwyn and the cottage,' Alan said. 'There's some pretty disturbing evidence inside the cottage. We think your brother was holding young girls against their will.'

'I wouldn't know anything about what he got up to there. He kept himself to himself most of the time,' Dewi said, casually. 'He's always been a bad one. I'd have nothing to do with him if I could. You can't pick your family.'

'You can tell me all about him when we get to the station,' Alan said. 'I need you to come out and speak to me face to face.'

'What has he done?' Dewi asked, matter-off-fact.

'We think he murdered the girls we found at the lake,' Alan said. The line went quiet. He could almost hear Dewi thinking. 'Are you still there?'

'Yes. I'm here. That wouldn't surprise me.'

'Where is he?' Alan asked.

'Hospital. Where he belongs.'

'Do you know which hospital he's in?'

'No. He didn't say. But it will be a nuthouse.'

'Did he go in by ambulance?' Alan asked.

'No.'

'He drove himself?'

'He must have.'

'What was wrong with him?' Alan asked.

'What was right with him?' Dewi said. 'He wasn't right in the head, you know. He's always been trouble ever since we were little kids. He used to drive my mam and dad around the bend; always blamed me for everything.'

'So, he had mental health problems?'

'I don't know about mental health problems, but he was fucking mental all right. Always has been.'

'Did you know what he was doing at the cottage?'

'No. But I had a feeling he was up to no good.'

'What made you think that?'

'There were always young girls about. They used to come to see the horses,' Dewi said. 'The horses were like a magnet. It's not healthy a grown man being around young girls all the time. I told him so many times, but he wouldn't listen. 'Don't put yourself in that position,' I used to say to him. And then there were all the rumours too. Once rumours start, there's no stopping them.'

'Rumours about Alwyn?' Alan asked.

'Yes. That was years ago, mind you but people never forget.'

'What were the rumours about?'

'I heard he'd touched a young girl where he shouldn't have. When she was mounting a pony,' Dewi said. 'I pulled him about it and asked him what had happened, but he denied it. He said he was just helping the girl into the saddle.'

'Maybe he was just helping her,' Alan said.

'I would like to believe that but there was more than one, you see,' Dewi said. 'It happened and then it happened again and again. Girl after girl complained to their parents. In the end, we stopped locals from coming onto the farm. It was the only way to stop the rumours. But then I heard he was still allowing some of them to ride the horses behind my back.'

'And where did you hear that?' Alan tried to keep the conversation going.

'In the local pub in Bodedern. I used to go for a pint in those days. I ended up in a punch up arguing about Alwyn with a local man who was mouthing off. The landlady took his side. She said she'd heard stuff about Alwyn before and that I was barred. She said she didn't want either of us in there ever again. That was thirty-years ago. I bet she's dead now a long time since. She was getting on then, you know.'

'We could have this conversation at the station,' Alan said. 'You can tell me all about Alwyn and we can get to the bottom of this in no time.'

'I'm very busy, Alan,' Dewi said. 'I've got animals to feed and a farm to run. I really need to get on. I haven't got the time if I'm being honest with you.'

'You'll have to make time. This a very serious matter, Dewi,' Alan said, sensing a lack of reality in his voice. 'I need you to come out of the house.'

'You'll have to take it up with my brother,' Dewi said. 'Look, I've been helpful. I've let you look around the farm. Now I need to get on.'

'Do you know if your brother knew Rachel Evans?' Alan tried to bring him back to reality.

'Who?'

'Rachel Evans. The missing girl from Bodedern.'

'No. He wouldn't know her.'

'Did you know her?'

'No.'

Kim gestured to Alan that she had information.

'Stay on the line,' Alan said. 'I won't be a minute.' He put the call on hold. 'What is it?' he said to Kim.

'Emily found a record from the old Gors Maternity Hospital in Holyhead from nineteen fifty-three,' Kim said. 'Bethan Pugh gave birth to twins, Dewi and Alwyn. Alwyn was born with spina bifida. He never walked and died at home from meningitis, age four.'

CHAPTER 43

Dewi waited for the detective to come back on the line. He looked out of the bedroom window. Some of the policemen were putting on helmets. He could see big plastic shields being carried by others. They were heading past the pigpens to the rear of the farmhouse and they were all carrying firearms. Another group made their way across the farmyard towards the front door. He lost sight of them as they reached the porch. They appeared to be preparing to enter his home. This was his fault. He'd fucked it up and Dewi would get the blame again. Just like always. He heard the line click on again.

'Hello, Dewi,' Alan said.

'Why are those policemen at my door?'

'Because we need you to come out and talk to us, Dewi. It would be so much easier and safer for everyone if you would leave your shotgun and open the front door. We can take you to the station and sort all this out.'

'I don't want to go to the station,' Dewi said. 'If anyone tries to break into my farm, I'll give them both barrels. I'm well within my rights to protect my home.'

'We don't want anyone to get hurt, Dewi, and no one is going to force their way into your home, while you have a loaded shotgun.'

'They're not?'

'No. That would be foolish. It would be simpler if you come out. No one will hurt you, but we do need to talk to you.'

'Have you found Alwyn?' Dewi asked.

'No, Dewi. We haven't found him,' Alan said, humouring him.

'Fucking typical,' Dewi said. 'He always gets me into trouble and then buggers off and leaves me to take the blame. He's done it again, hasn't he?'

'I'm not sure we can blame Alwyn,' Alan said.

'No. You can't blame Alwyn. No one ever blames Alwyn. Blame Dewi. It's his fault. It always is,' Dewi moaned. 'Fucking Alwyn gets away with everything. Dewi did it every time. If in doubt, blame Dewi.'

'We're not blaming you for anything, we just need to talk to you.'

'You can ask me questions here,' Dewi said. 'I'm not leaving here. I've got a farm to run.'

'I need to ask you questions face to face, Dewi,' Alan said.

'About what you found at the cottage?'

'Yes.'

'About the girls?'

'Yes.'

A light came on in Dewi's brain. He sat on the bed, put the shotgun in his mouth and pulled the trigger.

***

Monkey woke up with rocks in his head. He'd drunk most of a bottle of vodka with Amie and Walter. Walter left about four o'clock in the morning, leaving himself and Amie to have one more drink. They chatted about business and how they would progress their relationship over the coming months. The price of cocaine was about to increase tenfold and Smithy had organised shipments in advance. Monkey would make sure the shipments went ahead and arrange more. Amie would take over once the drugs were ashore and they would be fifty-fifty partners. He had been offered one of the spare bedrooms to sleep in and he slept like a baby. When he woke up, the sun was shining through the window. He got dressed and used the bathroom. The walls were tiled with grey marble and the bath was big enough for three people. It had cost tens of thousands just for the tiles. She had good taste and a lot of money. More money than Monkey would have earned in a hundred years if he hadn't cut a deal to take control. She offered him the choice, work with her or work against her. The second option came with a death sentence. Monkey had a wife and three children. There was no choice in the matter. He had no feelings of empathy for Smithy or Ghoul or their families. It was nothing personal, just business.

He went downstairs and looked into the living room, where they'd drunk the night away. There was no one there. The house was quiet. He thought Amie might still be in bed until he saw a note on the front door.

'Let yourself out. I had an early meeting. Speak soon, Amie.'

Monkey left the house and closed the door behind him. the drive home would give him time to think about what he was going to say to the others. With Smithy and Ghoul out of the way, he was the natural successor. No one would argue against him and if they did, he would have to sort them out. He walked down the drive and opened the gate which was magnetised. It could only be opened from the inside unless you had a key. It slammed closed behind him. The Mustang was a hundred yards down the road. It was a pleasant morning. The sky was blue, and the sun was shining. It would be a nice drive home through the mountains. He loved the scenery as the road climbed out of Betws-y-coed to the heart of Snowdonia.

He reached the Mustang and climbed in. The engine growled as he pulled away. He reached the end of the road and turned onto a treelined avenue. A police cruiser blocked the road. He thought they were taking the lockdown a bit too seriously until two more interceptors screeched to a halt behind him. The Mustang was blocked in. He turned off the engine and wound down the window, ready to explain why he was driving his car. Armed officers surrounded him, screaming and shouting orders. Monkey laughed nervously as he opened the door and climbed out with his hands in the air.

'Fucking hell, boys,' Monkey said. 'What's the problem?'

The police officers took him to the ground and cuffed him roughly. They pulled him up and marched him to the back of his car.

'What is your name?'

'Sam Pemberton,' Monkey said. He was confident this was a mistake and a massive case of overkill. 'What is the problem?'

'Is this your vehicle?'

'What is the problem, officer?'

'Answer the question. Is this your vehicle?'

'Yes, it's my vehicle.'

'Open the boot.'

An officer reached inside and opened the boot. The officers looked inside. Monkey saw what they were looking at. It was the body of a man wrapped in clear plastic sheeting. Ghoul's dead eyes stared at him through the polythene.

'There are two weapons in here,' an officer said. 'A sawn-off shotgun and a Colt revolver.'

Monkey didn't hear them reading him his rights. He closed his eyes and wished he could go back in time but there was no going back. His future had been bright for a few stolen hours and now he didn't have one. He felt sick inside and he wondered how he could have been so stupid to trust a shark like Amie Muir. His dad always told him that the life he'd chosen was a dangerous one. Monkey could hear his voice in his mind. 'If you swim with sharks you'll get bitten.'

CHAPTER 44

On hearing the shotgun blast, both armed units entered the farmhouse. They cleared the building room by room. They found what was left of Dewi Pugh in the main bedroom. Only the lower jaw remained. The rest of his head was gone. Alan and his officers went through the farmhouse, inch by inch, looking for evidence that would help to find Rachel Evans. Alan heard Kim calling from the kitchen. When he got there, Kim had rolled back a threadbare rug and opened a hatch which led into the cellar.

'Rachel Evans,' she called into the darkness. There was no reply. 'Pass me a torch,' she said.

'Let us check it out first,' an armed officer said.

'After you,' Kim said, standing back. Two armed officers descended the stairs. They were gone several minutes.

'Clear,' one of them called. 'You need to see this. We've got a body.'

'Oh no,' Alan said, shaking his head. They walked down the stairs. The cellar floor was concrete, and the walls were brick. 'It's a seed store,' Alan muttered, looking at the rows of sacks and boxes. The atmosphere was dry and warm. They made their way to the far side of the cellar where the armed officers were standing. In the corner, hidden in shadow was a coffin. It was old and dusty. Alan looked at the brass plate. The body inside was wrapped in a white linen shroud, the grinning skull was the only part they could see. 'So, this is Alwyn Pugh,' Alan said. 'There's no sign of Rachel Evans?' he asked.

'No.'

'The only person who knows where she is has just blown his head off,' Alan said.

CHAPTER 45

Three Days Later

The press were calling the farm the 'house of horrors'. Evidence was found linking Dewi Pugh to the kidnap and murder of at least seven females, although Alan thought the true number was in double figures. The cottage was a treasure trove of trophies belonging to young foreign girls lured to the farm with the offer of paid work as stable hands. Emails exchanged with the victims showed they were promised a wage, free food, and accommodation and the opportunity to teach children how to ride horses. It was a teenage girl's dream, which fast turned into nightmares. The passports and purses had identified each victim and early findings on a laptop found in the spare bedroom at the farmhouse were helping to fill in the blanks. There were more passports than bodies.

The team were called to a recap meeting to discuss the findings and plan how the case could move forward.

'When we first spoke to Dewi Pugh, he said he had no internet and no television,' Alan said.

'He lied. He had both,' Emily said. 'Actually, he was quite proficient on the internet. He had a website for the riding school, which he used to entice his victims to travel to the UK. In most cases, he communicated with them over an extended period. He was clever,' Emily said. 'He showed them photographs of the riding school and the horses, telling them their names and describing each of their personalities. He made the girls feel like they were going to be part of a happy family.'

'He groomed them,' Kim said. 'Excuse the pun.'

'Without a doubt. Once he had them convinced, which in most cases didn't take very long, he paid their airfare to Manchester airport and had a taxi waiting for them.'

'That's smart,' Alan said. 'There's no traffic camera footage of him travelling to Manchester, picking up the girls, no CCTV footage of him at the airport. He thought it through.'

'He did. From what we've found on the girls' phones, it looks like they lived in the cottage and worked with the horses for several months in some cases before anything untoward happened. Their phone calls and messages home were positive, and they looked healthy and happy on their pictures. Some of them sent money home to their families. At some point, Dewi closed the trap, they're attacked and held captive.'

'Do we know why their parents didn't report them missing when contact stopped?' Kim asked.

'Initial searches show none of them had parents or if they did, they didn't live with them. He was very selective in picking girls who lived with friends, their extended family, or lived alone. The pattern was the same with each girl. After a few months, they all sent messages home telling family and friends that they'd met someone and fallen in love and that they were going travelling around the world together for a few years and then the messages stop. Obviously, those messages were sent either by Dewi Pugh or they were written under duress. The messages are identical, probably copied and pasted. No one was any the wiser. He had all the time he needed to keep them prisoner until a new victim caught his eye.'

'Then he killed them and buried them near the lake where he can see their graves from the farm,' Alan said. 'He still has them under control where he can see them.'

'A classic psychopath,' Kim said. 'Narcissist to the end.'

'Some of the local farmers who bought livestock from him said he lived in the cottage from being a boy and worked the farm with his parents. They both grew old and sick and he put them into a home in Menai Bridge. He moved up to the farmhouse,' Alan said. 'I wonder at what point he dug up his twin brother?'

'Clearly, he had mental health issues, which appear to have worsened as the years went on, but he had the ability to function normally when necessary,' Emily said. 'The riding school was in the perfect position. He could operate his trap invisible to the world outside of the farm.'

'Then Rachel Evans went missing and he panicked. That set off a chain of events, but why?' Alan asked.

'Hypothetically, because he still had a girl tied up in the cottage and he knew that the search would widen and widen and that sooner or later the cottage would be looked at, so he killed the girl and disposed of the body in the lake in a rush before the police came knocking on his door,' Kim said. 'But he was scared. He panicked and didn't do things as thoroughly as he normally would. He couldn't take his time.'

'He dumped the body in the lake but he knew he hadn't done a thorough job and when the storm hit, she floated to the surface and Meredith Robson found her body,' Alan added. 'So, he had to shut her up but then Netty Owen went looking for Meredith and stumbled into a murder scene.'

'That all makes sense. Okay,' Kim said. 'We know Rachel Evans going missing was the catalyst to make Pugh unravel and pushed him over the edge, but did he take her and if he did, where is she?'

'Is there anything on Pugh's laptop to suggest he was looking at her pictures?' Alan asked.

'No. He doesn't appear to have any social media platforms,' Emily said. 'That was the first thing we checked. He had a website and used email.'

'So, have we been too focused on Dewi Pugh or are we looking for someone else?' Kim asked. 'Have we been looking in the wrong direction?'

'How long will it be before we get the information from Evolve, Emily?' Alan asked.

'It should be in anytime now.'

'Until it does, we work the Rachel case as if Pugh never existed. The dogs have been all over that farm and found nothing,' Alan said. 'We have to assume the two cases are separate until we can prove otherwise.'

CHAPTER 46

Ricky and Norman were watching the news. The coverage of the house of horrors was extensive. Speculation whether Dewi Pugh was responsible for every unsolved murder ever committed was rife. He was being linked to every young girl missing from the North Wales area going back decades. Reporters and victims' families were bringing up cases from way back. The police were being inundated with enquiries. For many grieving parents, Pugh had become the possible answer to many unanswered questions. Rachel Evans was being included in the list of his victims, despite there being no evidence that she was ever at the farm.

'This is good news for you,' Norman said. 'It is definitely going to take the pressure off you.'

'I'm not sure how you work that one out,' Ricky said. 'I've got people shouting paedo at me across the beach.'

'Because people will leave you alone while they're talking about the farmer. He'll be blamed for Rachel going missing.'

'Do you think so?' Ricky asked, hoping his dad was right. 'I haven't been online, so I don't know if I'm still getting death threats.'

'Have you come off Facebook?'

'Yes. I deactivated my account. I hardly used it anyway,' Ricky said. He stood up and went to his bedroom, grabbing his leather jacket and helmet. 'I'm going for a spin. I need some fresh air.'

'Okay. Don't be long. They're being strict on the lock down. If the police stop you, tell them you work with me and we're self-employed.'

'I'm not lying to them about anything,' Ricky said. 'They've got it in for me as it is. I'm not giving them anymore excuses to have a go at me.'

'Fair enough,' Norman said. 'Where are you going?'

'I'm going up to South Stack. There will be no one up there.'

'Okay. Don't be too long and be careful.'

Ricky used the lift to get to the car park. The golf course was closed, and it looked odd to see the fairways empty. He put on his helmet and started the engine and coasted down the access lane to the road. He turned right past the Sea Shanty which had the shutters down. The village streets were empty of tourists and locals alike. He turned left towards the beach, riding by the Black Seal and the Trearddur Bay Hotel; both were in darkness. He passed Craig-y-mor doing less than forty miles per hour. His dad always called it Scooby-doo house because he couldn't pronounce the Welsh name for it. From behind the house, there was a strong breeze blowing off the sea and he could see the waves crashing onto the rocks. He opened the throttle and increased his speed. As he rode uphill towards Porth Dafarch, he changed gear on the crest of the hill. The bike picked up speed as it travelled down the other side. He steered towards the centre of the road, hurtling towards the sharp bend at the bottom of the hill. He leaned into the turn and realised he was going too fast. The front wheel began to judder, and the handlebars began to twitch violently. His bike was misbehaving. He touched the back brake to slow the machine down, but nothing happened; the front brake failed too. It was too late to slow the bike using the gears. Ricky closed his eyes as the bike hit the wall head on and he was catapulted into the air. He hit a rock outcrop and then dropped onto the road, his body broken and twisted.

CHAPTER 47

Kim was sitting at her desk, catching up with her emails. One was from the drug squad in St Asaph. The subject was Walter Dallow. She hovered over the tag but then saw another message from Emily and debated which one to open first. The Dallow arrest had been a gift. Tip offs were few and far between. It was obvious the information came from a rival. She had no doubt about that. It wasn't often a dealer was dropped into her lap with so much evidence to hand. Dallow was arrested with drugs and cash in close vicinity. Someone had set him up and she had the distinct impression it was Michael Smith and his outfit. They were in control of the supply of drugs in the area. The faces changed now and then but Smithy appeared to have a chokehold on the island. Walter Dallow had stepped into someone else's domain and got burnt for it. She wondered what the St Asaph drug squad were mithering her for. She'd handed the case over to them and they passed it on to the Merseyside division. There was no obvious reason why they needed to contact her about it. Curiosity won the day and she opened the email. It was originally sent by a Matrix officer from Liverpool. He was a Detective Superintendent by the name of Paul Pulson. The subheading was Criminal Exploitation of minors. She read the email twice and then looked up at Alan across the desk.

'This is interesting,' Kim said.

'What is?' Alan asked. He took off his glasses and rubbed his eyes.

'St Asaph have forwarded on an email from a DS in the Matrix unit in Liverpool,' she said. 'Do you remember the Walter Dallow arrest a few weeks ago?'

'Was he the clown in the park toilets who had his pants pulled down?'

'That's him,' Kim said.

'That has got Michael Smith written all over it,' Alan said.

'Definitely. But listen to this. To cut a long story short, Matrix released Dallow on bail the next morning. He was in a cubicle when we found him, and his clothing was in a sink outside the cubicle. The CPS said the fact the money and drugs were in his clothing and not on his person was not going to look good in court; he was naked apart from his boxer shorts, for heaven's sake. They wanted to wait for the evidence from his phones to back up the charges. Since then, Matrix have had his phones dumped and came up trumps. They've rearrested him for criminal exploitation.'

'That's a biggy these days. He'll get more time for that than for dealing.'

'According to Pulson, he's built a considerable network of teenagers along the coast,' she said. 'They've got names, dates, times, phone numbers, and all of these kids are under sixteen. But he's not the top of the tree. Apparently, he works for a woman called Amie Muir.'

'I've heard of her,' Alan said. 'Her name came up in the Jamie Hollins investigation. She is a very dangerous lady.'

'Dallow has refused to implicate her in any of this,' Kim said.

'He will do if he wants to live. He'll be going down for that. The courts are jumping all over CE,' Alan said. 'Why are they emailing you with it?'

'Because two of Dallow's little workers are here on the island,' Kim said. 'And when I tell you who they are, one of them is going to make your jaw drop.'

'Now I'm interested. Come on, spill the beans.'

'We've got a fourteen-year-old girl called Louise Lee in Holyhead and a fifteen-year-old boy.'

'Called?' Alan asked. 'Come on. Don't wind me up.'

'Robert Evans from Bodedern,' Kim said, shaking her head.

'Rachel's brother,' Alan said.

'Yes.'

'Well, I never expected that,' he said.

'What are you thinking?' Kim asked.

'I'm thinking about the eight-hundred pounds in Rachel's bag,' Alan said.

'So am I,' Kim agreed. 'Shall we bring them both in?'

'No. Let's go and speak to them off the record at their homes. We may have been looking at this all wrong,' Alan said.

CHAPTER 48

Bob Dewhurst arrived first at the scene. A local fisherman had found a badly injured motorcyclist on the road near Porth Dafarch beach. Bob could hear the ambulance siren in the distance. They were coming from Holyhead and would be a few minutes. At an RTA, minutes could mean the difference between life and death. He left the blue lights flashing on his vehicle and went to take a look at the injured biker. He was unconscious. His visor was down, and the helmet was intact. A quick assessment told him the man's legs were broken in several places; his feet were facing the wrong way. The left arm was sticking out at the wrong angle, but he was breathing. There was nothing even an experienced first aider could do until the paramedics arrived. He checked his pockets for ID and found his wallet and driving licence. Richard White from Bodedern. Bob Dewhurst knew he'd been interviewed at the station. He was the stepbrother to Rachel Evans. Bob put his belongings into a bag.

The ambulance crew attended, and it took them fifteen minutes to stabilise their patient, so they could move him. They put him into the ambulance and then set off on the journey across the island to Bangor accident and emergency. Bob had called the garage who recovered vehicles involved in accidents. The owner was a local man known as

George Bike, for obvious reasons. Bob remembered his real surname was Jones. When he arrived, Bob called him over.

'Hello, Bob,' George said, touching his cap. He was wearing one-piece overalls covered in motorcycle racing logos. 'This looks like a nasty one. How are you?'

'I'm okay, thanks, George,' Bob said. 'Can I get your opinion on something? Take a look at this and see what you think.'

'What are you looking at?'

'It looks to me that the motorbike came down the hill from the bay and struck the drystone wall over there.'

'Okay.'

'There's not a single skid mark on the road,' Bob said, pointing. 'He either didn't try to brake, or they didn't work.'

'It's a Honda 250. He's riding a relatively new bike,' George said, shaking his head. 'Honda don't make bikes with dodgy brakes and they don't fail at that age. Either he was trying to kill himself or someone else was trying to kill him.' George went over to the broken machine. The front wheel was buckled in half. He studied the back brakes. 'Someone has tampered with the brakes. I'm not a hundred per cent sure until I get it back to the garage. Do you want me to strip it and tell you?'

'No. I'll have it picked up by forensics tomorrow. Don't let anyone touch it until then but I appreciate your opinion, thanks,' Bob said. He had a pretty good idea what had happened and why. Bob called Alan.

'Hello, Bob,' Alan said. 'What's up?'

What Happened to Rachel?

'I've been called out to an RTA on the Porth Dafarch road. A motorcycle has crashed into the wall at the bottom of the hill,' Bob said. 'The rider was Ricky White. I thought you would want to know.'

'Bloody hell,' Alan said. 'How bad was he?'

'He was banged up, broken legs, broken arm and he was unconscious. It took the paramedics a while to stabilise him. George Bike came out to pick up the wreck; we both think his brakes were tampered with.'

'What makes you think that?'

'There were no skid marks on the road. He either didn't brake, or they didn't work when he did.'

CHAPTER 49

Louise Lee and her mum Jen looked worried when Kim walked into the house. Louise looked like a ghost. She was pale and agitated. Her eyes were sunken with dark circles beneath them. She had a haunted look on her face. From her experience, Kim knew Louise Lee was a young girl with something to hide. Teenagers tended to display their emotions more than adults. They were easier to read.

'Do you want a drink, tea or coffee?' Jen asked. She looked uncomfortable allowing Kim into her home, but it was better than going to the police station.

'No. I'm fine, thanks,' Kim said. 'This won't take long. I have a few questions for Louise and then I'll leave you in peace.'

'Sit down,' Jen said, pointing to a leather armchair. 'What is this all about?'

'I want to ask Louise about a man she knows called Walter Dallow,' Kim said. Louise didn't look surprised to hear his name. Her reaction was odd. If anything, she looked frightened.

'Walter Dallow. Who is he?' Jen said. She glanced at her daughter, but Louise didn't flinch. She kept her eyes on Kim.

'He is a man from Liverpool who has been arrested on charges of criminal exploitation,' Kim said. Jen looked confused, so Kim explained. 'That is the use of minors in the pursuit of financial gains through criminal activity. It's mostly coordinated by organised crime families from the cities, targeting rural areas like ours. You may have heard about it on the news. They call it County Lines.'

'I have heard that. There was a piece on the news but that was about drug dealers,' Jen said.

'That's right,' Kim said. 'Walter Dallow is a drug dealer who specialises in the recruitment of teenagers along the North Wales coast. He uses them to sell drugs to their friends and Louise is in his list of contacts.'

'Are you sure?'

'Yes. We have recovered messages between them from his phone.'

'A couple of text messages doesn't mean much,' Jen said.

'There are more than a few and the conversations were communicated over a period of weeks.'

'What type of conversations?' Jen asked.

'They discuss the sale of drugs in Holyhead on his behalf. I can't show you the content because they may be used as evidence against him, but I can show you the number. This is your number, isn't it?' Kim asked Louise. Louise nodded.

'Yes. That's mine.'

'What are you doing messaging a drug dealer?' Jen asked, angrily.

'He was messaging me. I was just chatting.'

'Just chatting to a drug dealer and pigs might fly over Newry beach. Have you been selling drugs?' Jen shouted at Louise. 'If you've been selling drugs, you'll be through that door, young lady.'

'Don't make this a drama, Mum. It always has to become a drama.'

'A drama. I've got a policewoman in my living room telling me my daughter has been selling drugs,' Jen said, angrily. 'Don't tell me not to make it a drama because it is a fucking drama!'

'I don't think shouting at her is going to help,' Kim said, calmly.

'Oh really?' Jen asked. 'And how many kids have you brought up?'

'None,' Kim said. 'I haven't come here to interview Louise about selling drugs because I have no evidence that she has. All we have is circumstantial. If we had evidence that she'd sold drugs, we would be having this conversation at the station.'

'You haven't got any evidence that she's been dealing?' Jen said, looking relieved.

'No. We would have to catch her in the act to do anything about it.'

'Oh, thank heavens.' Jen pointed at Louise. 'You should count yourself very lucky, young lady.'

'If it's not about dealing, what have you come here for?' Louise said, ignoring her mum. She looked like she was about to vomit. There was something behind her eyes that Kim couldn't put her finger on. It looked a lot like fear.

'First, I want to ask you about your cousins, Rob and Rachel Evans,' Kim said.

'Rachel and Robert. What have they got to do with anything?' Jen asked.

'I'll explain. We know Rob was speaking to Walter via text,' Kim said.

'Rob told me Walter had messaged him.'

'What was the arrangement between them?'

'There was no arrangement,' Louise said. 'It never got that far.'

'We have the messages.'

'Then read them properly. Rob wasn't working for Walter. Walter was asking him if he would work for him.'

'And according to the messages, Rob said he would.'

'He did but Walter didn't get back to him. He never actually worked for him.'

'But you did, didn't you?'

'I did for a week or so,' Louise said, glancing at her mum. 'It was only a week and I wish I hadn't. It was the biggest mistake of my life so far. I got suckered into it, without thinking about what I was doing. Walter is very persuasive.'

'You are joking,' Jen said. 'My daughter has been dealing drugs. What will people say about me as a mother?'

'Don't make this about you, Mum,' Louise said, turning to face her. 'Because it isn't about you.'

'I beg your pardon?'

'Everything is always about you.'

'How dare you?'

'You make everything about you, so you can justify being pissed, morning, noon, and night. You're such a victim,' Louise said. Jen was shocked into silence. Her mouth hung open, but she couldn't forge a reply. Louise turned back to Kim. 'This is about Rachel going missing, isn't it?'

'Yes,' Kim said.

'It's about the money you found in her room?'

'Yes. We think it might be something to do with why she went missing?' Kim said. 'Do you know anything about it?'

'Yes. I do,' Louise said. 'It's nothing to do with Rachel or her going missing.'

'What do you know about it?' Jen asked, becoming increasingly angry.

'Shut up, Mum,' Louise said. She turned to face Kim. 'This is about Rachel.' Jen looked like she'd been slapped. 'The money belonged to me and Rob. There was eight-hundred pounds.'

'That's right,' Kim said. 'Tell me about it.'

'Rob took some weed from me to sell to his friends,' Louise said. Jen was going to speak but Kim held up her hand to stop her. 'He sold it all in a week. We had eight-hundred pounds, which was hidden in Rob's room. Aunty Pauline said she was going to clean his room, which means she would pull it apart, empty every drawer, sanitise them and put everything back together again. She's a bit OCD,' Louise explained. 'Rob knew she would find the money, so he waited for Louise to go to school and hid it in a handbag which she never used. It was in a shoebox in the wardrobe. Rachel didn't even know it was there.'

'Thank you for being honest with me,' Kim said. 'That's been bothering us from day one, now we can rule it out of the investigation. Thanks.'

'You're welcome. We wanted to tell you earlier but I'm glad it's out there now.'

'Can I ask you about something else?'

'Yes. You're a police officer. You can do what you like.'

'Were you in the park when Walter Dallow was arrested?'

'Yes.'

'Did you see what happened?'

'Yes.'

'Can you tell me what you saw?' Kim asked. 'You won't get into trouble. I'm just curious. There are some things which don't add up and you might be able to help me to piece things together.'

'Okay.'

'Tell me how you came to be there in the first place,' Kim said.

'Mike Smith found out I was selling weed at the skateboard park. He went mad at me. He was really scary. They put me in a van and drove me to the quarry. I thought they were going to hurt me, but he said if I helped him, he would let me off. He wasn't going to let Walter trade on the island. Mike Smith and his goons made me set Walter up,' Louise said. 'I didn't want to, but I didn't have a choice.'

'OMG!' Jen said. 'Is that why those two idiots that hang around with him were knocking on my door the other day?'

'Will you please be quiet, Mum,' Louise said. She took a deep breath and carried on. 'Smithy made me arrange to meet Walter in the park. That's where we always met. He told me to get him into the ladies' toilets, which I did. They were waiting for him. They jumped him and then he slapped me around the head and told me to leave. He took all the money I had for Walter.'

'I thought Smithy was probably responsible for the tip off we received but thank you for confirming my suspicions,' Kim said, smiling. 'You were right to be scared. Smithy is a frightening guy.

Walter isn't a nice man either.' She noticed Louise flinch visibly at the mention of his name. Her expression changed.

'What will happen to Walter?' Louise asked. She looked shaken to the core.

'He's been remanded to HMP Walton awaiting trial.'

'How long will that take?'

'It could take twelve months before he even goes to court. There's a lot of evidence to process. He had a lot of teenagers like you working for him. We have to investigate each one individually,' Kim said. 'Are you worried about something?'

'No. Not really. I'm just interested,' Louise lied. 'How long will he get?'

'That depends on the judge,' Kim said. 'You don't need to worry about him. He won't bother you again. Tell me how you became involved with him in the first place?'

'He approached me on Facebook,' Louise said. 'He liked some of my photos and posts and then he started chatting about skateboards. I thought he was a dirty old perv at first, but he knows his stuff about boards. He was a bit creepy, but he was funny too.'

'Creepy in what way?' Kim asked.

'You know. He didn't actually come onto me, but he left a few comments open, hoping I might flirt a bit. We had a laugh and then he dropped into the conversation that he sold a bit of weed on the side. He asked if me and my friends smoked it. I said we did. It went from there really. The next thing I knew, I was talking about meeting up and selling it to my friends for him. It was easy to make a lot of money and my friends thought it was sick that I could get weed. The rest you know.'

'Does he recruit a lot via Facebook?' Kim asked.

'Yes. I think so. That's how he got hold of Rob's number,' Louise said. 'He was always on there, commenting on stuff and making stupid jokes.'

'He sounds like a weirdo to me,' Jen said. 'It's called grooming.'

'Did you friend him?' Kim asked.

'Yes. He sent me a request and I accepted.'

'So, once you accepted, he could see all your friends and family?'

'Yes. I know he friended a few of my friends. He even chatted up one of my mates and asked her out. She told him to fuck off and blocked him, but she does look older to be fair,' Louise said.

'How old is she?'

'Fourteen,' Louise asked. 'Why do you ask?'

'Oh, nothing important. There'll be a wider investigation that will look into who he's been contacting and how many minors he's recruited to sell drugs. The more kids he's exploited, the worse it will be for him. It will have a big impact on his sentence. He will go away for a long time.'

'Good,' Louise said. 'I hope he goes down for life.'

'I thought you said he was okay?'

'I thought he was. I was wrong.' Louise seemed to drift in thought. 'Will they arrest his boss too?'

'You know who he works for?' Kim asked, surprised.

'Yes. Amie Muir,' Louise said.

'That's right.'

'She's a headcase.'

'She is, from what I've heard about her,' Kim said. 'How do you know about her?'

'Smithy told me about her.'

'Why did he tell you about Walter's boss?' Kim asked, frowning. 'Most drug dealers keep their business to themselves. I'm surprised Smithy would share something like that with a young girl like yourself. No offence.'

'He was trying to calm me down. I was upset because she threatened me,' Louise said. 'After Walter was arrested.'

'Who threatened you?' Jen asked. 'No one threatens my kids.'

'Jen,' Kim said. 'You're not helping. You go and make us all a brew. I'll have a coffee, white with two sugars.' Jen was reluctant but did as she was asked. Kim waited until she'd gone out of the room. 'Tell me about how she threatened you?'

'She sent me a text message the night he was arrested.'

'From Walter's number?'

'No. From a different one.'

'Did you keep the message?'

'Yes.'

'Can I see it?' Kim asked.

'Yes!' Louise scrolled through her inbox. 'She said she was going to cut my legs off.' She paused. 'With a chainsaw.'

'Yes. I can see that,' Kim said. She made a note of the number and took a photo of the message. 'So, what did Smithy say about it?'

'That he was going to talk to her and smooth things over. He told me not to worry about it.'

'Good. Let's hope he has smoothed things over,' Kim said. She saw a flicker in Louise's eye. 'You look very apprehensive to me, Louise. Are you afraid of Amie Muir?'

'Of course, I am.' Louise said. 'At some point, you're going to ask me to make a statement about working for Walter. I'm not stupid. You're going to need all the kids who worked for him to give evidence against him. She'll try to shut us up. I'm not saying anything.'

'You're very frightened of her. I can see that. Do you think she's going to try to hurt you?'

'Yes,' Louise said.

'Has she threatened you again?' Kim asked.

'Yes. She told me if I say anything, she will get my mum and cut her up with a chainsaw. Said she knows where she shops, where she drinks, and who she fucks, and I believe her.'

'When was this?'

'A few nights ago.'

'How did she do that, text?'

'No. she called me,' Louise lied. Kim saw the lie on her face.

'From the same number?'

'No. It was withheld.'

'And what did she say?'

'She said I was a little rat and if I say anything, she was going to hurt me and my mum.' Kim saw another lie.

'Have you heard from her since then?'

'No.'

'You're sure you haven't heard from her since?'

'Yes.'

'I don't want you to worry. You shouldn't take her threats too seriously,' Kim said. 'Some of these gangster types like to blow their own trumpets a bit too loudly. It's all about reputation. She goes around threatening to cut people's legs off with a chainsaw and people are intimidated by her threats. That is the way they work. She's angry because you set Walter up, but she'll get over it. I'm pretty sure nothing will happen to you.'

'That's what Smithy said, and he was a gangster too,' Louise said. She started to cry. The floodgates opened. Kim was taken aback by the reaction.

'What do you mean, Smithy was a gangster?'

'I can't tell you,' Louise cried. 'She'll kill my mum.'

'Who will kill your mum?' Jen asked, carrying three cups of coffee and a packet of biscuits. 'What have I missed?'

'No one is going to kill your mum,' Kim said.

'Who's going to kill me?' Jen asked, concerned. She put the drinks down and sat next to Louise, hugging her. 'Don't get upset. Tell me what you're talking about?'

'Walter Dallow works for a very nasty woman called Amie Muir,' Kim explained. 'She's threatened Louise, but I think it's all bluster. I'm not taking her seriously.'

'Well, you should take her seriously,' Louise said.

'Why is that?' Kim asked.

'Because you should. Are they going to put her away when Walter goes down or not?' Louise asked, sobbing. Kim didn't answer.

'Come on now, Lou,' Jen said. 'Don't get so upset.'

'Answer me,' Louise said. 'Are they going to send her away too?'

'The investigation into Walter is being handled by the Matrix unit in Liverpool,' Kim said.

'What does Matrix mean?' Jen asked. 'I've never heard of it.

'It's a unit on Merseyside that specialise in tackling drugs and organised crime. They are very well respected,' Kim said. 'I don't know what evidence they have on her. They know she's linked to Walter but just because he's been arrested isn't enough to arrest her as well. They need specific evidence on her to arrest her. If they had enough, she would already be inside. Walter is very unlikely to testify against her, so the answer is no.'

'That's just great.'

'If you know anything about them at all, you need to talk to me.'

'No. I'm not saying anything,' Louise said. 'I want you to leave. I'm not saying another word.'

'Louise,' Kim said. 'If you're in trouble, I can help you.'

'That's what Smithy said. You can't do anything. Go away and leave me alone,' Louise said. She stood up and ran up the stairs. They heard her bedroom door slam shut.

'I need to speak to her,' Kim said.

'No. She said she doesn't want to talk to you anymore.' Jen gestured to the door. 'You need to leave.'

'I can see she's scared. I can help her.'

'Get out of my house, please,' Jen said, opening the front door.

Kim left the house, her head in a spin. She got into her car and took out her phone. She called Richard Lewis.

'Kimio,' Richard answered. 'What can I do for you?'

'I think something might have happened to Michael Smith,' Kim said.

'Michael Smith. Smithy?' Richard said. 'The drug dealer.'

'Yes. Will you send someone out to his flat?'

'What for?'

'I want to know if he's alive.'

'That sounds like you don't think he is.'

'I need to know one way or the other.'

'Okay. I'll send uniform there now.'

'If they don't get a reply, I want to know about it.'

'No problem.'

Richard hung up and Kim thought about what Louise had said about Walter Dallow. She put the phone on hands-free and dialled the station. She asked them to connect her to Detective Superintendent Paul Pulson in the Merseyside division. It went straight to voicemail. She was going to disconnect the call when he answered.

'DS Pulson.'

'Superintendent Pulson,' Kim said. 'This is DS Kim Davis from Holyhead. I'm calling about your email regarding Walter Dallow.'

'Oh yes. I was expecting a call from you. How can I help?'

'It's not about the CE directly. One of the teenagers on the list is a fifteen-year-old boy, Robert Evans,' she explained. 'His fourteen-year-old sister, Rachel went missing from a village on the island, on the day Dallow was arrested in Holyhead. It's only a few miles away. She was very active on social media, a bit of a selfie queen. I know Dallow used Facebook to recruit kids, so I'm curious if he ever came across Rachel Evans. I'm wondering if you've looked through his social media yet?'

'We have but there's a lot of it. We haven't finished yet. There's a lot to go through,' the DS said. 'I can tell you off the record, from what we've seen so far, Dallow is a very unsavoury character with an unhealthy interest in teenage girls. I can't really give you any specifics yet. Is there something you want us to look at? I can ask the techs to check and get back to you.'

'Yes, there is. Can you look at his Facebook and messenger and see if he ever communicated with Rachel Evans or Caz Marino, which is her alter ego?'

'Rachel Evans and Caz Marino?'

'Yes. If I get her mobile number to you, can you check if he ever contacted her directly?'

'Yes. I will do that. Can I ask why?'

'It's just a hunch. He was in touch with some of her family and friends on Facebook. He was on the island the day she disappeared. One of her friends was asked out on a date by Dallow. She's fourteen. There're enough reasons for me to include him in the pool of possible perpetrators.'

'I see.'

'Some of Rachel's pictures were a little provocative. She'd attracted attention from undesirables. I'm wondering if Dallow was one of them.

There might be a connection. It's a long shot but worth checking it out.'

'It's better to cover all the bases. I'll get back to you as soon as I can about that subject.' He paused. 'I actually thought you were calling me about the shooting.'

'What shooting?' Kim asked.

'You haven't heard about it?' Pulson said. 'You would have had a call today at some point. We arrested a Holyhead man by the name of Sam Pemberton last Thursday. He was arrested driving a Ford Mustang with a dead body in the boot.'

'An old Ford Mustang?'

'Yes.'

'OMG,' Kim said. 'He's part of a local outfit. His nickname is Monkey.' Her brain was running at a million miles an hour. 'The outfit is headed up by a guy called Michael Smith, better known as Smithy. We know he was responsible for the tip off which got Dallow arrested in the first place.'

'Okay,' Pulson said. 'That is a coincidence of epic proportions. I don't like coincidences, especially around dead people.'

'Me neither. Where was Monkey arrested?'

'The Aigburth area of Liverpool. It's an affluent area. You'd need half a million or more to live in that street. But let me tell you how the arrest happened,' Pulson said. 'We received a 999, call identifying the Mustang, the street, and the fact there was a body in the boot. The murder weapon, a sawn-off shotgun was next to the victim. The victim was a male called Emeriss Walsh. His ID was in his pocket. He was also from Holyhead.'

'Emeriss Walsh was known as Ghoul,' Kim said. 'They were thick as thieves. He was part of the same outfit. I can't understand why they would be in Liverpool and how one of them was shot. Could there be anyone else involved?'

'There's no evidence of that so far. Pemberton's prints were all over the shotgun and he has residue all over his hands. He's the killer.' Pulson paused to let Kim process the information. 'If they were in the same outfit, why would Pemberton kill Walsh?'

'I have absolutely no idea,' Kim said. 'Where is he?'

'HMP Walton. He's made a no-comment interview. We've got nothing from him at all.'

'I'm concerned this is connected to Michael Smith setting up Dallow in Holyhead. It has to be. I'm also concerned about the whereabouts of Smith.'

'Why?'

'The teenager who Dallow recruited in Holyhead, received threats from Dallow's boss.'

'Amie Muir,' Pulson said. 'She's a nasty piece of work.'

'Muir has made threats against the girl and her mother. I've just spoken to her and she looks terrified but the key thing for me is that she was talking about Smithy in the past tense before she clammed up completely. I need to run this by my DI. Thanks for info. Can I call you back if we need to?'

'Definitely. One more thing before you go. Did you know Dallow has a property on the island?'

'No. Where?'

'A place called Pentraeth.'

'The other side of the island from here,' Kim said.

'We've got a warrant to search the place. You might want to send a team of officers over there and I'll have some of my detectives there too, if that's okay with you?'

'Yes. No problem.'

'It's a belt and braces search. Anything extra we can nail Dallow with is just a bonus.'

'Brilliant. Let me know when they're going in.'

CHAPTER 50

April Byfelt drove the patrol car along the coast road to Pentraeth. Bob Dewhurst was her passenger. Together, they'd been tasked to attend the search of Walter Dallow's holiday home. Merseyside police were about to execute the warrant. When they arrived, Todd Gaskell and a team of detectives were waiting for them. A locksmith was sitting in his van ready to gain access to the bungalow. It was a small one-bedroom building with leaded windows and leafless roses growing over a trellis above the front door. It had a small lawn and a garage to the side. They parked on the pavement and joined the Merseyside officers with a minimum of introductions; everyone was keen to get in and get the job done. The locksmith opened the front door and then went to open the garage.

'Bob. Can you and April take a look in the garage, please?' Todd asked.

'No problem,' Bob said. 'At least we've got something to do,' he whispered to April. 'I thought we'd be standing around waiting. I'm glad we've got the garage. There might be something juicy in there.'

'Like what?'

'A body?'

'Another one?' April said. 'Surely, there can't be any more. We don't need any more for a while.'

The locksmith drilled the barrel and pulled the door up. It rattled loudly as it slid into place. Bob and April exchanged surprised glances.

'You know who that belongs to, don't you?' April said.

'I do.' Bob went inside and walked around the vehicle. 'It could be that Smithy has sold his Capri to Walter Dallow but bearing in mind, it was probably Smithy who got Dallow arrested, that's highly unlikely. Will you check if it's been reported stolen, please? Dallow might have stolen it out of spite.' April made the call.

'No. It's not been reported stolen,' April said.

'That's a strange one,' Bob said. 'Why hasn't Smithy reported it stolen?'

'Shall I call the DI?'

'Definitely. He'll want to know for sure.'

***

Kim and Alan were discussing the developments. Events were snowballing and several cases were blending into one. It was difficult to see the wood for the trees. Alan was listening to her talking but not saying much. He was a thinker and liked to mull over the evidence before he gave his opinion. The phone rang and he answered it. He spoke for a couple of minutes and then hung up.

'Ricky White is out of surgery, but he still hasn't regained consciousness,' he said. 'Uniform are there. They'll keep us posted.'

'What's the prognosis?' Kim asked.

'He's badly banged up. His brain is swollen. There's a chance he might not wake up at all,' Alan said. 'We'll have to wait and see. At least we know where he is.'

Alan shrugged. 'So, Pulson said Dallow was using Facebook to recruit teenagers?' Alan asked.

'Yes. But it seems he preferred approaching girls.'

'Let me get this right. I don't do Friend-face.'

'Facebook.'

'That too. Because he'd communicated with Robert Evans, you think that he may have come across Rachel before she blocked the rest of the family?'

'It's possible. He has an eye for the girls and there were plenty of posts from Rachel. If he had friends in that circle, it would be highly unlikely if he hadn't seen her. I've asked Pulson to get the techs to check if he ever contacted Rachel Evans directly, or messaged any of her other profiles.'

'You've got one of your feelings, haven't you?'

'Yes. He was on the island the day she went missing. He was active on Facebook and he has an appetite for teenage girls. It could be something, it could be nothing, but it's got to be looked at. There's something niggling at me about him. He had the opportunity, right?'

'Without a doubt.' Alan sipped his coffee. He wanted to lace it with whisky, but it wouldn't be appropriate. 'Tell me what Pulson said about Pemberton and Walsh. I can't get my head around it.'

'He thought I'd called him about the shooting and when he started telling me about it, I didn't recognise Pemberton's name at first but when Pulson mentioned the Mustang, I knew it was Monkey. Emeriss Walsh was shot dead and wrapped in clear plastic and put into the boot of Pemberton's Mustang. The murder weapon was in the boot next to the body, covered in Pemberton's prints and he had GSR all over his hands and clothes.'

'That's careless at best. I wouldn't have thought Sam Pemberton was that stupid, would you?'

'Never in a million years. He definitely killed Walsh, no doubt about it but we don't know where he killed him or why he killed him and he's not talking. He made a no-comment interview and he's lawyered up. His lawyer is unlikely to advise him to speak to us. We might never know what happened. The fact they were in Liverpool bothers me. After the Dallow arrest, surely that can't be a coincidence.'

'I don't think it's a coincidence,' Alan said, shaking his head. 'But I can't explain it.'

'Me neither. When I spoke to Louise Lee, she spoke about Smithy in the past tense which worried me,' Kim explained. 'She was absolutely terrified. I get the distinct impression she knows that something has happened to Smithy. What that something is, I don't know. I'm sure Louise knows more than she's telling us. She's frightened of Amie Muir.'

'Pemberton and Walsh were in Liverpool, which just so happens to be the stomping ground for Walter Dallow and Amie Muir. That can't be chance,' Alan said. 'Michael Smith, Sam Pemberton, and Emeriss Walsh were all in school together. I can't see them turning on each other. Do you have a theory why they were in Liverpool?'

'Nope. Not a clue.'

'I'll give Pulson a call later on. They might have a better idea after they interview Dallow.'

'Do you think we need to go and speak to Rob Evans about the money?'

'In light of what Louise Lee told you about the cannabis, I don't see the point. We know where the money came from and we know it has no bearing on Rachel's disappearance. Pauline Evans has got enough shit to deal with. I think we should leave her in peace. We can have a word in his ear at some point in the future when his mother isn't around.'

'You're a big softy inside, aren't you?'

'There's nothing in there but whisky and Guinness.'

'And wind,' Richard added. He came into the office and went to Kim's desk. She was chewing on a pencil and typing up the conversation she'd had with Louise. She looked up as he approached. 'He has always had terrible wind, you know. I've spent a lot of time sat next to him in a patrol car many moons ago.'

'Thanks, Richard,' Alan said.

'Any news?' she asked.

'Yes. I have two pieces of news. Neither of them overly concerning if looked at individually but when they're put together with what has happened in Liverpool, they underline your concerns about Smithy,' Richard said. 'There's no sign of Michael Smith at his home and his car isn't there. The second bit of news answers that quandary. Bob and April are over at the search of the Dallow property in Pentraeth. They want me to tell you that Smithy's Capri is parked in Dallow's garage.'

'Why would that be?' Alan asked. 'I can only think of one reason. We need a warrant for Smithy's apartment. And we need to bring

Louise Lee and her mother in here and get her to talk to us. Tell me again what she said.'

Kim sat back in her chair and sighed. 'Louise told me she was scared of Amie Muir. I said everything would be okay and not to worry. She said, Smithy said the same thing and he 'was' a gangster,' she paused. 'Was a gangster, past tense. When I pushed her on it, she had a meltdown. I wasn't sure at first but now we know Pemberton shot Walsh, I'm one hundred per cent sure she does. Let's search his home and bring her in and ask her.'

CHAPTER 51

Alan and Kim waited for the armed unit to confirm the flat was empty. Two CSI officers accompanied them up the stairs and into the property. There was a sour odour in the air. Alan recognised it from other crime scenes and none of them were pretty. They looked around the flat room by room, their instincts telling them something had happened there; something bad. They had to find the evidence to prove that their instincts were right. The simple fact was Michael Smith was missing. His car had been found somewhere it shouldn't be, in the possession of a dangerous rival. All the alarm bells were ringing.

The flat was very nicely decorated. There was a seventy-five-inch flat-screen television on a white high-gloss unit and a settee that would fit a dozen people on it. A granite breakfast bar separated the living room from the kitchen. The kitchen was fitted with integrated appliances, marble worktops, and granite floor tiles; it looked like something from a magazine. Everything screamed money. Pots and pots of money. Alan noticed the wicker chair in the bedroom where it shouldn't be. It didn't belong there. A metal eyehole welded to the frame, indicated it should be hanging from the ceiling somewhere. The flat was too neat and tidy for anything to be out of place. Whoever put the chair there, didn't live there.

'We've got something in here,' one of the CSI officers called.

Alan went into the living room. He spotted the anchor point where a chain would have been fixed to a roof beam. The chair had been removed at some point. The CSI's were working directly beneath it.

'What have you found?' Kim asked.

'Sticky residue. You can see where something has been taped to the floor here and here and on the walls there and over there.'

'What are your first thoughts?' Alan asked.

'I would say a protective layer was fastened to the walls and floor. Under normal circumstances we might say someone has been painting and decorating but nothing has been painted. In truth, it was probably to minimise forensic traces being left behind.'

'I would agree with that,' Alan said, looking up at the beam above them.

'I'm going to test the floor beyond the protected area with luminol.' She sprayed the floor beyond the sticky residue and illuminated the surface with UV light. Blood spots glowed like stars in a pink sky. 'We've got blood spatter and lots of it. It has fallen like a mist.'

'Which suggests what?'

'The only time I've seen blood mist was at a workshop in Llangefni. The victim had a heart attack and fell onto a circular saw while the blade was running. The blood is catapulted by the blade and turns into mist. It travels quite a distance. This would suggest some type of power tool was used.'

'Okay,' Alan said. He sighed and looked at the beam. He envisaged a man hanging from it by a chain, broken and bloody. 'It looks like you were right.' Kim nodded, but she didn't look pleased to be right about

Smithy. 'There's a lot of blood spray down there. The killers may think they've cleaned up after themselves but from a forensic standpoint, they've tripped up.'

'They didn't expect us to get here so soon,' Kim said. 'They killed him and took his car, locked the door, and walked away. If Sam Pemberton hadn't killed Emeriss Walsh, we wouldn't be here at all.'

***

Emily clicked open an email from the Evolve lab. She opened an attachment and downloaded the results. The analysis of Rachel's social media was far from over, but she'd asked for the results to be sent to her, as and when they came in. There were three IP addresses identified as hostile towards Rachel's profile. Two of them were on the island and one was in the Chester area; she disregarded the Chester address straightaway. She looked at the addresses on Anglesey. One was in Beaumaris and needed to be looked at. They had been in frequent communication with Rachel's images on Instagram and the comments were aggressive and suggested violence. At this point, everyone was a suspect, but the third address stood out and grabbed her attention immediately. The messages were sexually violent. They were threatening and perverted. The user was clearly a sexual deviant. The IP address showed the network provider and the area and from that information, Evolve had then traced the bills and found the customer's name and direct postal address. She stared at the details for longer than necessary. The name and address were staring back at her. She needed to tell the DI immediately.

***

Todd Gaskill was searching the bungalow. They had found a laptop and two mobile phones, which they turned over to the Matrix officers. They would be useful in building their case against Dallow, once the information, contacts, messages, and pictures were analysed. He found a carrier bag in the kitchen next to the door which led into the garage. He could see a pair of black leather shoes, some trousers, and socks and a shirt. It was a complete outfit stuffed into a Tesco carrier bag, probably destined for the bin. A CSI officer took it from him and bagged the contents individually. The kitchen was dated but tidy. There were several cups washed and left on the draining board. He opened a cupboard which was well stocked with soup, beans, and pot noodles. The fridge was full of Stella Artois, Coke Zero, and sparkling water. There didn't appear to be anything remarkable about the cottage, at face value. It didn't look like Walter used it as anything but a holiday home. Even drug dealers need to take time off.

Todd opened the back door and looked at the garden. There was a square lawn surrounded by bushes and a potting shed at the far end which was painted green. The paint was cracked and peeling. There was a brass padlock on the door. He went back into the kitchen and recovered a hammer from a drawer. He walked across the lawn and opened the door with a powerful blow to the lock. It fell to the ground. Inside, there was an assortment of plant pots and grow bags, a wheelbarrow, and a hoe, all covered in cobwebs. Disappointed, he closed the door and went back to the bungalow. Finding the restored

Ford Capri was a bonus. The search had been a success, although it had left more questions than it had answered.

CHAPTER 52

Alan was driving across the island from Michael Smith's apartment to Walter Dallow's cottage. Kim was quiet. Her hunch about Smithy had been correct and she was troubled by the nature of his disappearance. It appeared he'd been restrained in his home, probably tortured for the whereabouts of his drugs and money, then murdered and disposed of. The perpetrators had done a reasonable job of cleaning the scene but reasonable wasn't enough. They clearly weren't expecting the scene to be scrutinised by CSI's. If Pemberton hadn't murdered Walsh, they wouldn't have obtained a warrant to search Smithy's home. He would have been missing but there wouldn't be any crime to report. Many adults get into their vehicles one day and keep driving. It could have been months before anyone showed concern about his whereabouts. The fact his associates were killing one another, didn't bode well for him. They had to assume he was dead. Guessing who had killed him was simple, proving who had done it was a different matter.

'Finding his Capri in Dallow's garage is absolute gold dust,' Alan said.

'It answers a lot of questions,' Kim agreed. 'From the CPS point of view. The facts are simple. Smithy is missing. There is blood in his apartment and the vehicle he loved is hidden in a rival's garage. That was a huge mistake. Why hide it there?'

'Let's say they killed Smithy and decided to hide his car so we would think he'd gone away somewhere,' Alan said. 'Dallow probably thought it was too dangerous to try to cross the bridge in a stolen vehicle with patrol cars everywhere and a lockdown being imposed. Despite having a holiday home here, he didn't have enough local knowledge to dump a vehicle where it wouldn't be found. He obviously wasn't anticipating being rearrested for Criminal Exploitation. If he hadn't been arrested, the Capri could have stayed in his garage for the next ten years and no one would have known any different.'

'That mistake will cost him the next thirty years of his life,' Kim agreed. 'There's enough circumstantial evidence to add murder to his list of charges, even without a body.'

They arrived at the cottage. The Capri was being loaded onto a flatbed truck and covered over. It looked like the search was winding down. Alan parked up and they walked the short distance to the cottage gates. It was a quiet part of the island. The nearest neighbour was three-hundred yards away down a narrow, treelined lane. Most of the properties in the area were owned by tourists and the lockdown was preventing second-home owners from visiting. The steady stream of caravans crossing the bridges was quelled, for the foreseeable future. Todd saw them through the window and waved. He went to the front door to greet them.

'It's not looking good for Michael Smith,' Todd said, gesturing to the Capri.

'No. It's not,' Alan said. 'There's a lot of blood trace at his apartment.'

He spoke to one of the forensic officers. 'We've found blood at an apartment in Trearddur Bay. Tell your guys to check the pedals for trace. I think whoever drove that car here was also present at a murder scene. There will be blood on his shoes if he was.'

'No problem. I'll make it a priority,' the CSI said.

'It looks like Smithy took on more than he could handle,' Kim said. 'He bit the wrong dog and it bit him back harder.'

'It happens. Taking on an outfit from Liverpool wasn't the best idea. Still, on a brighter note, the car will go a long way to putting Dallow down for good,' Todd said. 'Do you want to look around?'

'Yes,' Alan said. 'Have you sent all his clothing off to forensics?'

'Yes. Once we knew there was trace at the flat, we bagged up all his footwear and outer garments. There's nothing in the washing basket or washing machine but there was a bag near the garage door with shoes, trousers, and a shirt in it. It could have been left there with a view to dispose of later, just like the Capri. I've labelled them as urgent. Dallow might have left us some irrefutable evidence to nail him with.'

'Let's hope so,' Alan said. 'We're liaising with Paul Pulson at the Matrix unit. On the back of what we've found today, he's raising a warrant for the arrest of Amie Muir too.'

'That's good news,' Todd said.

'I know a young girl who will be relieved,' Kim said.

Alan's phone rang. He looked at the caller ID. It was Emily.

'Hello Emily,' he said. 'Give me some good news, please.'

'I'm not sure if it's good news, but it's definitely important news,' Emily said. 'Evolve sent me some IP addresses. There are two on the island and one in the Chester area. One of the Anglesey addresses is disturbing.'

'Okay. I'm listening.'

'They traced the IP address, which took them to a Virgin network. Virgin use their own hardware. They don't piggyback on other networks. So, it was simple to identify the customer and access their bills and their data.'

'You're waffling again. Give me the name, Emily, please,' Alan said.

'Sorry. The billing address is, The Brook, Bodedern.'

'Rachel's house?' Alan asked, confused. All his theories and maybes came crashing to a halt. 'Whose name is on the bill?'

'Norman White,' Emily said. 'They traced the user profile to a fake profile. The fake profile was stalking Rachel and had been for a while. There are some very shocking exchanges. He threatens rape and violence in most of his comments.'

'Can we trace the fake profile?' Alan asked.

'There's no need to do that. There are two Facebook profiles operated from one device. Evolve tracked some of the user's posts and it took them to another set of logon details. They belong to Ricky White.'

CHAPTER 53

The team were in the operations room at Holyhead station. Emily had sent the entire Evolve file to them. Alan had distributed the information for his detectives to analyse. Ricky White had been systematic in his pursuit of his stepsister. He had set up a profile using the name Paulo Vicente. His profile picture was a handsome young man, topless to the waist with pecs and washboard abs. He looked of Italian origin, akin to the name. Ricky clearly enjoyed catfishing females online, chatting them up, and luring them into sexualised conversations. Using Paulo as camouflage. He stalked Rachel incessantly. They were combing through the communications looking for anything that could link him to her disappearance.

'I think it's significant that the Paulo profile was deleted the day after Rachel went missing, don't you?' Kim asked.

'Definitely. Ricky White has got a lot of questions to answer,' Alan said. 'Number one is what he did with Rachel.'

'You're convinced he's our man?' Kim asked.

'All the evidence points that way. What do you think?' Alan asked.

Alan's phone rang. It was a call from an exchange.

'DI Williams.'

'This is PC Harris at Ysbyty Gwynedd. The consultant has just told me that Ricky White died from a bleed on the brain ten minutes ago.'

CHAPTER 54

Abby was sitting in her armchair. Two detectives were sitting opposite her on her settee. Lucy and Helen were detective constables from Merseyside, there to take a statement on behalf of the North Wales Police. Her anxiety was through the roof. All the years of feeling dirty and guilty and blaming herself for what had happened had ground her down. She was an emotional and physical wreck. Her bones were visible through her skin. She was dangerously anorexic, and her mental health had suffered for decades. It had been impossible for her to enter relationships. Watching the news about the serial killer on Anglesey had brought it all back. Dozens of women had come forward and admitted that Dewi Pugh had abused them at the riding school. Abby knew that with him dead, it was time to speak out about what had happened to her.

'Have you lived here all your life?' Lucy asked.

'I was born in Whiston hospital. My parents lived in Prescot at the time I met Dewi Pugh. We moved to Speke when I was a teenager and I've been here ever since.'

'It's a nice area.'

'It's been much quieter since the airport closed. I sort of miss the planes going over.'

'Tell us why you called us,' Helen asked.

'I saw the news,' Abby said. 'About the farmer on Anglesey, who killed all those young girls. I read online that a lot of other women have come forward too.'

'We believe so,' Lucy said. 'Were you a victim of Dewi Pugh?'

'Yes,' Abby said. 'My family had a caravan on the island. We used to go there every school holiday. I liked horses and I went to the riding school whenever I could. I would spend all my holidays there. Dewi Pugh groomed me from the first day I went there.'

'How old were you?'

'Thirteen the first time I went there. I loved it. Dewi was nice to me and he let me help out, mucking out the stables, feeding the horses. I would spend most of the holidays there. My parents liked Dewi. He was nice to me at first.'

'But he assaulted you?'

'Yes. It went on for years. He told me it was our secret and he let me ride the horses for free if I did what he said. I knew it was wrong, but I did it, anyway. Looking back, I was stupid. I should have spoken out the first time he touched me, but hindsight is a wonderful thing. I've kept it quiet all my life for the sake of my son.'

'Your son?'

'Yes. Dewi made me pregnant at sixteen. I was a silly young girl and I thought I could have a baby, and everything would be fine. I did my best to bring him up and Dewi gave me money every month.'

'What is your son called?'

'Walter.'

'Does he have the same surname as you, Abby?'

'Yes. Dallow. He goes to Anglesey all the time. He loves it there.'

Helen wrote the name down in her notes. Walter Dallow. 'Does he have a caravan there?'

'No. He has a good job working in imports and exports. He has two houses there. One's a cottage. The other is a detached house near Holyhead. He uses that one for fishing because it's near the harbour.'

CHAPTER 55

Alan and Kim followed the interceptor through Holyhead, towards the mountain. A convoy of vehicles were close behind them. They reached the detached property that Abby Dallow had mentioned in her initial statement. The house was set back from the road and was surrounded by leylandii hedges. They parked up and an entry team approached the front door. Armed officers readied themselves.

'Break it down,' Alan said. The uniformed officers smashed the lock and the door bust open. 'Search every inch of the place.'

Police officers swarmed into the building. Alan and Kim followed them inside. Within minutes, the bedrooms were called clear. The curtains were closed, and the house was gloomy. They searched the entire property but found nothing. Alan opened the kitchen blinds, which looked onto the back garden. There was a small orchard of cherry trees and a garage.

'Search the garage,' Alan said. He opened the kitchen door and stepped outside. There were no outbuildings that he could see. 'I was so sure we were going to find something. I could feel it in my bones.'

'Do you want me to call the dogs in?' Kim asked. Alan nodded. 'We could be looking for a body.'

'Over here,' an officer called from the other side of the house. Alan ran around the building. Two officers were standing next to wooden doors, which were fixed to a sunken coal bunker, beneath the house. They were fastened with a heavy-duty padlock. 'The lock is new, sir.'

'Cut it off,' Alan said.

The entry team arrived and used bolt cutters to remove the lock. They opened the doors and shone their torches inside. Plastic water bottles and cereal bar wrappers littered the floor. The smell of excrement floated upwards from below. Coal dust glistened in the light, with iridescent hues of blue and purple. Lying in the dust in a foetal position was Rachel Evans. Her skin black with coal.

'Get the paramedics in here now!' Alan shouted. The green clad ambulancemen rushed down the steps and checked her vitals. One of them turned around and made a thumbs up sign.

'She's alive,' he said. 'She's dehydrated and hypothermic. We need to get her to hospital.'

CHAPTER 56

One Week Later

Alan and Kim were guests at the Matrix unit in Liverpool. Superintendent Pulson was taller than Alan remembered, and he had more grey in his hair. It had been five years since they worked on the Hollins investigation. His suit was Hugo Boss whereas, Alan's was Asda George.

'Thanks for coming,' Pulson said. 'I bet watching Dallow being charged with kidnap and murder was worth the trip.'

'We wouldn't have missed it for the world,' Alan said. 'When do you think Muir will go up before the judge?'

'A couple of months at best,' Pulson said. 'We have Michael Smith's blood on her shoes. It's invisible to the human eye, but it's there. We also have traces from Emeriss Walsh in the basement of a house she owns. It's registered to a limited company that she owns. It's in the next street to where Sam Pemberton was arrested. We think Pemberton killed Walsh on Muir's order with a view to taking over the operation in your neck of the woods. He didn't realise he was getting into bed with a rattle snake.'

'He turned on his friend,' Alan said. 'Karma is a bitch.'

'How is Rachel Evans?'

'On the mend and happy to be at home,' Alan said, 'Her mother is the happiest woman on the planet. We were lucky Abby Dallow came forward when she did, or we would have been too late. She was nearly out of food and water.'

'Did he harm her?' Pulson asked.

'He didn't get the chance to,' Alan said. 'But he would have. The apple didn't fall far from the tree with Dallow. He inherited the same appetites his father had.'

'I can't believe he had a relationship with his father and didn't know what he was up to at the farm, can you?' Pulson asked.

'I don't suppose he'll be in a rush to answer that,' Alan said. 'There's a chance they were in on it together. Whatever the truth is, he won't be a danger to anyone else and Rachel Evans is safe with her family.'

EPILOGUE

One Year Later

It was the first week into her life sentence. Amie had done over a year on remand and she genuinely believed she would walk away with a not guilty verdict. Her defence team had cost over a million pounds and they were winning the battle in the courtroom until the prosecution presented Louise Lee as an eyewitness. Amie was distraught. Louise had presented as a confident and articulate young girl, who gave her evidence as convincingly as it could be. She told the jury how she witnessed the dismemberment of Michael Smith. The courtroom had been stunned into silence while she gave her testimony via a video link. Her evidence convinced the jury that Muir was a murderer and because of the nature of the crime, the judge gave her a full life term. Amie didn't think she could do life. Before the verdict, she'd hoped that she might walk free again but now there was none. She would never be released. Once the news of her sentence reached the streets, the grip she had on her business evaporated. Her properties and assets were confiscated by the state. She had no money and no power anymore. She was a no one.

It was her turn for a shower. The water was always lukewarm, and the landings were cold and drafty. Amie turned the hot water up and stood beneath the shower. She closed her eyes and thought about another life. The life she'd enjoyed before she ventured too far away from home. She'd pushed the boundaries too far and too hard. Walter Dallow hadn't helped the situation. It turned out he was the son of a psycho killer and a paedophile. It had been no wonder he enjoyed recruiting young dealers so much. She should have buried him and Louise Lee when she had the chance. It was too late now. The time when she wielded the power of life and death was past.

'Amie Muir,' a voice disturbed her thoughts. She felt a hand yank her hair back sharply, tearing the roots from her scalp. There was a sharp pain across her throat, and she watched her blood splatter on the tiles and run towards the plughole. Arterial spray arced across the shower room. 'The man you fed into a shredder was my dad. Say hello to him when you get to hell, bitch.'

Amie collapsed onto the tiles and watched her blood run down the drain until the darkness moved in and surrounded her.

***

Walter Dallow tried to eat his meal but couldn't. It wasn't that he didn't have an appetite, they'd put shit in his food again. Human shit. It was broken glass the day before. He cut his lip and gum. When he reported it, the prison officer smirked and said he would look into it. It was clear that his investigation into who had put the glass in his food had been thorough. He had to eat in his cell because he was a convicted paedophile. The police had found thousands of images on his phones and computers. Although he was serving life for the murder of Michael Smith and the kidnap and imprisonment of Rachel Evans, his other misdemeanours had been taken into account and broadcasted to the world by the press. They were in a feeding frenzy when it was revealed Walter was the illegitimate son of a serial killer. It would be written about and debated for decades. Nature or nurture. Was he born evil or was he taught to be evil?

On the inside, he was a dead man walking. He was trapped inside concrete and barbed wire with a target on his back. It was simply a matter of time before they got to him. Someone would get him. Walter had received a note telling him that what had happened to Richard Huckle at Full Sutton prison was nothing to what they were going to do to him. Huckle was serving twenty-two life sentences for abusing kids in Malaysia. They'd stabbed him to death and removed his testicles with a razor blade stuck to a toothbrush and stuffed them into his mouth. He didn't want to suffer any pain. There was another forty-years or so do until he died. That's over fourteen thousand, six-hundred days of looking for glass or turds in his food. There was no one to visit him, no one to write to and no one inside would talk to him. What was the point in existing?

It wasn't a difficult decision to make. It had crossed his mind a hundred times a day since he was arrested. He thought about Rachel Evans and why he'd gone to her school that day. She'd been driving him insane posting her pictures in her uniform. The bitch was begging for it. He'd approached her many times, but she brushed him off cruelly. She said he was too old, too fat, and too ugly. He wasn't taking no for an answer. That was a red flag to a bull. He told her he was coming to her school to talk to her face to face. He thought he'd missed her until he spotted her running across the rugby pitches towards the wood. When he followed her, he found her unconscious in the grass. He called Dave and told him to pick him up at the other side of the wood. Dave didn't ask questions although he wasn't happy when Walter put her into the boot of the Range Rover. They'd taken her to his house near the harbour and he locked her in the coal cellar. If he hadn't been arrested, he would have gone back to get her later that night. He would have kept her there for years, just like his father had. It was all ifs and buts.

Walter took his sheet and ripped it in half. He fashioned a noose and tied it to the bars on the window. He climbed onto a chair and put the material around his neck. His mind was resigned to what he was about to do. He kicked the chair away and the noose tightened. His feet twitched and danced in the air for a short while and then he was still.